The
Orange
Cat Bistro

The
Orange
Cat Bistro

Nancy
Linde

Kensington Books

KENSINGTON BOOKS *are published by*

Kensington Publishing Corp.
850 Third Avenue
New York, NY 10022

Kensington and the K logo Reg. U.S. Pat. & TM Off.

Library of Congress Card Catalog Number: 96-076015
ISBN 1-57566-050-4

First Printing: July, 1996
10 9 8 7 6 5 4 3 2 1

Printed in the United States of America

For my parents, Ruth and Alfred Linde, who gave me the love of learning and the arts which has sustained me.

Leaving her unsympathetic husband to pursue a career as a novelist in a tiny Greenwich Village apartment, Claire pours all of her own fears, doubts, dreams, and pain into a fictional character who begins to take on a life of her own.

CHAPTER ONE

When my husband left me, suddenly there was enough air. For three years, no matter where I went, the walls pressed in on me. Even jogging around the Reservoir, the sky folded down around me and made walls. My brain screamed for open spaces, but no space was open enough. If we were in an East Village restaurant with pressed tin ceilings, the ceiling lowered itself crazily and pressed the air out of my chest. It only made me cling to him more tightly. I was convinced that without Aaron I couldn't breathe. I never realized he was the one stealing my air. I like to think it was an innocent theft, but he stole a lot more than air from me in our thirteen years together. He had my sex encased in plastic and tucked away in his battered wallet. My sex, which had flowered like a Riverside Drive windowsill full of plants, now smelled like spilled beer, stale smoke, and rancid french fry oil in an old man's bar. If that salty-sweet part of me had to smell like a public house, at least it could have been a bistro where stock simmered all day, and a cat slept in a window full of geraniums.

The very day he left, in the middle of the shock and panic, I
could feel myself coming back to life. I could feel this stream of
lost me trickling through what had become a blighted country,
through what I had come to believe would always be a blighted
country. Quickening, real energy, not the hour or two of false
hope that coffee brings. It was my breath coming back—a silver
living stream. Suddenly there was enough air in the room, the silver living thread that was my soul, and I thanked God for its return even though the price of getting myself back was losing my
husband. I thanked God, and we agreed that it was a good bargain
and I could afford the price.

The price was high, the price was very high, but I could afford it. Economics of the soul—I hadn't had the freedom to make
my own decisions for thirteen years. Now a decision had been
made for me, a decision I was ashamed I hadn't had the courage to
make, and suddenly I had the opportunity to heal the sick empty
place in my life that was born out of lack of courage. Lack of heart
if you take it literally from the French. Obviously I needed to visit
the bistro on West Tenth Street where the fat orange cat slept
under geraniums and order beef heart, coeur de boeuf, dripping
with heartening blood—eat it raw, accompanied by a glass of
house red, and stain my heart red with courage. Take courage
from Madame, perched behind the cash register, stout in widow
black, warm, imperious, an empress, her son-in-law in charge of
the kitchen but under her. She eats men like french fries and buys
a bigger girdle each year. I should be ashamed of my lack of courage in front of her, but I breathe her in—her faint aroma of soap
and sweat and mothballs—and take heart from her enormous
presence. I skip the beef heart and order cassoulet.

I arrive at the bistro at three-fifteen every day, after teaching at the cozy overheated private school on Bank Street and settle myself at my corner table with a pile of papers to grade. Madame's granddaughter brings me café au lait and brioche. Drops spatter the marble table as I dip the cake into the milky coffee, but I manage to keep the essays clean because I'm a professional again. I'm surprised to find myself a virgin again, too, delighted to no longer be obliged to open my body. I'm as self-contained as Madame, my back straight and solitary and strong against the iron bistro chair, the back of a virgin warrior. I feel my back solitary each night against sheets that are unstained and crisp as a fresh sheaf of typing paper. My bed is as narrow and virginal as if I were a daughter in Madame's house, under her protection, under the protection of my own virginity. I'm under the protection of my straight shoulders, my breath, my white cotton panties hung out to dry in the yard where lavender grows. The cotton smells sweet from the sun and wind, and the wild onion growing tall in the unmown grass gives it a virgin tang.

It's a good thing to have the protection of Madame's beef heart, her red wine, my sweet-smelling cotton panties, because these are not easy times. Splintering off from my husband made me feel like one of those broken hearts in an old illustration. The wind blew through the crack, howling at night, but I was tired of being afraid, tired of letting fear be my master, tired of caving in, tired of making my fear a cave in which I would hide, smelling its scent—fresh sweat over stale sweat, the chemical perfume of my deodorant giving out, a chalky feeling in my armpits.

I've heard there are people so agoraphobic that their bed is their only island of safety. Even stepping out into the kitchen makes them reel. Imagine being so dependent on your husband, you have to wait for him to come home to take you to the bathroom! I never got that bad, but my bed became a cave, the mussed sheets full of crumbs, collapsed piles of books in my husband's place.

How it stank in the labyrinth. And how fresh the air was at Madame's. In my room above the bistro with its white iron bedstead, I sat at the mahogany desk drinking coffee as powerful as God, proud to be upright and not huddled in the cave of the bed, proud of the normal relationship I was developing with air. I typed away at Madame's prehistoric Underwood, giving all my pain and fear to my heroine, Nevada. I made her strong as Madame's coffee and as vulnerable as I had been. Though she was my creation, I hoped she would serve as my guide. Torch flaring, she'd lead me into the labyrinth and show me the sacred paintings on the walls. Maybe if we could find the intersection of sacred and scared, I would no longer be afraid of that old stink reattaching itself to my clothing. I didn't understand how I, the true spiritual heir to Madame's peasant health, had ever let herself get this crazy. With Nevada I was going back into the labyrinth to find out.

CHAPTER TWO

Nevada crawls out of her sculpture, pausing at the lip to see if anyone has invaded her studio while she was carving birds on the walls of the inner chamber. No one is there except for the luminous blue-and-gold creatures in Alec's paintings. She croons to them as she struggles out into the world, resisting the oceanic pull of her Nautilus Shell. After ten years of working on the Thing, she never tires of crawling in and out of it. Why would she want to sell it? How often does a straight woman get a chance to crawl back into the womb? She wishes people would stop hassling her about it.

She should never have let Alec talk her into giving that party. Everyone, all his friends anyway, had insisted on crawling into her Thing, even though she kept insisting it wasn't finished. She still thinks Alec set her up. He's never spent more than three months on a painting, and he thought that was way too long.

Grouchy critics, haughty gallery owners, her competitors all came out glowing, claiming her Thing was better than LSD, better than a flotation tank, better than ten sessions of past-lives regression therapy. After their immersion, everyone refused her champagne punch. They just floated around, smiling into each other's eyes, touching each other's faces. She hadn't heard of such a bliss-out orgy since the Maharishi held an audience for the Tri-State disciples back in 1969. There was a lot less backbiting, a lot more generosity in the art world in the week following her party. A number of unknown young artists got their start that week. Probably she would be doing a public service by letting the Thing be put on display, *but it's just not finished yet.*

Alfred Munford, the collector, had been particularly insistent, and each time she emerges, she expects to see him sitting on her decrepit sofa, ogling her Thing, checkbook in hand. But money's not the issue. The issue is that there's always more polishing and carving to do inside. Outside the Thing looks smooth, simple and seamless like a shell, a monolith, a spaceship, but inside she's carved hun   tiny figures—birds and be ts and goddesses and gargoyles,   g o her back, her skin warm against the warm skin of the Thing her chisel an organic extension of her hand.

Second, what would she crawl i   he Thing go? It's not as if she has any ideas for new pr   vould feel unfaithful to the Thing if she started fantasizing about other sculptures. And anyway, her old clawfoot bathtub doesn't do it for her anymore. Once she could crawl into it and be perfectly happy with a green, fragrant Vitabath froth, but after she realized she could stretch a hose from the kitchen sink and half flood the Thing, she stopped using the tub for anything but ritual cleansing.

But the trouble is Alec is getting jealous of the Thing, which sits in the center of their loft, screwing up the traffic flow (only because there's a drain there, left over from the industrial past of the loft. She can't very well leave the Thing flooded with scummy water, can she?) Alec claims she spends more time with the Thing than she does with him, which is approximately true, but then he doesn't provide her with the feeling of security the womblike Thing does. But it's more than just a womb, much more. She knows its fleshlike contours better than she knows her own body. If she tended her body as obsessively as she tends her Thing, people would think she was an incredible narcissist.

What would she sleep in if she let them have it. True she could stay in bed all night with Alec, but she doesn't really feel safe there, in a world she hasn't created. After Alec has gone to sleep, she slips out of bed and wriggles into the innermost sanctum of the nautilus-chambered Thing, where sometimes she thinks she can hear a river running over rocks as she drifts in and out of sleep; sometimes she thinks she can hear her mother's voice singing to her. In the morning the first dawn light filters into her chambered shell, obliquely, subtly, not strident and buxom the way it does Outside and caresses her body, caresses the tiny sculptures of birds and beasts and goddesses that cover part of the inner skin of her Thing, caresses the cave paintings of deer and fires and sacred mountains.

From the outside, her Thing appears no bigger than a spaceship, but inside infinite space opens out. There are three-layered ancient forests—the massive oaks reaching to where blue sky turns black, the delicate white birches dancing just above her head, the forest floor strewn with Queen Anne's lace and edible mushrooms. Farther in there's an inland sea so intensely salty, she can float for hours, even sleep, cradled in bloodwarm water. In her Thing she always sleeps lightly. Even at night, a pearly glow emanates from the stone walls, filling her with calm, happy energy. Who knows what she might miss if she indulged herself in a deep sleep, the kind Alec enjoys in the outside world. Slipping in and out of sleep, she's been so sure sometimes that the carved goddesses are dancing with the deer and lions, that just behind her head, they're all drinking thick red wine made for them by shepherds who are just waiting for her to paint them.

I take a sip of cold coffee, which amazingly enough, still tastes good. I like Nevada. I haven't liked anyone this much since I met Allegra, wandering through a Magritte exhibition at the Museum. We were both pretending we weren't fifteen and just off the New York Central. Recognizing each other as sophisticated City women, Mesopotamian sorceresses, doomed poets, we quickly became inseparable. Our parents marveled at how we never ran out of things to say. We could spend all Saturday shopping, discussing all the boys we knew, reading poetry, our own and the poems they didn't let us read at school, talking about the amazing things we'd learned in physics—quarks! black holes!, telling each other stories about the mythical lovers who were sure to be knocking on our doors soon, soon, soon. And we'd still tie up the phone all night, till one of our fathers, claiming bankruptcy, forced us to hang up. Or if we had a sleepover, we'd make up stories till we drooped with exhaustion. Our mothers would come in to scold us, not realizing that we weren't little girls anymore, but WOMEN. Why *were* we in such a hurry?

Now Allegra and I write a couple of times a year. And that's good for the nineties. She's got a job, kids, a neurasthenic cat.

I start getting my clothes ready for the morning—ankle-brushing navy skirt, crisp striped shirt. Allegra would tease me about being such a schoolmarm. She'd insist I wear feathers and rhinestones, at least show a little skin. I miss her. I hope Nevada doesn't have a neurasthenic cat.

CHAPTER THREE

"Nevada! Get your butt out here now!"

Nevada jerks awake, her forehead grazing the inner skin of the Thing. She runs her finger over the spidery tracing of blood. The Thing likes blood sacrifices. She could marble the granite with her moon flow, but how would she keep it from turning as unappetizing as old apple cores?

Mulling that over, Nevada barely hears Alec's threats to come in and drag her out by the hair. It's not until she hears his feet scrabble against the entrance tunnel that she realizes she's awake and has a situation to deal with.

"Coming, dear," she calls, aiming for TV wife, circa 1955. When Alec takes that tone, placating him is the *only* way. She'll show him her compliant hindquarters like a proper female monkey. That might buy her enough time to get a cup of coffee before Alec launches into his rant. Once he's started, her only option is to let herself be flattened by the juggernaut of his rage. Her feminist friends don't have to know how low she sinks to keep the peace. Her feminist friends don't have to live with Alec. They would probably say she doesn't either, but what do they know about the careful adjustments that make her life (just barely) workable?

Reluctantly Nevada starts crawling toward the entrance. It's amazing how she reconstitutes herself each time Alec's rage shatters her into tiny pieces. She could get a job as a cartoon mouse. And it's Alec's rage, not Alec, she reminds herself, pausing at a particularly comforting twist in the tunnel. Isn't that what they taught in Sunday school? Hate the sin and love the sinner. Turn the other cheek. She's offered every single one of her cheeks to Alec and where has it gotten her but black-and-blue? She just hopes this morning Alec's not going to tie her up and humiliate her while he gets off. She strokes the Thing's inner skin. She can barely take that when she's half-awake and it seems like a dream. Other women might prefer that, but a dream penetrates the interior. Reality is a whole lot easier to ignore.

Nevada starts crawling again when she hears Alec's growl. As she nears the entrance, a cold breeze raises goose bumps on her bare skin. How she longs to stay inside forever, luxuriating in the Thing's soft stone caress! A little rudimentary plumbing wouldn't be difficult to install—a composting toilet and a rainwater catch basin, maybe a seawater recovery plant. Alec growls again. Reluctantly she pulls herself away from the delights of technical problems to solve. Though they're sacred objects she can fondle like blue-grey river stones, they distract her from the all-important task of placating Alec.

Pushing through the pile of rough boulders that shield the Thing's entrance, Nevada squints into the strident light. There's a strange man sitting on her sofa, staring at her nipples as they harden in the cool breeze.

"My wife, Venus," Alec announces with a flourish. "On the half shell."

I'm hardly your wife, you jerk, Nevada thinks, scrambling for something to cover herself. And the Thing is more like a shell and a half. Doesn't Alec have any sense at all? He knows she always sleeps naked Inside, though in their bed she covers herself with as many layers of flannel as she can get away with. Draping herself in a paint-spattered drop cloth, she offers her hand to the balding stranger wearing perfectly pressed jeans and a crested blazer.

"Reginald Hassiloff," he says, smiling at her. "At your service. Don't mind your dishabille, my dear. I'm used to the models at the Institute running around without a stitch."

At least they're awake and have agreed to be the center of everyone's visual field, Nevada thinks, but all she says is, "Coffee?"

"That would be charming, my dear. Just a tiny splash of cream and a half teaspoon of sugar. And you do make that with filtered water, don't you?"

"Triple-filtered," Nevada assures him as she heads toward the kitchen. At least Alec won't be able to build up to one of his major rages with a guest in the house. Her hide, if not her pride, is safe—for now.

Alec catches her arm as she swishes past him in her drop cloth. "Don't change," he says in a low voice. "You're perfect just as you are."

Nevada gives him an incredulous look. Unwashed, her petite, bouncy body barely concealed beneath dirty canvas, she feels at a decided disadvantage. Reginald Hassiloff looks as if he's taken at least three showers today and has a valet who does nothing but iron his boxers. Alec smells a little ripe, but he's covered by his usual floppy layers—poet shirt, baggy khakis, embroidered Afghan vest. But when he grasps her arm hard enough to leave bruises, she gives him a bright, false smile and nods.

At least she can throw some water on her face and brush out her ringlets while the coffee drips through. That perks her up a bit as does the rich, dark aroma. Fresh coffee is one thing she *can't* get in the Nautilus Shell. Could she run a 120-volt line without ruining the Thing's delicate ecosystem? Maybe a small wind-powered generator would be less disruptive.

As she sets out terra-cotta mugs, she wonders why Alec brought Hassiloff here. For the Thing? He certainly has the old money stink that serious collectors give off.

Pouring out the coffee, Nevada notices a tiny naked woman squirming in the bottom of her mug. Nevada stands very still. She barely notices the hot coffee dripping on her feet. Is major league insanity what she has to look forward to if Alec forces her to sell the Thing? The just-workable lunacy she lives with has served her so well. She's grown almost fond of it.

Quickly Nevada finishes pouring the coffee. She puts a splash of cream and half a teaspoon of sugar in Hassiloff's, four teaspoons and no cream in Alec's, and the same in hers. She's heard that coffee is a hallucination antidote. Hopefully she takes a sip, then spits the black syrupy stuff into the sink. This isn't at all how she likes her coffee! And she has no idea how she does like it. Nevada looks questioningly into the cup. Does her hallucination know? Hallucinations could be the repository of all sorts of lost things. The little figure reappears from beneath a wave, doing the backstroke. She spits a spume of coffee unhelpfully at Nevada and disappears beneath the surface.

Nevada takes a deep gulp of coffee. In the long run it's easier to like what Alec likes. She carries the tray out to the living area.

Alec's got his arm around Hassiloff's shoulders and is saying something in a low voice. They laugh. Nevada blushes and puts the tray down on the coffee table. She suspects the joke is on her.

"I've heard so much about your wonderful Nautilus Shell, my dear." Hassiloff picks up his cup, sips, and smiles. "And if it's as good as your coffee, I'm sure I'll just adore it."

Uh-oh, here it comes, Nevada thinks, gulping her teeth-jarringly sweet coffee. What can she possibly do to discourage him? Spill coffee in his lap? Alec would make her pay for that later, but it might be worth it to see Mr. Moneybags squirm and clutch his crotch.

"It's not for sale." Nevada stands up abruptly and starts putting the coffee things back on the tray. She tries to grab Hassiloff's cup, but Alec gives her a warning look. She sits down. "It's not for sale," she says in a chastened tone. "But you can look at it. Briefly."

"You're quite the negotiator, my dear." Hassiloff smiles. "But I'm sure we can come to terms. I think you'll find me a very generous person."

If you were a truly generous person, you would go away, Nevada thinks, but she merely adjusts her drop cloth. The gritty canvas makes her long for a bath in a rainwater pool, deep in the rocks of the Thing. There she could talk to seabirds about the meaning of life. She loves to hear them cackle derisively when she philosophizes. "I'm not negotiating," Nevada says. "I don't want to sell."

"Your husband seems to think you can be persuaded."

Nevada tugs nervously at her drop cloth. Alec has the power to make her do things no woman in her right mind would even consider. And after the visitation in the kitchen, she doubts she's anywhere near her right mind. It *would* help if she weren't half-naked. If she had on a red power suit with Joan Crawford shoulder pads and a perfect armor of makeup, she might be able to resist Alec's bullying.

Alec tosses her a boyish grin. If she ever becomes a mother, she's going to teach her daughter to be excruciatingly careful about the choices she makes. What starts as the kind of wild ride that rock songs celebrate can deform your life into stranger shapes than you could ever imagine. And she has a very good imagination.

"Well let's get it over with," Nevada says as she clears the table. "You'll have to take off your clothes, Mr. Hassiloff. Don't worry." She laughs at his look of alarm. "I'm not going in with you. If I don't take a shower soon, I will spontaneously self-destruct." Luckily the Thing is self-cleaning. A good storm will wash all traces of Hassiloff off the inner walls.

"I've heard you can get lost in there without a guide." Hassiloff straightens his tie nervously. "And that at the bottom of certain cliffs, you can see skeletons picked clean by the buzzards."

"Really?" Nevada says. "How interesting. I've never seen any skeletons, though there are wild places even I haven't explored. Of course, if you would rather not go in . . ."

"Hogwash," Alec says. "The only time anyone's been inside was at our Halloween bash. Everyone who went in came out."

"Did you do a body count, dear?" Nevada asks. "I know I didn't. Anybody could have vanished in there. I didn't know half the people you invited."

"It sounds like a good place to get rid of—enemies," Hassiloff says, and coughs.

"But we're all such good friends in the art world," Nevada says. "Aren't we?"

Alec gives her a warning look. "I'll go in with you," he says, starting to shed his clothing. Nevada turns away. Alec's pale bony body used to fill her with lust and tenderness, but now all she can see in Alec's nakedness is pain. And she certainly doesn't want to see Hassiloff strip. That much cleanliness is obscene.

Drop cloth trailing, Nevada heads toward the shower. She doesn't want to see them drop to their knees and crawl through the Thing's entry hole, Alec's mouth in perfect position for a little discreet ass-kissing. When he's intent on a sale, Alec is capable of anything. And he hasn't sold anything of his own for a long time. She doesn't know how he's been paying the bills. But she's not going to worry about any of that. She's going to take a long hot shower that will drown out the sounds of whatever they get up to in there. With any luck, they'll both end up as buzzard food.

I think I need a glass of brandy after *this* chapter! Alec is some piece of work! I thought Aaron was bad. One thing I can say about my ex-husband—he never laid a hand on me, though I think there are times he was sorely tempted. At least he had that much self-control. I was always aware of his size and strength and the energy crackling beneath his controlled demeanor. Aaron would have been happier in more primitive times, when he could have dominated hundreds of terrified serfs instead of just me. Being a petty tyrant in the nineties is not PC, and Aaron is nothing if not PC.

Why *did* I marry Aaron? I longed to perfect myself and my life, which were slipping out of control. Who better to help than a psychiatrist? At that time I would have done anything to feel safe. Living in New Rochelle, so green and safe and boring, protected by my parents and Allegra's love, I never guessed at the chaos that lies beneath the fragrant, grassy lie of the suburbs. Until a certain incident, which I don't want to discuss at this time.

And there was nothing Aaron wanted more than to perfect

me. I would let him mold me into his Ideal Feminine, and he would make me safe. That was our bargain. But instead of bending, I broke. That's what he said when he left me for one of his graduate students who was, presumably, more malleable: "I did my best to mold you (and when he said best, he was talking about years of Ivy League education) but instead of bending, you broke." He hated weakness. He hated my agoraphobia. It drove him wild that I couldn't take a supermarket in stride, that I stopped being able to drive, that I couldn't make witty cocktail party conversation with his supervisor because I was too busy having a panic attack. It didn't reflect well on him as a health care professional.

It didn't reflect well on me as a maker of contingency plans. Where was Allegra during all of this? Doing her junior year abroad. In an ashram in Baja. Having children in Michigan. I don't think I could have told her, anyway. My parents were right where they were supposed to be, and I never said a thing to them. All they knew was that I married a bit young, but Aaron was a parent's dream.

It's only now that I might be ready to talk. I hope Nevada is a good listener.

CHAPTER FOUR

Reginald Hassiloff emerges alone and dazed from the lips of the Thing. He blinks in the bright daylight and stumbles over to the couch where Nevada, finally showered and dressed, is drinking her second cup of coffee. She still can't remember how she likes it, but Alec's way is starting to taste alarmingly good. If she's not careful, she's going to start liking it when he beats her.

Hassiloff has that Thing-dazed look about him. He seems unaware of her presence and his nudity has obviously become a non-issue. Nevada sighs. The Thing will do that to people. "More coffee?" she asks.

Despite her soft approach, Hassiloff startles like a deer in a clearing, then pulls a pillow over his nakedness.

"Don't mind your dishabille, my dear," Nevada says. "I'm used to running around without a stitch, myself." But she doesn't have it in her to get up a full head of nasty. It's hard not to like someone who loves the Thing. "Did Alec fall off a cliff?"

"He'll be out shortly," Hassiloff says in a voice as rusty as a wilderness hermit's. Nevada can almost smell the nettles on his breath. "He wanted to get one last glimpse of the ceremonial fire stones—you know that lovely Stonehengesque tumble near the entrance."

"What do you mean, *'last glimpse'?*" Nevada sits up straighter. "Last glimpse" sounds ominous.

"Dear Alec said they were just the inspiration he needed to unblock—and since I'd like to take the Nautilus Shell with me today, this will be his last chance to visit with them."

"Today?" Carefully Nevada sets her cup down. "That's not possible."

"Oh but it is," Hassiloff says, his eyes gleaming with Thing-light. Nevada knows that look well. "I have a truck and crew downstairs."

"Do you plan to display it?" Nevada tries to fight down the panic rising in her chest. It is her sculpture. He can't take it without her signature. And Alec has never been much of a forger.

"Oh no!" Hassiloff seems genuinely shocked. "I could never share the Nautilus Shell."

A tiny woman crawls out of Nevada's cup. Nevada watches her disinterestedly. What is a hallucination to her when her Thing is about to be shanghaied? If it were going to the Museum, she could at least visit. With her encyclopedic knowledge of the Thing's topography, she could find wilderness places no one else would ever stumble on. There she would lie, breathing in the mossy, loamy smells under the thick trunks of old trees.

The little figure pauses at the lip of the cup, panting for breath. Nevada eyes her with self-disgust. Even her hallucinations hyperventilate. But when she feels tiny fingernails on her wrist, she leaps up, frantically shaking her arm. No matter how hard she dances, she can't seem to dislodge the tiny hallucination. It crawls up to her shoulder, pauses, and leaps into her mouth. Nevada chokes and starts to cough. If her hallucination only had the courtesy to stay visual! The tiny woman slides down Nevada's throat, settles in her chest, and starts stealing her air. Nevada tries to breathe hard enough for the two of them, but there isn't enough air in the room, maybe not in the world. Nevada looks at Hassiloff breathing peaceful as a Buddha on her couch. *He* seems to have plenty of air. Is he the one who's been stealing hers all these years?

"Put on your clothes!" she screams. She can't kill a naked man. Hassiloff just sits and stares. She has her hands around his throat, when Alec wrestles her to the ground.

"Hey, hey, what's this?" he says. "Can't I leave you alone for a minute?" He waits till she's calm, then lets her up. "I know you'll feel better when you hear what happened to me. I'm simply *radiant* with inspiration. I see a series of fluid feminine forms in shades of grey, greys so subtle they're near silver, every shade of grey in the mineral world with patinas as fine as velvet, sun-drenched linen, well-sanded wood. It's sure to get me a one-man show." Alec looks at her expectantly. "You know how blocked I've been lately. Aren't you happy?"

Nevada wants to tell him just how not-happy she is, but Alec is into honesty only when it's his. And anyway she is happy that he's once again inspirited. The art-haunted Alec is the Alec she loves.

"Take off your clothes," he commands, slipping a pair of cut-offs over his long thighs. "You don't mind modeling, do you? Now that the Nautilus Shell is sold, you have nothing but time on your hands."

I'd rather have blood on my hands, Nevada thinks, unzipping. "I'd really prefer not to sell the Thing just yet," Nevada says, as she pulls off her jeans.

"You really don't have a choice," Alec says, adjusting his easel. "If we don't sell the Nautilus Shell, we're going to be in the street."

Nevada sits so she won't fall. "What happened to all that money from your last big sale?"

"Babe, that was two years ago." Alec sets up a fresh canvas. "It's amazing how much granite costs. You're going to have to start pulling your weight."

"Couldn't you sell something else?" Numbly Nevada pulls off her shirt.

"My stuff hasn't been selling lately. You know that. You're the one who's hot. I don't see why you're making such a big deal out of this. You can always start something new."

But I have a relationship with my Thing, Nevada thinks. *I can't just abandon it.* She rubs her temples. "You know how hard it is to start something new. Look how long you've been blocked."

"And now I'm unblocked. It's part of the process. Do you want to be on the street?"

"Are we really that broke?" Her headache trickles down into her stomach.

"We're down to our last twenty."

Nevada looks at him dumbly. "Twenty dollars?"

"I don't mean twenty thousand." Calmly Alec takes a stick of charcoal out of a little wooden box.

Doesn't this man have nerves? The rent's due next week and the refrigerator's almost empty. Nevada's too scared to cry. "I trusted you to take care of things."

"I told you, I'm tired of pulling all the weight." Alec starts squeezing colors onto his palette. "It's your turn. I think I'll enjoy being a kept man."

Nevada arranges herself in a variety of postures until Alec nods. She could never handle being on the street. At times just being out in the loft terrifies her.

"I'm thinking of your career, too, you know," Alec says, setting a fresh canvas on his paint-stained easel. "You have to get your work out while you're hot. If you wait a couple of years, people will have moved on to the next thing."

"But why Hassiloff?" Nevada ignores the sweat trickling between her breasts. "He wants to hide it away on his estate. If we sell to the Museum, I could at least visit."

"He's offering so much more money, we really don't have a choice. Trust me. You know I have your best interests at heart." Alec starts sketching. "And if it's in the Museum, you'll just waste all your time visiting."

"At least it would get me out of the house."

"You should start something new. Ten years is too long."

Nevada stretches her right leg. Alec does care about her. He pushes her past her stuck places. Where would she be without him? She would let the Thing swallow her for good, never make another piece, never let the world share her vision. And that would make her as selfish as Hassiloff. She could make a real contribution if she listens to Alec.

"OK," Nevada says. "He can have it, but not just yet."

"That's just an excuse, dearie, and you know it. But if you agree to sell to Hassiloff, I'll give you another month. He'll agree to anything. Look at him." Alec nods at Hassiloff, who's still sitting on their sofa in deep stoned bliss. "I'll throw a drop cloth over the Thing and you can pretend it's gone. Start something else while you get used to the idea that the Nautilus Shell is history."

Gone for good, gone for good, gone for good. Her new mantra. She forces herself to stay in the realm of the practical. "How are we going to pay the rent?"

"I've got an offer to run an artists' retreat in the Catskills next week. That will cover us till we get Hassiloff's check. And I don't want you cheating while I'm gone. You know I'll know. As of today, the Thing is finished."

Nevada nods numbly. What else can she do? She'd never make it on the street. And presumably there *are* all sorts of new sculptures inside her waiting to be born. A tear runs down her cheek. Poor Thing. It's going to miss her terribly.

Typing a final period, I push away from my desk. What would Aaron think of this? I'm so used to his pedantic voice telling me what's what, even in bed. "Dear, you're not sleeping right," he would say when I scrunched up in fetal position. He insisted I sleep on my back, hands crossed on my chest—the way grown-ups sleep. I swear that's exactly how highborn ladies sleep on their stone tombs! When Allegra and I wandered through the Museum's Medieval Hall, we thought they looked so peaceful. But when I tried to sleep that way, my bed became a coffin. I guess that's OK if you're dead, which I wasn't, quite. But dead was starting to look pretty good.

Setting up the ironing board, I get out a pink shirtwaist for tomorrow. Aaron even told me I didn't dream right. He'd sit up for hours, watching my eyelids to time my REM sleep. It was always too long or too short or at the wrong time of night. I'm surprised he never had his graduate students move into our bedroom, glue electrodes to my head, and monitor my dreams by computer.

I pour distilled water into the iron. If Aaron read this, he'd probably have me committed. He insisted on reading my dream journal and then would tell me my dreams weren't Freudian enough. It got to the point where I started making up dreams, even stealing from Freud and Jung. I was a regular outpost of the collective unconscious. Amazingly enough, Aaron never caught on. If he read something that sounded familiar, he probably figured I was *finally* getting it right.

This book is the first private space I've had since I granted Aaron colonization rights to my mind and body.

CHAPTER FIVE

Nevada feels as empty as a newly wombless woman. Even the dust motes shining in the West Street sunlight mock her with their spinning silence. She prowls around the loft, looking for somewhere to settle, something to do, but the chairs seem inhospitable as cliffs. If she sat down, her perch would tilt and, shrieking like a bird of prey, drop her into the abyss. Which is probably where she belongs for allowing Alec to manipulate her into declaring the Thing finished. Isn't it just like him to leave her to deal with her loss alone? It would help if she had his bony shoulder to cry on. He can be sweet . . . when he wants to be.

When he threw the dust cloth over her Thing, she'd wanted to rend her clothes and wail, sprinkle ashes on her head. If there had been an open grave, she would have thrown herself in. But she has to admit that there was just no other way she was ever going to stop fiddling with the Thing, no way she was going to move on in her work. She is doing this, she tells herself, to prevent her perfectionism from driving her totally mad. A little madness may be good for the soul, but she's definitely reached the point of diminishing returns. Who knows what other pieces she has in her, struggling to get out? She will never hear them with the Thing blocking all her senses. Who knows what has died in her already? Sibling rivalry among the unborn—it's more than she can bear. All she wants to do is start working again. But her hands, so recently blessed with making, have become crone claws, whose barrenness is catching. Dust rags fly shrieking from her. The broom does a mocking little dance in its corner, inviting her to ride. At her approach, books gallop stiffly off on their spines and repile themselves just beyond reach.

Nevada puts a Laura Nyro record on the stereo and lets the sad sweet music fill her loft. Laura Nyro, scholar of sadness, turns the sadness sweet—a miracle. Enough of a miracle to allow her to settle herself into a sun-drenched corner of the loft. She puts her back into a corner and slides down to the paint-spackled floor. A wall at your back is good; a corner's better. There is comfort in a corner. A corner is cozy. A corner is a cradle. She can imagine brightening the corner where she is. If she doesn't think about anything larger than this corner, the world, for example, or the Museum, she can imagine surrounding herself with music and mobiles and big silk pillows. She could create a magic corner which she would never have to leave.

"So where is meaning, anyway?" she asks Laura Nyro, who's too busy singing about betrayed love to pay her any mind. Even if she weren't being ignored, she would feel foolish asking a question like that, though it seems an important question to keep asking. But she always hears someone snickering over her shoulder—her father, maybe, or legions of smart-ass undergraduates. To say,

"Meaning is in sculpting my Thing," seems like such an inadequate answer, though when she was sculpting it, the question never arose.

Is meaning just in making something, Nevada wonders, stroking the lumpy, shiny floor with work-roughened hands. The paint-streaked wood feels like the first thing she's touched since she covered the Thing with shrouds. It's as though Alec stripped away her fingerprints, leaving her hands as blind and blank as the eyes of Greek statues. How wonderful to see them quicken as they stroke the shiny-hard blobs of paint, the rough blobs of spackle! Her big, square hands look, even to her, like they could do anything—build a house, play the piano, make lace. They are the part of her she has faith in. If they are starting to work again, they will lead her to sanity.

Could she put them to work baking banana bread or sewing a dress? The bread would smell so warm and inviting, laced with lemon rind and walnuts, smelling like care. It wouldn't matter if she were taking care of someone or somebody were taking care of her.

And sewing a dress, even though it would be just for her, she would feel like her mother's girl again. Her mother, who taught her how to sew and iron, how to press the cloth out flat, smoothing the wrinkles away with her hand, the hot cotton smelling so much like home, would be proud of a party dress with finished seams. She has her mother's hands, hands that could make the world if God were busy. Much as she loves them, she has to acknowledge that her hands don't go with the rest of her. Her hands match her heart, her hands are who she is. The rest of her has a delicate classical prettiness that people mistake for her. Even her stone-cutting muscles are concealed under soft flesh. *She* would have shaped herself from granite, not porcelain. She would not have made herself a five-foot-high doll from the Franklin Mint. She's no doll woman. She's her hands. She's her mother's hands. If she looked more like a pioneer woman, men would be less confused by her, less apt to wrap their silly fantasies around her.

Her mother, who makes Cabernet Sauvignon from her own grapes, who cans peaches, beans, and tomatoes from her garden, who slaughters her organically raised turkeys, looks like a pioneer woman. Her mother's hands are covered with blood and good Nyack earth. Her own hands are covered with paint and stone dust. Should she follow in her mother's handprints and plant a garden on her rooftop? It would root her in thousands of years of women planting food, planting clothing, planting pretties. What demon voices from her psyche would dare say there was meaning only in sculpting, would deny the meaning of her mother's life? She'd press the seeds in the warm earth and trust that the Manhattan sun knew enough about agriculture to nurture her zinnias, her tomatoes, her arugula. She'd be like the women in illuminated medieval manuscripts, who look like flowers and vines themselves—fecund, eternally pregnant, faces turned up to the sun. She could be like the abbesses with their encyclopedic knowledge of healing herbs and white magic.

Or she could try making a baby. Considering how long it took her to hatch the Thing, she'd probably be pregnant—like an elephant—for two years. Her mother only needed nine months to create her. Is her womb as competent as her mother's? Would it be as clever at sculpting as her hands?

If it took Nevada only two years to hatch a baby, she would be lucky. It hurts so much when my students say I understand them better than their own parents. They send me corny cards and invite me to their recitals and awards parties. But this is *one* thing I can't blame on Aaron. My barrenness is a side effect of that incident I'm still not ready to talk about.

Aaron as a father is a terrifying thought. Or would a baby have deflected his attention away from me? Probably he would have started in on my breast-feeding technique. My milk flow would have been too fast or too slow, too magnesium-rich, too zinc-deficient. That intense, observing eye and me on the other side of the microscope like some kind of fascinating bug. The Scientist at work, ever vigilant, even in our most private moments. In bed, I felt as if he were collecting notes for his next book: *The Effects of Post Traumatic Stress Disorder on Female Sexuality*. At the moment of his climax, I was free. But after a brief swoon of release, he was once again practicing The Scientific Method.

I felt nothing but the futility of his sperm filling my barren places. That futility would build after lovemaking and fill me like dark water. The only thing that kept me from finding some dark water and throwing myself into it was the thought of those who loved me. My students would never understand why I wasn't there on Monday morning to applaud their poems. And I never did find a way to tell my parents that I wasn't happily married. They thought I was concentrating on my career before the right time to give them grandchildren. If Nevada had children, could my parents love them? Could they love Nevada?

CHAPTER SIX

Nevada is still sitting in her magic corner. It's a good thing Alec is in the Catskills, leading that artists' retreat. If he were here, he'd make her desert her safe, soothing corner and occupy the whole loft: sleep on the bed instead of this nice comfortable pillow nest, eat at the table instead of on the undemanding, companionable, paint-spattered floor, use the kitchen for serious cooking instead of kamikaze raids.

Nevada pushes her head deeper under her quilt, but she can't shut out the sunlight. Her magic corner is not nearly as sheltering as the Thing. Maybe if she made a tent . . . The kind she played under as a child would be easy. All she'd have to do is make a quick foraging trip into the loft for a tablecloth and chairs. If she were feeling ambitious, she could make a medieval tent with a minaret roof and banners. But that would mean venturing beyond the front door for supplies. If Alec were here, if she had his tall bony body to ground herself on, the street would be just bearable. Without him, the street is a minefield of leaning buildings whose purpose is to squash her flatter than a painting. Alec's beard is a waterfall of hair she can hide behind. In the cave under the falls, she's in her own portable sanctuary.

When she was at Pratt, going out into the world each day was exciting—who knew what might happen, who might talk to her, touch her, fall in love with her, what sculpture ideas might appear in the sky as she walked up Atlantic Avenue, what inspiration might speak itself out of cool flame in a dusty classroom. But now it's hard to find a good reason to leave the house. Most of what she needs, D'Agostino's and UPS deliver, and Alec's willing to haul home the rest. He likes feeling needed.

Her friends don't mind coming to her; she loves to cook and bake for them, and they love to gaze out her windows at the ever-changing light on the Hudson. Paula even cuts her hair when it starts looking like the weeds on the abandoned West Side Highway. She can dance and do yoga and Tai Chi alone or with company. She does miss walking through the cool evening streets of the Village when Alec's away. It's not that her friends wouldn't walk with her and hold her hand when she shakes with fear. She just doesn't feel comfortable letting them see her that crazy. She and Alec have full knowledge of each other's loony depths. She knows he'll accept anything she does, as long as it's not meant to hurt him. He'd better, considering the goods she has on him.

If people knew what went on in their bed . . . Would it ruin Alec or guarantee his reputation if it were known that he paints with his penis (at least he's found a legal outlet for his exhibitionism), that painting is the only useful thing that he can do with it although he certainly enjoys titillating himself with her body, that he gets his inspiration from her curves, but can take his satisfaction only in his paintings? Maybe that's what give his colors their luminosity. Nobody else gets whites like Alec. At least he creates beauty out of his sickness, which is more than she can say for most people.

Ten years ago she would never have dreamed of putting up with such epic weirdness, but ten years ago her own weirdness had yet to bloom. Back then she believed lovers should follow a ballet script geared to an audience of twelve-year-old girls. Her scenario of the perfect art world marriage collided with her ex-husband's *On the Road* story line. She doesn't need to make the same mistake with Alec. How would she manage without him?

If she hadn't been dazed by the breakup of her marriage, she never would have allowed Alec to waylay her at the Cloisters. She'd always thought museum pickups were tacky, and she'd hardly talked to a man in her two years of mourning for her ex. Since Jim had left her for redheaded twin art models, she'd enjoyed thinking of herself as the celibate saint of the art world. Hanging out with the painted saints at the Cloisters was her only comfort till Alec plucked her out of her thornbush.

When she saw Alec, lurking among the ancient wooden Christs and eyeing her hungrily, her impulse was to flee. With his Christ-like expression, his mix of boyish shyness and aggressiveness, his holy man beard and Hollywood blond hair, he was beyond weird. But there was something about his neediness and urgency that drew her out of her vacuum of sadness. He'd eased her away from her martyred virgins into the medieval courtyard and engaged her in a frenzy of kissing before she even knew his last name. It was years since she'd last engaged in public necking and never in a place where ancient monks might suddenly appear with scourges. But he'd wanted her so much, her self-consciousness had dissolved.

Alec soon had her soaring in a high, hot cloud of desire. If he had tried, she might have let him take her on the low stone wall overlooking the medieval herb garden. But he was, in some odd way, a perfect gentleman. Before he plunged his hands into her clothes, he'd taken her, supporting her in a swoon of desire, to a cave in the bushes just beyond the cloister walls. There, like a highwayman in an old ballad, he'd ravished her. If she thought his reticence at the climactic moment was quaintly chivalrous, chivalry seemed most appealing after Jim's betrayal.

When she and Alec emerged from their cave in the bushes, she'd expected him to disappear wraithlike into the hot July evening. But holding her tightly around the waist, he'd escorted her to his favorite Cuban-Chinese restaurant, where he'd fed her arroz con pollo, café con leche and flan. He was oddly shy after their recent intimacy, but they *were* practically strangers. Though he didn't say much, she felt both soothed and stimulated by his presence. He was the first person in two years who'd penetrated her sadness. After dinner they walked down Broadway to Dyckman Street where, ignoring her laughing protest, he'd bought her a corsage of pink tea roses. How could she resist a man who would pin a birthday corsage on her blouse after she had effectively eliminated any need for courtship? But he kept right on courting her—escorting her home on the subway, calling for dates, bringing her lilacs and peonies. He hid his mean streak very well in their courting days.

Even though she can no longer attribute Alec's reticence to quaint chivalry, even though she feels sometimes that she would kill for a good fuck, Alec is endlessly inventive. He's certainly more fun in bed than Jim, who prided himself on his abilities as a cocksman. She really doesn't know what she would do without Alec. He's big enough to toss her over his shoulder and cart her home if she really loses it. It never has come to that, but it's comforting to know she wouldn't have to make it home under her own steam. Her other friends are almost as short as she is and strong only in their paintbrush-wielding fingers. The irony is, with her stone-carving muscles, she's the one who should be carrying herself home. If she could only figure out how to let her physical strength seep into her psyche!

Maybe it would be comforting to be even more loony than she is. She could get herself checked into a nice cozy insane asylum, the kind with big, old-fashioned chintz-covered chairs, and retreat into madness. She'd have meals brought to her on a tray—chicken croquettes and mashed potatoes with pools of gravy, cubes of red and green Jell-O shimmering on her plate like an acrylic sculpture, never her favorite medium, but who would want to eat food that looks like granite? She'd sleep, protected from reality by dragon nurses, on crisp white sheets. And she would sculpt in the art therapy room, or would they make her weave baskets? They'd probably medicate her so thoroughly, she wouldn't know reality if it tried to bum a quarter off her.

What she really needs to do, Nevada thinks, trying not to pant, is give up hyperventilating, hallucinating, and fantasizing asylum. The forlorn hope that Alec will rescue her is obviously just that. It's high time she thought about rescuing herself. But how? There's so much to be terrified of—the crowds in the street, the air-sucking hole that follows her around like a pit bull terrier, hallucinations whose appearance are dictated by some mysterious logic of their own.

Could the answer be *in terror*? Nevada gets up and starts to pace. Trying to stay safe has made her nothing but a prisoner. Maybe what she needs to do is seek sanctuary Outside! Her refuge would be the streets and the sky; her body would be her home, her portable shelter.

It's spring but still cold. Nevada wraps herself tightly in her quilt, made by her from sewing scraps—velvets the color of night sky, chintzes from a dress that looked like an overstuffed chair in an English country house, some of her mother's old dresses, stitched together by her in the evening while Alec read aloud or played his flute.

Her quilt, with its intricately stitched strata of memory, is what she has to give up. Her skin has to be open to the world—no quilt, no loft, no Thing. Her skin would be open to the street, the weather, the emotional climate, would lose its pale, cared-for smoothness. Her glossy hair would get snagged and dirty. Only her hands would stay the same, her hands that are rough and old-looking already, her hands that are strong enough to carve stone surely will see her through.

You have to admit Nevada's got moxie. Aaron had to kick me out of the nest. If I'd had Nevada's courage at that crucial moment when I lost my nerve, what would I have done? If I hadn't lost that esprit that Allegra and I had adventuring our way through the City?

When Allegra and I were fifteen, the City was an illustrated fairy tale opening its pages for us. We arabesqued through the streets, too full of happiness to walk, sure that our high spirits would bring nothing but smiles. And if people thought we were spoiled suburban girls who knew nothing of life, we were moving too quickly for their criticism to stick to our golden skin.

What would I have done if I hadn't lost that young girl certainty I had when the Museum distilled its riches through my tiny body? While my mother shed her heels and my father rubbed her feet, I would go on solitary rambles through the Impressionist rooms, lost in a dream of sun-struck gardens. I could stand for hours, staring at the face of a Spanish courtier, more vivid by far than anyone I knew. My parents, after cocktails in the fountain room, knew they would find me sitting by the limestone fountain in the Spanish courtyard, mesmerized by the whiteness of the stone. I wondered for years how the artisans captured summer in that cloistered, indoor space.

If I hadn't lost my nerve, maybe I would have become an artist. But how could someone too scared to buy a can of tuna at the A&P find the courage for that path? Art is a lot more complicated than tuna. It's even more complicated than the A&P. But words are good. I can hide behind words even as I use them to explore the delights and terrors of this world.

CHAPTER SEVEN

Gathering up her things, Nevada heads for the door. But her courage starts to fail when she's face-to-face with the impenetrable black-painted metal, dense as an imploded star. Walking out the door suddenly seems as impossible as walking through it. Doors are there to keep certain things out and other things in. Maybe she should listen to the wisdom of the door and stay inside where she belongs.

Nevada slides down to the floor and plants her back against the door. Is the door starting to lean in on her? Is it shoving her slowly and inexorably across the room? If it doesn't stop until it has squashed her against the opposite wall, not only will she cease to be viable, so will her loft. When she's on the street, she'd like to know that her asylum will still be there for her. Cautiously Nevada stands and the door rights itself. What wisdom is the door trying to communicate? If it gaped open invitingly, if it reached

out a doorknob and led her courteously into the hall, things would
be a lot clearer. Still there's not a lot to be gained from dawdling
here. Resolutely Nevada grasps the doorknob, which doesn't
shrink from her. Encouraged, she turns it and pulls open the door.

Outside the hallway gleams white as a skull. The black-and-
white tiles whisper tales of nightmare kitchens—roaches scurrying out of cereal boxes, refrigerators swarming with baby rats.
Closing her eyes, Nevada gropes for her backpack and denim
jacket. The lock clicking shut sounds like a finger breaking.
Squeezing her eyes shut, she makes her way down the hall. If she
doesn't see it, it doesn't exist. Using her hands as eyes makes her
feel a little more in control. The shiny enameled walls feel like
nursery rhymes, like bowls of cornflakes and cream and strawber-
ries, but when she opens her eyes, the hall assaults her with its
harsh fluorescent glare, known to cause fits in epileptics. Is it possible to become epileptic this late in life? Nevada examines her
body for telltale shakes, finds nothing but the usual hyperventilation and dizziness. Hyperventilation, her old friend. She's glad
she's not alone.

The hall seems to be stretching into infinity, but there's
something wrong with the perspective. Is the corridor tilting? Is
she on the wrong side of the fun house mirror? Already she's
drenched with sweat and she hasn't even made it to the elevator.

She knows what the trouble is—she's forgetting to keep her
eyes closed. Resolutely she squeezes them shut and gropes onward.
Onward Christian Soldiers, she thinks dubiously, but really what
is she if not a pilgrim warrior or, for that matter, a sheep in need of
shepherding. "The Lord is my shepherd. I shall not want," she
recites aloud. "He maketh me to lie down in green pastures. He
leadeth me beside the still waters. He restoreth my soul." Nevada
takes a deep breath. God does seem to be restoring her breath,

which is practically the same thing as her soul, according to her Buddhist friends. This is the first unconstricted breath she's taken all day. And between God and her hands, she's managed to grope her way to the elevator.

The elevator button feels both hard and soft, like licorice. When the car comes, she fumbles her way through the door, straight into the barrel chest of a fellow pilgrim. Before she can even consider opening her eyes, the door closes behind her.

"Are you OK?" the man says in a deep voice, putting out a hand to steady her. If she were a sensible person, she would open her eyes. That's what her mother would tell her to do. But her mother is a sensible person who isn't afraid of supermarkets or museums. And she's already in a moving elevator with a stranger. With her eyes closed and her hands on the shiny speckled walls, she feels relatively secure. Who knows how terrified she'd be if she saw a pair of drug-crazed eyes or a dirt-caked leg where his pants have surrendered to wind and weather?

"I'm fine," she says firmly, amazed that her voice doesn't shake. Even if she is a total loon, the whole world doesn't have to know it. "Could you push lobby for me? I'm conducting a little experiment—I'm trying to see what being in the world without eyes is like."

"It's dangerous enough out there with eyes. How are you going to manage? You don't even have a cane."

"I didn't think of that," Nevada says sheepishly. "I'll just have to open my eyes if I get in trouble."

"You'd better open your eyes *before* you get in trouble."

What is it that Paula said about men with voices like this? They sound as if they have an extra gonad? This man sounds kind, but Nevada thinks she hears, "dippy dame," in his meta-masculine voice. Her ears, however, have never been as good as her hands at picking things up. She'd love to touch his face and see what she could learn. But what if she found him full of boozy violence, pumped full of TV images of what men do to women when the ratings wars rage? She would rather not know. She has thrown herself on the mercy of the universe. She's Out.

"I can walk with you as far as Hudson and Christopher," the stranger offers as the the elevator bumps to a stop. "If you're going that way. My voice coach had to end our session early today."

"It doesn't matter *which* way I go, as long as I go," Nevada says, delighted to have a shepherd, terrified to have him witness her craziness.

Tucking her hand under his arm, which feels both strong and fat, he steers her toward the courtyard. He's wearing an itchy but comforting wool jacket. She imagines that it is houndstooth check, the kind of jacket a Barbara Pym anthropologist would wear. A man wearing a houndstooth jacket is more likely to take her for a cozy tea than a fatal stroll by the river, she assures her absent mother, and keeps her eyes defiantly closed. Of course salesmen don't check your police record before they take your money. "Oh no, sir, I'm sorry. With *your* rap sheet, you'll have to buy sharkskin."

As they walk out of the courtyard, the river wind assaults her with gritty energy. She was hoping for more of a caress—after all it is a fine April morning and the Hudson has been her household God for so long. Through her windows the wind would have whispered enticingly of the pleasures of Outside. Talking to the wind about the world seems more appealing than letting the wind carry her into it. If she were alone, she'd cling to the wall of Westbeth for support, taking comfort from the sun-warmed brick. She can just see herself spread-eagled against the wall—a public lunatic, afraid of falling off the edge of the earth. If she did start acting like lichen, would her guide desert her? Is he already regretting his kindness? Stumbling along hesitantly beside him, she probably looks like a voyager from the Planet of the Loons. She's never been able to tell how much of her craziness shows. For all she knows, she comes off as normal as a TV anchorwoman on her maintenance dose of Valium.

It's amazing how much concentration it takes to keep her eyes closed. The foolish things long to fly open and let in the reality lurking, waiting to snare her in its net of immanence. On the street, even with her eyes closed, her imagination feels overpowered, faint. The smell of garbage cans and fossil fuels, the roaring trucks, are more real than any comfort she could dream up. Nevada edges in closer to her shepherd who narrates the sights to her, just as if she were a real blind girl. He describes the green of the apples and the purple and white of the irises in the Korean market with obvious relish. How blessed he is to be able to take such pleasure in what is, Nevada thinks wistfully. Is it a skill he could teach her?

Depending on this stranger, trusting him not to walk her into a wall or under the wheels of a truck, is softening her armor. "What's your name?" she asks her guide, stroking his sleeve.

"Nicholas," he says in his deep voice. "What's yours?"

"Nevada," she says. "Would you mind if I touched your face? I have no idea what you look like."

"What do you think you can see with your fingers?"

"Everything." If she discovers anything terrible, there's still time to make a run for it.

"Well if you can see everything." He takes her hand and puts it up to his face, right there on Hudson Street.

Nevada shuts her eyes tighter and pretends she's alone with him in a grotto, as people brush past impatiently. His skin feels soft, pale. He's an indoor person, like her, with a well-trimmed Vandyke beard, a prominent nose, a broad face. A kind face.

He takes her hand and squeezes it closer to whatever suffering hides behind his face. "No one's touched me in such a long time," he says. "You really do have eyes in your fingers."

She can feel tears on his face, just a few, trickling onto her hands. How had she forgotten about other people's suffering? She strokes the tears into his skin, softening it, irrigating his suffering.

Nevada shivers. How long has it been since she's touched anyone? Alec won't let anyone touch him, *ever*. He likes to tie her arms behind her when he makes love to her. He dreams, he says, of women without arms, women who are all breasts and mouths and cunts, women who can't pin him down. She was surprised at his eagerness to live with her, but he seems to think she's necessary to his work. Anyway he's the one who's got her pinned down, lying in their bed with her hands touching only each other, night after night for the sake of his art. Not that it's been bad for her art. On the contrary. Her art has flourished at the expense of her body.

Nevada moves in closer to Nicholas, her eyes still tightly closed. How beautiful men are in their bodies, underneath their clumsy clothes that disembody them as effectively as Alec disembodies her. How blessed she is to have hands to touch the small of Nicholas's back. The roar of the street has faded. There's nothing but his body and her body. They could be in a grotto. The distant trickle of water on rock is the only sound other than the beating of their hearts.

Her hands have been cut off for so long; she's been listening to voices saying, "You've made your crazy quilt, now lie under it," for so long. What kind of country do we live in, Nevada wonders as Nicholas's hand makes her arm remember it's part of Nevada, that there's so much touch starvation? Why has she had to rely on the Thing's granite embrace? Alec's touch freezes her into marble, his pornographer's touch that delights in turning a sculptor into a sculpture, his own personal disarmed Venus de Milo. Alec is disarming, with his boyish eagerness, and his lovely, lonely art, his tall skinny boyishness that she used to find so irresistible. It always seemed as if he were going to grow up, grow beyond, with her tender ministrations, his adolescent solipsistic sexual obsessions.

Healing does seem possible, perhaps not for Alec, but for her, she thinks as Nicholas kisses her.

CHAPTER EIGHT

The light is turning violet over Madame's garden. I leave Nevada captive inside the filigree machine that was once on the cutting edge of technology. The coffee is starting to wear off, leaving me tired and jumpy. It's worth it though. There's nothing like a cup of coffee to get up a good head of creative steam. I thank God for legal drugs and being healthy enough to use them. At the height of my agoraphobia, a cup of coffee would set off a full-fledged panic attack, even if I were safe in bed.

Sitting on the dusty velvet window seat, I watch the fireflies starting to flicker on in Madame's hollyhocks. Are they God's promise of real magic or a sideshow come-on? I'd ask Nevada, but she's as confused as I am. That's one of the things I like about her.

I envy Nevada. If I had as seductive and exquisite a refuge as she does, I'm not sure I would venture out into the world. If I were Nevada, I would never sell my Thing, no matter what my stupid boyfriend said. And I envy her hands. My strength is in evanescent things, things that disappear as quickly as fireflies and leave me wondering who I am. Things like what happens in a classroom when I'm there. A writer can get lost beneath the words, a teacher erased with the chalk dust on the blackboard. Sometimes I feel like a cloud of chalk dust being clapped out of two erasers. I rise over the schoolyard and gaze down at the little boy in blue tie and polished saddle shoes who's happily launching me into oblivion. I don't even have hands to wave good-bye to him.

But a sculptor has hands. She leaves something that tells the world she was there. She can look at it and remember who she is. Nevada can crawl into her sculpture; she can live in it. It's a portable womb; it's her whole universe if she wants it to be.

In the classroom at Bank Street I produce grade books, attendance records, lesson plans, notations in the margins of my students' papers in a language no one even wants to understand: COH, AGR, U,—coherence, agreement, unity—all things there aren't enough of—SUB—subordination—which there's too much of, scrawled hieroglyphics from the land of FB—fractured bureaucratese.

They used to call the women who worked on typewriters "typewriters." Imagine being a typewriter! At least you would know who you are and where you are—in front of a typewriter. Which is where I am, but sometimes I feel as if I'm in deep space without a star map, trying to pull Nevada's story out of my guts. I wonder if a star map could help me in there. I don't think there's anything that can make you feel more alone than sitting in front of a blank sheet of paper. No one else can do it for you. And you have to invent a whole universe. I wonder if God felt lonely when She invented this one. Is that why She did it? And where was Her husband?

In my agoraphobic days, I became used to depending on my husband for everything. He was so fused into my circuitry, that I could do nothing without him. To embark on the creation of this universe makes me feel like a heroine. I'll have to fill my backpack with everything I need to survive my journey—flashlight, candles and matches, sleeping bag, spare shoes, enough of the money of the countries I'm headed for to buy everything else. But I'm not sure what kind of money they use and I don't know if there's a universal coin, maybe a little iron disk with a hexagonal hole in the middle, that I could wear around my neck. That was always the kind of thing I would ask Aaron. If he didn't know, he would make it up.

But on this journey I have to do everything—invent the laws of physics, create a universal currency that I can make a necklace of, propitiate any preexisting gods, see if I need any licenses, learn how to navigate the bureaucratic license maze.

Another thing I envy about Nevada is her awakening sexuality. Playing the ceremonial virgin daughter of Madame's house is really starting to pall.

CHAPTER NINE

Sitting in a corner of The Orange Cat Bistro, I drink chamomile tea to try and calm Nevada down. Maybe if I can get her to relax, she'll come out and sit with me. The air's a bit smoky from the Gauloises of the regulars, but the black-and-white-tiled room is clean and spacious. We could be in Saratoga Springs, taking the waters.

"God is in the details," Nevada says to me, although she won't come out into the bright air to say it. She's quoting somebody she just read, but she won't tell me who it is. Or maybe she can't remember. When she gets too close to the dizzying air of Outside, her mind gets foggy. She stumbles on the stairs, breaks glasses, forgets her name. That never happens to me. Even when the pounding of my heart deafens me, my mouth amazingly keeps saying the right things.

Right now Nevada's taking her strength from my body. My

skin is the only thing separating her from Outside. You could say I'm a portable Thing. Still, she's not ready to come out and sit with me, though she would like her own cup of tea. It will be a long time before she'll be ready for a cup of Madame's espresso, strong enough to cause heart palpitations in the dead. But she's happy to be here.

"What do you mean, 'God is in the details'?" I ask.

Shyly she says, "I don't think you're fair to yourself about the value of what you do. It may be ephemeral compared to driving heavy earth-moving equipment, but that doesn't mean it's not real. I envy you for having such a powerful effect on people. People start reading because of you. They live their lives differently. You'll never know how many of your students' children you'll live on in. All I do is hang out in my sculpture and perfect my navel."

"You have an exceptionally lovely navel."

"You never could take a compliment, Claire."

"You know how hard it is for me," I tell her. "You hear the terrific things my students say to me. I hear them, too. Somehow they just don't get past my skin."

"Open up your skin." Nevada takes a sip of my tea.

"Do you want your own cup?" I ask. "I'm buying."

She disappears further inside. "I can afford my own tea." Her voice tickles me where I can't reach.

"Could you please scratch," I say. I'm too proud of my new-found normalcy to do any weird wriggling in front of the Bistro regulars.

"If you truly acknowledge the value of what you do."

"OK, OK, I acknowledge it. Now please scratch me wherever you are and rise. I promise I won't try and lure you out any farther than you're ready for. I hate itching where I didn't even know I had places. Ahhh, that's better. Thank you."

"And another thing," Nevada says, coming so close to the surface, I can almost see her. "Writing may not be what people think of as value, you may think writing is just words, but you can create worlds from words. 'In the beginning was the Word . . . and the Word was God.' You know that. Don't you remember anything important, or do you just think about all the bad things that have happened since you were twelve?"

I have to laugh. Nevada's got me there. I spend way too much time in my mind, stroking the bad memories. It feels so bad, it feels good. How can you stop peeling off the scab once you've lifted the edge?

"And another thing, what is all this about you envying my emerging sexuality?" Nevada says. "I thought you adored being the virgin daughter of Madame's household."

"When my ex-husband wanted to have sex, my reaction was a seriously bewildered: Why?" I say. "Can you imagine me coming from a place like that? And that was the problem. Not only didn't I come, I couldn't even imagine wanting to."

"If we're going to talk about sex, I think we should eat pastry," Nevada says, taking out a little gold compact and painting her lips red.

"Napoleons?"

"I had my mouth set for whipped cream, but napoleons would be appropriate."

Madame's granddaughter doesn't even blink when I order two napoleons. "Does this mean you're coming out?" I ask Nevada.

"We'll see."

"You know, I still miss him," I say. "I'm ashamed to admit it after what he did to me. It's not that my heart is open to him. It's just that it isn't closed."

Madame's granddaughter deposits two napoleons in front of me. I thank her and don't ask for an extra fork.

"I'm so ashamed of being left," I say. "I'm ashamed of turning into the kind of woman who gets left. I'm ashamed that I didn't love him enough, that I didn't make him happy, that I couldn't be satisfied by what he had to offer me, that I couldn't satisfy him."

"Maybe he couldn't be satisfied. I never thought your ex-husband had a talent for happiness," Nevada says. "But I thought we were going to eat pastry and talk about sex. Don't you want to have fun?"

"I don't know if I'm ready to have fun." I lick custard for her off my spoon. "If you really want to have fun, come out and eat your own pastry. There's a man over by the espresso machine who looks just like Gérard Depardieu."

"I can ogle him perfectly well from here, thank you. And I am enjoying the napoleon. Eat one for me."

"I'm going to get fat as Madame! If you want custard, you're going to have to come out and eat your own. Anyway, you were willing to go outside with Nicholas. Why not with me?"

"Actually, now that you mention it, I felt like a little baby bird being thrown out of the nest. You just thought nobody would want to read a novel about a woman who never goes out. Do you really think I'm crazy enough to go off with a stranger without even opening my eyes?"

"You like living on the edge," I say weakly. I had no idea Nevada was so strong-minded.

"The hell I do," Nevada says. "You know perfectly well what I like is being safe. What do you think Madame would say about such asinine behavior?"

I don't say anything. I know perfectly well what Madame would say. "All right, you don't have to do it if you don't want to."

"Well, I did want to find out what happens," Nevada says. "He seemed like a nice guy. Safe does get boring. And I was getting sick of Alec. You really saddled me with a loser there."

"I promise you Nicholas will be a nice guy. You can trust him. Even though we both acknowledge that no one should go off with strangers, especially without opening their eyes."

"I'm not sure you have as much control as you think," Nevada says. "But it's comforting to know you have good intentions. If you want, we can talk about your ex-husband until we both die of boredom."

"Well thank you. I haven't wanted to talk about this with Madame. I find her a bit intimidating, don't you? She confesses her weaknesses and doubts only to the priest. I can't imagine doing that, even if he does play chess here every Thursday."

Nevada nods. I love her intelligence. She's one of the few people I don't feel too smart around. Aaron was one of the others. With him I felt my mind was a gift, not something heavy and awkward that I had to drag around in my backpack—a pickled brain in a jar spilling formaldehyde all over my teasing comb and autographed photos of TV doctors.

"It just seems like such a waste, what I had with him is gone, shriveled, dried up and blown away. The friendship, the understanding, the jokes only we shared. He was my first reader. I don't know who to show this to."

"You got very cranky when you did show him your work. Don't you remember? He always had twenty-nine suggestions for revision, each of which would have taken at least six months to complete. And they were always some brilliant, off-the-wall idea from some parallel, noncontiguous universe."

I have to laugh. "Nevada, you can make enemies being such

a truth teller. You'd better be careful when you're out on the street."

"I'll be careful, if you'll let me be."

"You seem to do pretty much what you want."

"Well why don't you?" Nevada asks. "You're not married anymore. There's nobody trying to rewrite your life according to some bizarre deconstructionist theory."

"I am doing what I want."

"Well I wish you'd stop moping around about him and get on with it. One of the best things that happened to me was getting out of junior high. Do you remember the endless hours we spent going on about boys who couldn't have cared less? We imbued them with all sorts of magical qualities and abandoned our own magic. Please don't make me go back to that no-exit place."

"Talking about hopelessness, do you know what it feels like not to have been touched for months? You had sex with Alec last week."

"If you can call it sex. After I broke up with my husband, there was a long period of celibacy—I felt inviolate. That was before you knew me. But my skin doesn't have that needy hunger that yours does."

"Nevada's famous granite skin," I say. "How can you not long to be touched? I don't think about it when I've got it, but when I don't have it, it seems to fill up the whole world. My skin feels grey, grainy, as if I'm an old black-and-white photo of myself, deteriorating in the album, the glue drying up and blowing away."

"Ughh," Nevada says. "That sounds disgusting. I'm glad I'm not that needy. Men are dangerous to need."

"That's true," I concede, "but what's the percentage in needing the embrace of a granite sculpture?"

"It's a lot more reliable. You can count on it being there and staying there. Some of my best friends are rocks. They've got more personality than many people *and* are a lot more giving. People don't give minerals enough credit."

"You mean like diamonds are a girl's best friend?"

"I prefer granite."

"I prefer flesh. And hopefully before mine shrivels away."

"Well then, why don't you find yourself a lover? Your husband had one before he even walked out the door."

I look over at the men talking and playing chess by the zinc bar. They seem infinitely desirable in their variety, in the solidity of their shoulders, the jut of their chins, the way their jeans fit, even the old ones with softening necks and grey in their five o'-clock shadows. What could they possibly desire in someone as ancient as me? They probably all want the models they see in magazines—nineteen and smooth as Spandex.

"I don't know how to date anymore." I take a sip of our tea. "It's not like riding a bicycle. You know how you feel not quite ready to come out and sit with me? Well, that's how I feel about sex. I feel more fragile than I did in junior high. At least then I had my dreams. Now I have thirteen years of disillusionment under my belt. I didn't know that I would never meet a boy who even remotely resembled Dr. Kildare. At least I had something to look forward to, a perfect love that would transform me, lift me out of the tedium of junior high into a sphere of unimaginable bliss. Even though it never happened, even though it was a fantasy that caused me great harm, there was a wonderful purity about it. I wish I could walk out into the world of dating, armored in that innocence, today."

"Give me a break," Nevada says, sticking a finger down her throat and gagging.

"Come out if you're so tough," I say. "I'm trying to get at

something important. There's no point in writing off junior high because remembering it is painful and embarrassing."

Nevada doesn't say anything.

I'm tired of talking to her anyway. I'm not even sure she's still there. I'm sick of the whole subject. When I remember how much of my self I denied to stay married, the whole thing seems hopeless, at least as hopeless as junior high. At least then I didn't have wrinkles lining my eyes and grey in my brown hair.

I'm going to let Nevada do it for me. I'm not ready to go out there with my fragility, my grey hair, my years of failures out into the world of AIDS and serial killers and momma's boys and weekend daddies, whose kids will see me as the Wicked Witch of the West, just for a chance to ease the hungry longing in my skin. I want to stay the virgin daughter of Madame's household a little bit longer, even if I die of touch starvation. Let Nevada do it for me. Since she's so tough.

CHAPTER TEN

Nevada shivers. How long has it been since she's touched anyone? She doesn't care if she is in the middle of Hudson Street with a man she's just met and may never see. She doesn't care if Claire is pushing her into this. Maybe Claire is her friend.

Nicholas's mouth tastes of mints and garlic. Nevada rubs her nose up against the roughness of his cheek and inhales his cologne. Men's colognes are so much less shrill than women's, Nevada thinks, snuffling into Nicholas's neck. Is that the only way women can claim territory, their scent filling up space like a scream?

Nicholas smells like Royal Copenhagen. The noises and smells of Hudson Street lap lazily into her awareness, the car exhaust not quite wiping out Nicholas's subtle spiciness. "Do you always smell this nice, or were you going out to meet your ladyfriend?" she whispers into his ear.

"I was going out to meet you."

"I needed to be met." If she can just get him to keep holding her! Soon he'll start walking, and the smell of burning will fill her nostrils. Nevada shivers. She's got to get him off the street before her thinking gets out of control. "Can we go back to your apartment?"

"You're a remarkably trusting young lady," he says, "considering the times we live in."

"This would have been no less crazy in the sixties. People just thought it was cool to be crazy then. Now we think it's crazy to be crazy," Nevada says. "But it's OK. I have a guarantee of safety."

"What are you, a Mafia princess?"

"Do you think I look Italian?"

"No, but you don't look crazy either. Are you?"

"I'm not sure," she says. "How would I know?"

"I'm no expert on craziness, but I do know you shouldn't be this careless. Do you know how much trouble you could get into? I doubt you've even opened your eyes yet."

"How do you know I'm not going to do something unspeakable to *you*?"

"I'll take my chances."

"There you go. I think you're being very foolish. I could be a renegade martial arts master. I'm five times as strong as you think I am. Don't you know it's the little old man shuffling along in canvas slippers you have to watch out for? He may be five feet tall and so Zenned-out, you think you could knock him over with your breath. But he's the one who'll send you flying with a flick of his pinky. Anyway, what kind of muscles do you think it takes to sculpt granite?"

"I'd like to find out," he says.

"Well, let's go. This is New York. Pretty soon someone will try to charge us rent on our square foot of pavement."

Nicholas laughs, a deep laugh that Nevada likes a lot. Maybe Claire is going to do OK by her. Claire had better, or she's going to catch hell the next time they're in the same place.

"If you want to pretend it's the sixties, you'd better keep on keeping your eyes closed," Nicholas says, steering her who knows where. "But aren't you a little young to remember the sixties?"

"I've always felt that was my era. The sixties was so much more interesting than disco and corporate piracy. Why don't you hum some Beatles' songs or something," Nevada says through the air-sucking hole that's suddenly sprung up around her. Without Nicholas's arms holding her, she feels tenuous, a crumbly leaf, windblown through the streets of Manhattan. Is that the crackling of fire she hears? For the first time in hours she longs for her Thing, its cool, still inner reaches, its whiteness, like bone, like alabaster, a prehistoric color, the color of nothing. How she longs for cool, quiet white and not this spinning darkness that bristles with shooting stars and shapes that continually form and re-form themselves. How she longs for Nothingness, for God to take her up now, out of this life where all she's capable of feeling is dizziness and terror. If only she could crawl into her Nautilus Shell and carve another tiny goddess and listen to water drip down the cave wall. How cool and damp it would smell! How can she let Hassiloff hijack her Thing and leave her this defenseless?

Nicholas starts singing "Norwegian Wood" to her in a low, rich voice. She puts her hand on his resonant chest and it grounds her, enough to keep her feet moving in tandem with his.

"Where did you learn to use your lungs like that?" she asks, when he finishes the song.

"I'm an opera singer," he says, and launches into a lieder version of "I Want to Hold Your Hand."

She smiles and lets him play with her hand as he leads her along. Imagine being brave enough to get up on a stage in front of hundreds of strangers! Could he teach her proper breathing techniques?

Nicholas guides her across a broad noisy street. Nevada hears the sound of coins jingling, then feels a paper cone thrust into her hand. She fills her nose with the spicy scent of carnations. The ferns tickle her nose and she sneezes.

"The pink ones have deep red centers." Nicholas puts his hand under her elbow and they continue east. "And the green ferns make them look like Christmas *and* summer. They look like Finland."

"Are you Finnish?" Claire's found her a man who not only buys flowers, but can talk about them.

"Do I look Finnish?"

"That's not fair," Nevada says. "You know I'm not supposed to open my eyes."

"Whose rules are we following?"

"Yours. Don't you remember. You said I should keep on keeping my eyes closed."

"Only if you want to pretend it's the sixties. Anyway you don't seem like the kind of woman who lets men set the rules."

"You're right. I don't. Or," she says, thinking of Alec's bedroom rules, "I shouldn't. I'll stop right now." She takes a deep breath. "I'm keeping my eyes closed because I'm agoraphobic. If I open them, the world will tilt and I'll slide off the edge."

"You're telling the truth, aren't you?" Nicholas says. He increases the pressure on her arm, but it doesn't begin to be enough support.

A wave of dizziness washes over Nevada. As she'd always suspected, talking about it only makes it worse. She'd rather Nicholas saw her as a madcap heroine from a thirties novel than as *damaged*. Why did she have to tell him? Claire made her do it. Wait till she gets back to The Orange Cat Bistro!

"Is there a tree around or something?" she asks. "I think I'm going to faint."

Nicholas leads her over to a spindly street tree. Nevada drapes herself around it and tries to stay upright. If she sinks down to the earth, which is what her spinning head wants her to do, she's going to end up covered with who knows what. She lets out a shaky laugh. "This isn't exactly a mighty oak, is it?"

"There's a nice café, nearby," Nicholas says. "It's quiet there. We could sit down and have a glass of wine."

"That sounds good," Nevada says faintly. "Only I don't know if I can cross any more streets. The traffic sounds so predatory."

"Pretend you're a hologram." Nicholas strokes her shoulder. "Then the traffic will flow right through you."

"Hmmm, that's not bad," Nevada says. She lets go of the tree and gropes for Nicholas's arm. He's right. If she lets the traffic in, it flows right out the other side. "I could make a sculpture of this," she says. "It's really a very good idea."

CHAPTER ELEVEN

I'm drinking café au lait at my usual table, shyly watching Madame's handyman replace damaged ceiling tiles. The way his muscles strain against his blue shirt makes me feel lonely. I'm about to take a bite of my croques monsieur when Nevada walks in the door with Nicholas. Staggers in, I should say. I hope I never looked that far gone. She looks as though she's going to implode if someone doesn't put her to bed. Although even bed, when you're feeling that terrified, is not the refuge you hoped for. I could take her upstairs to my room. My grass- and lavender-scented sheets might shift her emotional chemistry. But I don't want to take her out of the game just yet. She just feels like she's going to die. She won't. Believe me, I know.

Nicholas seats her at a table near the garden. The back door is open, letting in the scent of green things growing, fresh and damp and earthy. It smells as if the mushrooms Madame puts in her boeuf bourguignon grow wild out there. Nevada puts her head down on the cool marble table. I envy her, despite her dizziness and terror. I don't think I could conjure up a man to pay attention to me.

Nicholas is more handsome than I expected. His head is leonine with a longish blond mane. I could have sworn he would be dark. And he's not academic scruffy as I had imagined. It's obvious that he's a man used to being on stage. He's a bit archaic, a bit classical—not a nineties man. What other surprises does he have in store for us?

Nicholas fusses over Nevada, bringing her wine, rubbing her shoulders. Nevada's too far gone to appreciate it. All she wants is to be back in her loft. All I want is to be the one receiving Nicholas's attention or maybe to be young and stunning enough to bring the handyman down from his ladder. He would throw himself at my feet and declare his undying lust, risking Madame's wrath, or would she smile benignly? He would kiss his way from my feet up my legs, pushing my knees open, kissing ever onward, pushing his lean, muscular body in between my thighs. Nevada, of course, is prettier and thinner and younger and, for her, all is possible. *If* she can just pull herself together.

I sigh and push my sandwich away. To tell you the truth, I could do without this touch hunger. I liked it better when I was content with my narrow white bed, when I was thrilled to be doing what normal people do without thinking: walking through the streets of the city, cruising the supermarket, negotiating a restaurant. But a man's attention would bring such satisfaction to the craving in my bones. Did Crazy Jane get in as much trouble believing that as I do? Probably, if you can believe Yeats.

Still I'd rather be me than Nevada right now. There's nothing worse than feeling what she's feeling. Even being raped doesn't feel that bad. You get raped, it takes maybe twenty minutes, an hour, and it's over. You go home and take a bath, get the tests. If you think you can, you try to put the guy away. Then you put it behind you. The way Nevada feels, it's as if she's in a constant state of rape, as if the whole world could rape her at any moment. It's as if there are countless erect penises, invisible to everyone but her, leering at her from doorways, trains, the street, the sky. These are disembodied penises, you understand. They're not attached to men. It's as if the trains, the street, the sky themselves could rape her, and there's no way she can protect herself. No amount of being a good girl, placating men, trying to live a safe life can protect her. The penises are everywhere. And they never have enough, they never detumesce, they never come.

Nevada's sipping her wine now, looking a little better. The color's coming back into her cheeks. Am I guilty of character abuse? Should I have left her safe in her loft with that pervert Alec? But staying there would have been like entombing her alive with her fears and the stink of her fear-sweat. She should thank me for breaking into her bricked-in chamber. Surely the chance to come alive is worth feeling as terrified as she does. I don't care what she says. I'm not doing this just because people won't read about a woman who never leaves the house. I could make that an interesting book, if I wanted to. There's nothing I like more than a technical challenge. I'm risking far more writing all this peculiar stuff—a sky stuffed with penises? Everyone is going to think I'm weird.

I could have let her stay in her loft, making tea for her friends, potting pretty cups and vases, being a lady, being circumscribed, letting Alec disarm her forever. I'd rather give her bionic armaments than lady-arms, which can bear only cups of tea and comfort. I'd rather she bore arms, high-power rifles hidden under the ultraflesh. For fingernails, flesh-ripping hooks painted bright red. Would that be enough to give her courage? Or would that just be letting us be co-opted by a universe of testosterone gone wild?

Nicholas walks past me on his way to the men's room. He looks right through me, though I can't keep myself from staring at him. To him I'm just another middle-aged woman. It's Nevada he's fascinated by. If she weren't so young and pretty, would he accept her craziness? He would probably have left her on Hudson Street and walked on to wherever he was going. But I would have taken care of her. I will take care of her. She can't help being young and pretty and fascinating to men. She'll get over it.

CHAPTER TWELVE

"I'm not sure this is such a great idea," Nevada says faintly, as Nicholas leads her out of The Orange Cat Bistro.

"What, dear?"

"The whole thing. Being Out. I'm losing my focus. I can't remember why I wanted to be out here. The wine's making my head fuzzy." At the edge of the fuzz, greasy smoke curls into blue sky.

"Do you want me to take you home?"

Nevada thinks about that, taking momentary shelter in the doorway of The Orange Cat Bistro. How *does* Madame get the Manhattan sun to beat so powerfully on her plate glass windows? You would never believe you were in Manhattan if you chose not to look beyond Madame's white lace curtains. You would think you were in some small provincial city in France or even Belgium. Some boring but gloriously safe little city, still mired in the fifties.

Not that she's choosing to look at *anything* just yet. But she can feel the sun beating on her closed eyelids, clearing away the fuzz.

Does she want to go back to the loft like a retreating army, leaving the field to the conqueror? Who is? Her fear? The world? It would be one thing to let the world have a chance to conquer her. The world is so big and complex. But to let her own fear lay her low! The walls would close in on her so fast, her brains would squeeze out her ears. Where *did* she hear about people eating monkey brains right out of the skulls of live monkeys? They were supposed to be a great delicacy.

Nevada shivers. She doesn't need to think about people eating monkey brains or smell that swirl of smoke in the corner of her mind. She needs to make a decision. She doesn't want to make sweet Nicholas impatient. If she goes back now, it will only make it worse next time, if there even is a next time. She'll be making herself a meal for Alec to feast on. She'll pluck and spit and roast herself, lay herself on the platter and look up at him with big goose-girl eyes. "Eat me," she'll say. "Eat me up." And he'll be more than ready, tucking a napkin under his chin, his mouth shining with grease as he falls to. "Where's the peas?" he'll bellow. And she won't be able to tell him, because she'll be all eaten up. She's not a self-renewing resource. Someone has to start thinking about the ecology.

She's tired of not being allowed to touch him. She's tired of having her arms tied behind her back. *Why has she been consenting to this?*

"If I walk back in there, I might never walk out," she says. "Let's keep going."

"Did you ever consider doing this more gently?" Nicholas asks, leading her east. "Getting a quart of milk one day. The next day going to the park for half an hour. Taking the bus a couple of miles, the day after that."

"That would make sense," Nevada says. "But the walls are so thick. I'm afraid they won't budge unless I blast them with dynamite."

"I get the feeling you see yourself as a coward, but there's nothing braver than facing your fears," Nicholas says, squeezing her arm. "Even though it may not feel too good. You should give yourself a lot of credit for what you're doing."

"I don't feel very brave," Nevada says, smiling weakly. "I'm shaking and I can't even open my eyes. But I see your point. Tell me, do you pick up baby birds with broken wings?"

"Is it that obvious?"

" 'Fraid so."

"But there's not much call for it in Manhattan. In Yonkers, where I grew up, wounded birds were always dropping out of the sky."

"I guess I'm your wounded city bird. But don't make a goose of me."

"You have a great deal of natural dignity. I can't imagine anyone making a goose of you."

Nevada wonders why Alec never noticed her natural dignity. Or maybe he did, and it just made him want to humiliate her more. Some men find that fat white waddling goose butt such a turn-on. "That's the nicest compliment I've ever received," Nevada says, her cheeks glowing. Can Nicholas really be *this* good? It was amazing how Alec, the perfect bodyguard, became Alec, the perfect abusive boyfriend.

Nicholas squeezes her arm. "Tell me, what are you afraid of seeing?"

"I guess the way things are." She doesn't add, "your eyes."

"You're not big on reality."

"Are you?"

"If I could pick my times and places."

"In a way we aren't really that different." Nevada buttons her jacket up to her neck. "You're just willing to let in a little more of it. I like to create my own reality in my loft, in my art, with my friends. How do you handle the streets? There's so much suffering. It just keeps getting worse and worse—the homeless camping out in doorways, the addicts panhandling, wearing those fingerless gloves, but their hands are so filthy you can hardly tell where their skin leaves off and the gloves begin." Nevada takes a deep breath as she sees a pair of smoke-stained hands reach toward her. "It's as if their skin itself has turned into filthy matted wool. How can anyone let themselves sink that low? Even animals keep themselves clean. And I feel like such a bitch saying that, someone who doesn't understand how easy it is to fall off the edge of the universe. I'm not blaming the homeless—it's the addicts I can't understand. It seems as if they have a choice. And their choice would be to kill me for a quarter." She shivers. "It feels so overwhelming. How do *you* stay open and compassionate?"

"Some people cope with it by shutting it out," Nicholas says, steering her around a panhandler who smells so ripe she has to hold her breath. "They just shut it out of their minds and even out of their vision. Don't you think that's better than locking yourself into a prison the way you have? It's a way of coping."

"I can't shut it all out and stay open for my art. I can't shut myself on and off. I don't know how people do it every day, being Out with their eyes open. Maybe they numb themselves with booze or shopping or television. I guess there's a hundred ways to drug yourself. Anyway, on the street, you have to stay alert. It would be suicide to shut it out."

"You could try to help," Nicholas says, his clear, deep voice cutting through the panicky images in her mind. "That's how I deal with it—by volunteering at a homeless shelter when my performing schedule allows."

"I really admire you," Nevada says. "But even with people like you, there's *still* so much suffering. I'm afraid I'll drown if I let it in."

"You do what you can do, right where you are," Nicholas says. "I know I've helped people. I know their names. I know the dinners they've eaten because of me. I know the apartments that a few have found. If you wait till you think of a way to save everybody, you end up paralyzed. You don't have to be God. All you have to do is what you can. All you have to do is something."

"I wish I could bear the thought of even opening my eyes."

"Why not take it one step at a time? Give yourself credit for being out. Next time you can open your eyes."

"How did you get so sensible?" Nevada says. "I'm going to do what you say. I'll just keep putting one foot in front of the other. I won't even start thinking about the newspaper."

CHAPTER THIRTEEN

"You know, my plan was to stay Out for as long as possible," Nevada says to Nicholas as they get close to his apartment. "Sheltering in restaurants and apartments is going to defeat my purpose. I can cocoon just as easily in your apartment as in mine. I don't want to create islands of safety in a sea of fear. I want to get comfortable swimming naked in the sea. I want to be a drop of water in the ocean. I want to be a Zen mermaid."

"Don't you think you're making this harder on yourself than you have to?" Nicholas says as he puts her hand on the iron railing of his stoop. But he has to smile at the thought of Nevada as a Zen mermaid.

"Warriorship is the only possible path for a coward," Nevada says, feeling for the step. The concrete is a little cold, but it is almost stoop-sitting time. "Where are we?"

"East Sixth Street. Outside my building. And you're not a coward."

"Right," Nevada says. "East Sixth Street. A good place to be brave. What's that awful smell?"

"There's a meat packing plant on the next block. You get used to it. Unfortunately."

"Animal fear must be even worse than ours," Nevada says. "There's no way out of those pens. Animals can't lose themselves in fantasy and daydreams like humans can." The smell is almost unbearable, but she wants to lose herself in it. "I want to immerse myself in Outside until there's nothing left to be afraid of."

"When you're dead, there's nothing left to be afraid of." Nicholas pulls a handkerchief out of his pocket, spreads it on the stoop.

"Maybe," Nevada says. "Maybe you enter a realm where all your fears solidify like some campy old 'Twilight Zone' episode. But only if you allowed your fears to dominate your life when you were alive. I don't want that to happen to me. I don't want to be known in supernatural circles as the Coward of Eternity."

"What are you going to do," Nicholas asks, carefully sitting on his handkerchief. "Live on the street?" Nevada nods uncertainly.

"You know, Nevada, there are real things to be afraid of. They're not all in your imagination. There is a world. You could create the very things you're afraid of. You could make yourself dead in a hurry."

"There isn't anything specific I am afraid of," Nevada says. "Not even death. I wish there were—dogs or spiders or elevators or something. That I could cope with, some concrete thing to focus the full force of my anxiety on. Then the rest of my life could be an anxiety-free zone. I could put up 'Don't Exercise Caution' signs."

Nicholas smiles, then frowns. "I'm sure if you wanted to torment yourself with a fear of some rare breed of spider found only in one small village in Outer Mongolia, you'd be imagining them everywhere."

"Are you getting exasperated with me?" Nevada asks, running her hand along the rough concrete of the stoop.

"There really is a world out there and it really can hurt you. Do you have any idea what you're getting yourself into? You shouldn't be going home with a stranger. Didn't your mother teach you anything?"

"Haven't we been all through this?" Nevada says, pushing down her own doubts about this man she hasn't even seen. "Haven't you steered me safely through the streets? When you're blind, you have to surrender and trust. You should try it. It's what I need to do—surrender to life. I want to invite life to devour me. I want to stop preserving myself like some thrifty virgin whose time has passed. You know how people save their best clothes and china and even rooms, and never get the good of them? I don't want my life to be an unused parlor. I don't want to show up at God's door and say, 'Here I am, good as new.' God wants to see that life got some good out of you, that you let life eat you."

"You seem to be on very familiar terms with God." Nicholas shifts on the hard step.

"I'd like to be. I feel like I can hear God better out here, even with my eyes closed. I *have* to keep going."

"Isn't there someone who takes care of you? Someone who would keep you from doing something this foolish?"

"Well, there is someone," Nevada says. "But he's away. And he would never stop me from doing something foolish. He'd encourage me, just to see what happened. Then, if he found it bizarre enough, he'd paint it."

"Oh, an artist," Nicholas says.

"What's that supposed to mean?"

"Whatever you want it to mean."

"I'm an artist. You're an artist." Nevada leans against the iron railing.

"There are artists and there are artists."

"Stop being enigmatic."

"You should have told me you had a boyfriend."

"He's not exactly a boyfriend."

"What exactly is he?"

"He's what I've been letting devour me instead of life."

"Stop being enigmatic."

"I'll stop if you'll stop."

"That's mature."

"I don't want to be mature. Mature is preserving yourself. Mature is always wearing a watch and always checking it to see how your time is going. And it's going, believe me it's going." Nevada unbuckles her wristwatch and swings it in front of where she thinks Nicholas's eyes are. "I don't know why I didn't take this off when I left my loft. Time is draining away through this watch. You know how water circles the drain in the tub, then gets sucked down into some mysterious realm of dead time?" She swings the watch in wider and wider arcs until it flies out into the street. "There! My wrist is a thousand pounds lighter."

"That's the first sensible thing I've seen you do," Nicholas says. He unbuckles his own watch and tucks it in his jacket's innermost pocket. "I'm emulating you. Now we're time-free."

"Is that like being home free?" Nevada asks. "Let's be home

free in the park. I don't want to go inside yet." She feels drunk on the air, drunk on being Outside.

"On one condition."

"What's that?"

"We vow not to use any time references."

"I never use time references."

"You just said, 'just yet.' "

"Oh pooh. I just said that so you wouldn't get uptight about my wanting to stay out. 'Just yet' is so vague, it's practically meaningless. We could stay out a few 'moments' or for the rest of our many lives."

"You like to play fast and loose with meaning," Nicholas says. "How can I trust anything you say?"

"First of all, I already told you, you have as much to fear from me as I do from you. Surely you saw *Fatal Attraction*? Second, I'm a sculptor, not a writer. Language is not my medium. It's too plastic. It squirms around too much. I like stone. It's solid. You know where you're at with a block of stone."

"I suppose I should be happy that you want to go to the park rather than to a strange man's apartment. It *will* be light for a while. Come on. We can catch a cab on Third Avenue. I don't think you're ready for the subway."

Nevada scrambles to her feet. It's been a long time since she's been someplace green. "I could too handle the subway," she says. "I'm a warrior."

CHAPTER FOURTEEN

"Spring's afoot," Nicholas says to Nevada as he leads her into Central Park. "It's time to open your eyes."

"I don't need eyes to know that," Nevada says. "I can feel it on my skin. I can smell damp loamy earth and new grass. And in the nastiest city in the world!"

"New York's hardly the nastiest city in the world, my dear. I almost lost my voice when we toured Eastern Europe. The pollution there is incredible! And so sad for those who imagine Europe to be an illustrated fairy tale."

" 'And for all this nature is never spent./There lives the dearest freshness deep down things.' You know what I mean?" Nevada laughs and inhales the sweet park air.

"I'd like to believe it."

"You're my guide. You're the one who's willing to live in reality. Surely that means you're a hopeful, optimistic person. Don't you believe in life's continuing ability to renew itself?"

"I'm not sure I really think about it all that much." Nicholas steers her down a twisting path. The ground feels rough and rocky under her feet. "I do what I have to do and what I can do. When there's somebody in front of me who's suffering, I try to help them. I try to do the things that make me happy, like singing. Life is simple when you're singing. You just sing. Maybe it's a mistake to think so much."

Nevada's stomach lurches. Men are always telling her she thinks too much. Why don't they think more? What does Nicholas think she is—some piece of fluff he picked up in an elevator? Or is that what he wishes she were? Just when she starts talking about what most matters, some man tells her she thinks too much. Should she play Barbie doll when she emerges from her Thing? Or give up her fruitless efforts to relate and have herself permanently installed in her Thing. Hassiloff's so desperate to get his hands on it, he might agree to her becoming Priestess in Residence.

"You know if you think too much, you'll never do anything," Nicholas says. "If I thought too much about going onstage, I couldn't do it. So I just go out and sing. How many people could do what they do if they thought about it? How many people would have children, write a novel, get married, if they really thought about the consequences? No one would do anything."

"Maybe that would be an improvement. Just think of all the things that wouldn't happen—war, rape, committee meetings."

"Yes, but nothing good would happen either. And nothing necessary." He settles her on a bench near the lake. "There aren't many people around. We ought to have some privacy, for a while."

Nevada can smell pine needles and hear ducks. Probably no

one would accuse *them* of thinking too much. "So, you're one of those people who doesn't trust the universe to take care of itself," she says, determined to be as thoughtful as possible. If he can't take it, she might as well know now.

"You trust the universe to take care of itself?"

"I didn't say that. But it is a position I admire. It's a position I would like to emulate. Such a wonderful word—emulate." Nevada leans back, feeling the sun soaking through her denim. "Thank you for bringing it back into my life. Just imagine having that kind of high wire faith! Imagine having faith."

"It takes faith to do the smallest everyday things." Nicholas picks up a flat stone and sends it skipping over the lake. "It takes faith to breathe. It takes faith to keep putting food in your mouth and chewing it. And it takes highly developed, self-conscious faith to be a sculptor."

"I don't know," Nevada says thoughtfully. "I just keep on keeping on. I just keep on putting food in my mouth and chewing it. I keep on carving because it's the only thing that really makes me happy. And you know what's weird? It makes other people happy, too. People love to caress the carvings in my Thing and watch the light change."

"It sounds like we're coming from the same place," Nicholas says, putting his arm around her. Nevada likes the way it feels, solid and like maybe she's not alone. He's not really antithought. He just likes to be sensible. She snuggles into him and he kisses her face, he rains kisses on her cheeks and forehead and the top of her head. Everywhere but her mouth. When is he going to kiss her mouth? Her mouth is a strawberry with a terrible longing to be eaten—by Nicholas, not by the universe. And certainly not by Alec, who's eaten enough of her to last a long, very long, lifetime.

"I don't know if we're coming from the same place—that

would be too weird for words," she says. "But maybe we're going to the same place. I'd like that."

"And where would that be, my dear?"

She snuggles in closer. "Your apartment?"

"I thought you were thinking in more cosmic terms," Nicholas says as he stops kissing her.

Nevada's face feels cold and unloved as the spring wind blows over the spots Nicholas kissed. What is it with these nineties guys? They have to learn to let the universe eat them. He's more scared of her than she is of him. "I could be thinking in more cosmic terms," she says cagily. "What did you have in mind?"

"I was thinking about faith," Nicholas says. "Living a life filled with faith. Maybe living that life with another person."

"Now who's thinking too much?" Nevada says. She just wants to get kissed. She wants to shelter in Nicholas's arms, have his deep voice block out the flames that crackle constantly in the back of her mind. She gets back into kissing position. "Who wants to talk at a time like this? Especially about abstract stuff like faith."

"Faith isn't abstract to a Catholic," Nicholas says sternly. "Faith is a warm, living thing." He doesn't take his arm away, but it feels as if it's no longer really there. The crackle of flames grows louder.

"Don't you want to be my sex object?" Nevada says, wriggling up against him and breathing more easily as the flames recede.

"I thought I was making myself clear. No."

Alec would have laughed. Nicholas may be sweeter, if he's for real, but he doesn't have much of a sense of humor. And the flames are sucking up the air again. Nevada takes a deep breath, but it doesn't help. "Are you afraid I have a communicable disease, or something?"

"Yes, actually. But don't take it personally."

"Well, I doubt I have any creepy diseases. I never leave the house."

"What about your boyfriend?"

Nevada considers that. Should she tell him that Alec can't use his love toy for anything useful to a lady? "I really doubt Alec's gotten himself into that kind of trouble."

"But you don't know."

"No, I don't know. But what about your plea for faith?"

"There's faith and there's foolishness. And then there's blood tests."

Nevada thinks about that. Does she want to get the tests? Nicholas is right. But imagine getting a positive result and having to live with it. It isn't as if there's much you can do about AIDS. She'd really rather not know. Sex isn't worth all this trouble. She barely knows this guy. She doesn't even know what he *looks* like. He could be covered with scabs.

It's a long way home. How is she going to get there if Nicholas doesn't take her? Could she make it out to Fifth Avenue and catch a cab? She'd have to open her eyes and let in the full catastrophe. Maybe Nicholas is right, and the way to do this is gradually. When she's fifty, she might be ready to open her eyes. For now, since she's four traffic-snarled miles from home, she'd better be nice to Nicholas, who deserves it.

She touches Nicholas's arm. She loves the rough woolly feel of his jacket. "I'm sorry I teased you. I was just trying to make you laugh."

Nicholas lets his arm reconnect with her shoulder. His laugh is a little bit forced. "There. You succeeded. I *could* use a laugh."

"The whole world could," Nevada says. "And if I could make everyone laugh, a good deep belly laugh, I'd get them to throw away their watches. Especially those watches that beep when you're making love." She lets her hand linger on his jacket, keeping her touch light and limited to wool. "Did you ever think about the word alarm? Isn't it incredible that we allow ourselves to be 'alarmed' awake every morning? No wonder I find the world so alarming. Not that I wake up that way, but the ones who do set the tone for the rest of us. What a way to enter the world every blessed morning!"

"I agree with you, but surely you don't want to dictate the way everyone lives their lives." Lightly Nicholas strokes her shoulder.

"They try to dictate the way I live mine. Or at least they create a world I'm supposed to live in. The World as defined by the *New York Times*—if that's the world, I'd rather have myself bricked up in my Thing."

"You want to be a fascist of flow?"

"Sure. Only I'd make sure the trains didn't run on time."

Nicholas laughs. "That's fine for you—a solitary artist can live by her own rhythms, but a performing artist has to stay in synch with the rest of the world."

"So how come you threw away your watch?"

"Well," he admits, "I actually tucked it away. It was a gift."

"You don't have to explain," Nevada says. "But keep in mind, you have a ticking time bomb next to your heart."

"Don't you think most people want to throw their watches into next week?"

"Well why don't they?" Nevada says. "Why don't we start a grass roots movement—The Clock Punchers' Association?"

"Time isn't the enemy," Nicholas says, hoping it's true.

"Look at how much of music is about keeping time. And I still say there are things worth doing. If they're things that require more than one person, those people need a way to keep time."

"If no one did anything," Nevada says, "the newspapers would go out of business. Then we could create a world that wasn't defined by an insatiable appetite for disaster and gossip."

"And what would your *Clock Punchers' Journal* report on?"

"First of all I don't see why we need a newspaper at all," Nevada says. "But if you insist on having one, it could report on things like answered prayers, epiphanies, the triumph of love over cynicism, The Poems Written Today tally. You know, interesting stuff."

"Sounds like an award-winning paper to me." Nicholas takes some crackers out of his pocket and offers them to a squirrel. "And a big seller. The alcohol and tobacco companies are sure to take out big contracts."

"Laugh if you like, but wouldn't you rather live in the world as defined by my paper than in the world of the *New York Times?*"

"It sounds like a cross between the *Church Times* and the *Ladies' Home Journal.*"

"What's wrong with that?"

"What about evil? What about tragedies? Evil flourishes in secrecy." Nicholas succeeds in coaxing a squirrel to take a cracker from his hand. "If you don't know about tragedies, you can't help those in need."

"Maybe evil flourishes in a world that's obsessed with it," Nevada says. Why *is* Nicholas so interested in evil?

"So in the world as defined by the *Clock Punchers' Journal,* would you be willing to open your eyes?"

"Definitely."

"I wish I could create that world for you," Nicholas says, gently touching her hair.

"That's very sweet." She suspects most men would find the world of the *Clock Punchers' Journal* dull. Nicholas is really worth cultivating. She grasps the edge of Nicholas's sleeve. His jacket is starting to seem like home. She wishes she could crawl into it. "What color is this lovely woolly scratchy thing, anyway?"

"Tweed."

"Like those birds I hear?"

"Exactly," he says. "Greys and browns and flecks of green."

"Cool." She tries to feel the colors with her fingertips.

"You mean you haven't peeked?"

"Nope."

"With an iron will like that, you could do anything."

"Don't admire me," Nevada says. "I wish people would stop telling me how strong I am and what incredible things I could do if I would only own it."

"Maybe it is time for you to open your eyes. There's nothing horrible around; we're practically alone. There are some wonderful mustard gold seedpods."

"I don't know," Nevada says. "I'm enjoying my visionless quest. Who knows what will show up next? Why don't you bring me some seedpods? Maybe I can feel the color with my fingers. I'm not doing too well with your jacket, but with pods, who knows?"

Nicholas's arm disengages from her shoulder. The hollow sound of a rope striking a flagpole creates an echoing silence. Doves make mournful dove sounds, and then Nicholas's solid footsteps return. He opens her palm and deposits some tiny lozenges. They feel velvety, but her fingers are definitely color blind.

"You really should open your eyes," Nicholas says. "There

are some first flowers out—trees full of delicate yellow new growth. It's too good to miss."

"I can't open my eyes yet," Nevada says. "If I unwrap you now, what will I have to look forward to? I'm saving my first glimpse of you as a special present."

"I hope I don't turn out to be the coal in the bottom of your stocking."

"I'm sure you'll be the best present under the tree—an FAO Schwartz life-size lion."

"You're more than kind, my dear, but there's a whole world of things to look forward to."

She tries to roll her eyes, but it doesn't work when they're shut tight.

"If you're not willing to look at the ugliness of the world, you miss the beauty too," Nicholas says.

"Thank you, Dr. Brothers."

"You really ought to see this."

"What?"

"Take a look."

"It's easy for you to say. You're not a cripple."

"Neither are you."

"If you were my shrink, I'd be thinking of suing you around now."

"Good thing I'm not."

"Did you used to throw your little wounded baby birds out of the nest before they were ready?"

"Never."

"Well I'm more complicated than a bird."

"More stubborn, too."

"You don't know the half of it. Even if I *wanted* to open my eyes, I wouldn't give you the satisfaction."

"What happened to that sensible girl who threw out her watch? Why don't you do something I like again?"

"I stopped trying to seduce you."

"That's true. OK, I'll tell you. There's a black lace brassiere stretched around a tree."

"Demi or full cut?"

Nicholas looks closer. "It's one of those push-up things."

"Do you think it belongs to a naiad?"

"I'm sure of it."

"You're right," Nevada says. "That's definitely worth opening your eyes for."

"I don't see you doing it."

"I'm having too much fun."

"That's great." Nicholas smiles. "You're out in the world, and you're having fun."

"Yes, but I haven't opened my eyes yet."

"But you're not hiding in your Thing and you're having fun. With me! Why don't you acknowledge it?"

"OK, I acknowledge it. I'm having fun. This never would have happened if I hadn't left the loft. The truth is, now I *never* want to leave the park. Could we live here? Are we near one of those stone bridges, you know the kind poets slept under in French movies?"

"Yes, we're near an old stone bridge. No, we can't sleep under it, and we can't live here. This is not a movie, and it's going to be cold soon."

"I want to stay."

"You can't. I'm not sleeping in the park, and I'm not leaving you here alone. There are people living here who have nothing to lose."

"I thought it was your mission to rescue lost souls," Nevada says stubbornly. Why does he want her to leave just when she's starting to feel comfortable in public space? Is this some subtle game? She might even be ready to open her eyes if they stayed another couple of hours.

"My mission is to rescue wounded birds. I'm not a saint. Or a fool."

"Would you rescue a wounded vulture?" Nevada asks, fingering the velvety lozenges.

"Not if it's carrying a sawed-off shotgun."

"Are you going to force your protection on me?"

"If you want to put it that way."

"Where are we going to go?"

"My apartment."

"You trust me?" Nevada says.

"Yes, I trust you not to rape me." Nicholas takes her arm. "I like talking to you. I like your ideas. I'm not sure you can live by them, but they do make a twisted kind of sense. Come home with me and I'll make you the best pasta primavera you ever ate."

"Can we take the subway?"

"I don't think I can handle you *and* the subway. You'll probably like it so much, you'll want to sleep *there*. When you can open your eyes, we'll ride all the way from Coney Island to 241st Street."

"Promise?" Nevada gets up when he says yes. She prepares to start putting one foot in front of the other. She's going to be in a whole new place soon.

CHAPTER FIFTEEN

"Having fun?" I ask Nevada, turning away from Madame's elegant old Underwood. Nevada sits cross-legged on my iron bed, shaping her nails with an emery board. A week away from the Thing and her nails are already worth rehabilitating.

"Doing my nails is always a peak experience for me. Orgasmic, in fact."

"You know what I mean."

Nevada puts her emery board down. "Yes, actually, I am having fun. It was getting claustrophobic in the loft. There's a surprising amount of fresh air out here in the world. Your world, that is. And Nicholas is terrific. So far, anyway."

"Our world." I take the last page of Chapter Fourteen out of the typewriter and put it in a folder.

"Whatever," Nevada says. "How long do you mean to keep

up this blind girl thing? It's fun, but I can't wait to see what Nicholas looks like."

"He's cute," I say gloomily. "I don't know how long I'm going to keep it up. How long can you stand it?"

"I didn't think I could do it *this* long, but it's taken on a life of its own. Now I feel like I could do it forever. But I didn't know I had a say in this. I thought you pretty much did what you wanted."

"That's a horrible thing to say. I think of you constantly. Much more than I want."

"That's nice." Nevada takes a bottle of nail polish out of her bag, strokes some red onto her left hand, and holds it up to admire.

"I didn't think you were the nail polish type." Holding my breath, I run over to the window and throw it open.

"What's wrong with polishing your nails? The last time my nails looked this good was when I sprained my wrist rollerblading and couldn't sculpt for six weeks. I might as well take advantage of it. I mean sooner or later you *are* going to let me get back to work, aren't you?"

"I suppose." I stick my head out into the night and take some deep breaths.

"You wouldn't make it for five minutes in my studio," Nevada laughs. "Especially when Alec's painting."

"I like the smell of paint. At least you know it's in the air because art is being created."

"Well, *excuse me.*" Nevada starts on the nails of her right hand. "If you'd left me on my own, I'd be sculpting now. Now all I have to work on is my body."

"You look very pretty," I admit. "But I thought you were more of a plain Jane."

"Apparently not."

"You never used to be this way."

"This is the only canvas you've left me," Nevada says. "I miss working with my hands."

"Why don't you buy a sketch pad?"

"Maybe I will, when you give me a guarantee of sight." Nevada waves her nails in the air. "But I do have a date. Since I can't see, I might as well look nice."

I sit back down at my desk and let my head sink onto the typewriter. If only I could crawl into it the way Nevada crawls into her Thing. Nevada has all the luck.

"Why are you so down?" Nevada asks. "The book's going great. Isn't that what you wanted?"

"I wish I had a hot date."

"You can have mine," Nevada laughs. "If you'll let me have my Thing back."

"You'd rather crawl back into the Thing than go out with Nicholas?"

"Can't I have both?" Nevada says, taking a pair of false eyelashes out of her makeup kit.

"That is the age-old question isn't it?" The typewriter makes a hard pillow but is somehow comforting.

"How come you get to immerse yourself in your book, and I get to have the date? Why can't we both have both?"

"That's the contract," I say.

"Let's change the contract."

"It isn't done."

"Well then why don't you take satisfaction in writing your book and I'll take satisfaction in being with Nicholas?" Nevada walks over to the mahogany vanity to apply her eyelashes.

"Ah, taking satisfaction in what you have on your plate. A

neat trick." Idly I strike at the typewriter keys. "When you figure out how to do it, be sure to let me know."

"You just do it."

"Thank you, oh Wise Woman. Don't forget to put in a good word for me with the Goddess, the next time you happen to see Her."

Nevada ignores me. "So what's stopping you from going out and getting *yourself* a hot date?"

"You don't know anything about it, Nevada. You've got Nicholas falling all over you. Wait till you get to be my age."

"That's such a cop-out, Claire. You're not that much older than me. Go take a look at yourself in the mirror. You're a very attractive woman."

I walk over to the vanity and take a quick look. Next to Nevada's perky blond prettiness, I look as plain and colorless as an Anita Brookner heroine. With my flat light brown hair, I've got English teacher written all over me. "Not bad." I walk back to the desk. "For an old bag. Who cares about looks anyway? Isn't it the spiritual qualities that count?"

"You know what Bette Davis said about old bags—if you really need to get something done, get a couple of old bags to do it."

"Wasn't that old broads?"

"Picky picky picky," Nevada says. "Why don't you hang loose. Like me." She lets her head and arms go loose as a rag doll's. "I know what would cheer you up. Let's have a pajama party! When was the last time you did something silly? We can put our hair up in curlers, smear cold cream on our faces, and make popcorn. You do have an extra nightgown, don't you?"

"How can we do something so frivolous, when there are people on the street with no homes?"

"How is it going to help the homeless if we don't have a pajama party?"

"Don't you think they'd feel better if they knew we were suffering for them?"

"I think they'd feel better if they had some ideal of home to emulate—the pajama party ideal, for example."

"That's so callous."

"What good is it going to do anybody if you're miserable on their account? Especially if your misery paralyzes you. It would be different if it spurred you to action. Why don't you volunteer at a soup kitchen and be cheerful? Like Nicholas."

"If there's anything I can't stand, it's having my own characters held up to me as examples." I gather up Nevada's makeup-smeared tissues and crumple them into a ball. "Anyway, look who's talking about paralysis. If I hadn't pushed you out of your loft, you'd still be crawling around in your Thing like a geriatric fetus."

"I'd hardly call that paralysis," Nevada says. "I was creating art."

"Granted, but how was that helping the homeless?"

"Since when is helping the homeless *the* measure of value?"

"How do you figure out what's worth doing?" I toss Nevada's tissues into the wastepaper basket. "We were brought up to think relationships with men were the thing to do. In which case putting on all that nail polish and junk is also the thing to do. Then everything changed and work and careers and independence were the things to do. Relationships with men were secondary. Sisterhood was in. Now social action and charity are in. Careerism is out. Art's never exactly been in. But it's never exactly been out either. It's always been weird and solitary. How can anyone do all that? And I haven't even mentioned having children."

"And then there's weirdos like us who do art. That eats up time like a cranky baby."

"Do you remember the suntan imperative?" I say dreamily, stretching out on the bed. "All the time we squandered trying to achieve the perfect tan in the bad old days before skin cancer and UV rays and the disappearing ozone layer."

"Right," Nevada says. "You had to get a tan with no strap marks, which meant you had to lie around like a beached whale. Or you could wear a strapless suit, which meant you couldn't swim because it would slip and expose your breasts to the pack of boys praying for just that."

"But it was fun, giving yourself up to the sun," I say, feeling that old sun warm my limbs. "Listening to the waves, smelling the Coppertone—it was a great meditation. Until your brain started to fry, that is. I almost gave myself sunstroke a couple of times, trying to get really mahogany. Why did we do it? Just think of all the time we wasted, not to mention the wrinkles we acquired."

"Think of them as merit badges," Nevada says, perching on the foot of the bed. She starts on her toenails.

"But why did we do it? We could have all become Nobel Prize–winning scientists or solved world hunger or achieved world peace or *something*."

"It was the suntan imperative. We had to." Tiny toenail filings are drifting down onto my bedspread. Nevada brushes them onto the dark wood floor.

"Well I'm tired of having externally imposed imperatives running my life."

"What would you like to have running your life?"

"Nobody likes a smart-alec, Nevada."

"What about Woody Allen? Everyone likes him. Or they used to, anyway."

"Maybe men have an easier time figuring this out." I close my eyes. I don't want to see what Nevada's going to do next.

"I don't know," Nevada says, stroking red polish on the nails of her left foot. She's got her foot tilted up so the polish won't get on the spread. "I've never been a man, not in this lifetime, anyway."

"Why don't you ask Nicholas the next time you see him. He is our resident expert." I determinedly keep my eyes closed. I don't know how I'm going to explain red polish on the white spread to Madame.

"What about Alec?"

"Alec isn't exactly in the mainstream of male experience, charming though he might be."

"True enough." Nevada sighs.

"Maybe it's easier when you're working on a survival level," I say, "and you just do what you have to do each day to stay alive. Maybe it's a luxury to be as confused and miserable as we are."

"Well if you really want to be reduced to a survival level to focus your mind, I'm sure it can be arranged."

"Ha-ha."

"I've heard hanging concentrates the mind wonderfully."

"You're a veritable treasure chest of quotations, Nevada. Why don't you use your own words for a change?"

"I don't want to crowd your space. You are the writer. If you still think writing is worth doing, that is."

"You don't want to crowd my space? What do you think you're doing now? What am I going to say to Madame if you ruin my spread?"

"Chill out, Claire." Nevada strokes red on her last little toe. "I'm an artist. I have great little-muscle control. Do you see one drop of polish on your spread?"

"No, but look at the mess on the floor."

"I was going to clean it up." Nevada caps the bottle. "Do *you* clean when you're in a creative heat?"

"Only if I'm stuck. Then I find there's nothing more intriguing than defrosting the refrigerator." I spit on a tissue and wipe Nevada's nail filings off the floor. "You know what I hate about writing? Nobody wants to read a book without a love interest."

"Cranky old men hate all that love stuff," Nevada says. "My father always turns away from the screen when the kissing starts."

"I didn't know you had a father." I straighten up and stare at her.

"What do you think—I sprang full-blown from your forehead?"

"Actually, I never thought about it. I can't think of everything, you know."

"Well don't forget to let me go to the bathroom once in a while, OK?"

"OK, but I hope you don't mind doing it offstage. People don't like to read about that kind of thing."

"Why don't you stop worrying about what people think? What do you think?"

"I think I don't feel like writing about you going to the bathroom in any detail, whatsoever."

"You're so prissy. You'd never last with Alec for three seconds. Going to the bathroom is very interesting. If I were a writer, I'd write about it. Imagine how fascinating it would be to a Martian."

"You want to write this book? Be my guest."

"I want to go out with Nicholas. You stay home and write it. I've been home."

"So does that mean you like to read books with a love interest?"

"Why don't you write a book about careers and sisterhood and independence and volunteer work and religion and art and love. Now that would be worth doing."

"I don't know, I think people only want to read about love. And violence." I try some of Nevada's blue eye shadow. It looks more like violence than love and I wipe it off.

"You don't think very much of the human race, do you?"

"I think the human race is better in what they do than in what they read. After all, very few people eat their children."

"What a charming thought."

"You know what I mean. Raising children is a tremendously unselfish act."

"So what do you have against writing about romance?"

"Actually it's fun. It's just that I don't like externally imposed imperatives."

"Welcome to the universe."

I throw a makeup-smeared tissue at Nevada. "So do you think this book is as important as volunteering in a soup kitchen?"

"That's hard to say. It would probably do people good if you could enjoy writing it. The positive energy you'd be putting out would help the world, even if nobody ever read it. You know, as Meher Baba said, 'Don't worry. Be happy.' " Nevada does a few crazy dance steps around the room.

"Please don't talk about people not reading my book," I say through clenched teeth.

"Well, it is possible," Nevada says. "It could happen. If you can't get your mind around that, you probably shouldn't be writing at all. You'd be writing for the wrong reasons."

"Must you keep lecturing me? It is absolutely insufferable to be lectured to by my characters. Especially characters who don't exactly have it all together themselves. Although the truth is, you have it easy. You've got Nicholas and Alec, too, if you want him. You've got buyers lined up for your Thing. What do you know about how hard life is?"

"You know perfectly well what I know about that," Nevada says, brushing her hair with my brush. "Listen, I've got the perfect solution to your problems. Volunteer at a soup kitchen. Maybe you'll meet a nice homeless man you could date. You could kill two birds with one stone."

"That's got to be the most disgusting expression in the English language."

"Oh, stop being such a writer."

"Why don't you have an anxiety attack?"

"Get a life. Stop feeding off mine."

I snatch up the Nautilus Shell folder off the desk. "What do you think would happen if I tore these pages up and threw them out the window?"

"You'd probably disappear."

I laugh and put the folder down. "You're probably right."

"I think it's time to have a pajama party," Nevada says. "Before we do some serious damage."

"Before one of us says something unforgivable."

"So what do you think? Want to make banana bread?" Nevada asks, combing my closet for nightgowns.

"Why not?"

"Is it worth doing?"

"Definitely."

CHAPTER SIXTEEN

"I hope Madame isn't up," I say as Nevada and I walk into the kitchen of The Orange Cat Bistro. It's cramped, cozy, professional, intoxicating. I gaze with awe at the professional mixer, big as a pickle barrel.

"Don't worry. It's after midnight," Nevada says, boldly turning on all the lights. In my plaid flannel gown, she looks like a camp counselor. "Doesn't Madame have to get up early to go to market?"

"She is at Hunt's Point at dawn, but it's not clear to me that she sleeps." I'm wearing Victorian floral. At least The Orange Cat Bistro isn't haunted by white nightgowns.

"We'll make two breads and leave one for her," Nevada says, rummaging in the cabinets for loaf pans. She emerges, triumphantly waving two battered tin relics. "Just imagine how many people these have fed over the years!"

"I don't know what will happen if Madame catches us fooling around in her temple." The subject of kitchen privileges has never come up. "I hope she likes banana bread. If I have to move again, I will go out of my mind."

"Everyone likes banana bread. Anyway, who would be cruel enough to throw out a poor divorcée for making a loaf of bread? We're not living in a Dickens novel, for heaven's sake."

"It's too bad I'm not a widow." I open the double doors of the refrigerator and take some eggs out of a huge carton. "I bet people are a lot nicer to you. Divorcée suggests illicit sexual knowledge, something seedy, big overblown breasts, and too much makeup . . . having been left. It makes me feel like leftover meat loaf."

"Your ideas about divorcées are completely out-of-date. Everyone's divorced. Everyone who's anyone, anyway." Nevada roots under the sink for mixing bowls. "I think you read too much. Anyway, day-old meat loaf is one of my favorite foods. It just keeps getting better."

"You know how much you hate being told you think too much? That's how much I hate being told I read too much."

"Sorry." Nevada plumps down a twenty-five-pound sack of flour on the stainless steel island. "As far as I'm concerned, you can read till your eyes drop out of your head."

"Another disgusting expression. But I just might." I pull some wooden spoons out of a crockery pitcher. "Couldn't you find any whole wheat?"

"I don't think the French are too big on health food," Nevada says.

"I bet the idea that divorcées are desperate to have it hasn't gone out of date."

"Everyone's desperate to have it. If terror hasn't completely squashed desire. Aren't you?"

"Technically speaking, yes."

"And nontechnically?"

"I'm not ready. Or, more precisely, I'm past ready, a gone to seed rose, overblown and red as an out-of-date divorcée's lipstick."

"You'd think you were eighty-five, the way you talk. If I were a man, I'd want to go to bed with you." Nevada rips open the flour sack.

"Thank you, I think." I put water on for tea. "But do men have us so much under their control, that we can't talk, or even think, about anything but them for more than thirty seconds?"

"You started."

"I started? No way."

"You said everyone thinks divorcées are desperate to have it." Nevada puts two yellow mugs on the counter.

"That's about how the world perceives divorcées."

"It's not about how the world perceives divorcées, sweetie. It's about how you perceive yourself."

"Don't call me sweetie. Especially not in that tone of voice." I find some peppermint leaves in the back of a cabinet. "And don't psychoanalyze me. I'm perfectly capable of psychoanalyzing myself, *when I happen to be in the mood.*"

"Aren't we touchy today," Nevada says, breaking eggs into a crockery bowl.

"Well, it's bad enough to have to write about you and Nicholas and you and Alec without having to listen to your half-baked psychoanalytic theories about my nonexistent sex life. Isn't it me who's supposed to be having half-baked theories about you?"

"Be my guest."

"Pass." I laugh and pour boiling water over the tea. "I guess I'm not in a psychoanalytic mood today."

"Are you in the mood to make banana bread?" Nevada throws me a lemon.

"Grating lemon rind is my favorite part." I find a hand grater in the crockery pitcher and start rubbing the lemon against the rough side. "What a great smell!"

"You know what's even more incredible—the smell of cut lime."

"That's an exotic smell—the smell of wind on a tropical island. Lemon smells like you're in your mother's kitchen, the safest place in the world, the smell of baking is in the air. There's nothing that could hurt you there."

"Is that what you think?"

"What could break into that enclosure? It's the closest thing I know to sacred space."

"I hate to burst your bubble, sweetie," Nevada says, "but don't you know most accidents happen at home?"

"I bet you're not talking about slipping in the tub."

"You know I'm not, girlfriend."

"Don't be mean, Nevada. I want to bask in kitchen. I want to fill my nose with the smell of lemon peel. I want to fill my hand with the weathered wood handle of this grater, which is just like the one my mother inherited from her mother. I want to revel in the old technology—not plastic, not microwave, not even electric. Human-powered technology makes *me* feel human, softer, grandmother soft in those floor-to-ceiling aprons they used to wear. I feel as if I have those huge, soft, powdery grandmother breasts. What do you suppose ever happened to them?"

"You want to fill your nose with the scent of lemon peel so you can't smell the stink of the world?" Nevada says, ignoring my question. "You want to fill your hand with the feel of weathered wood so you can't feel anything else?"

"*You,* the poster child for Agoraphobics Anonymous, are saying that to me?" I rub the lemon so hard, I break through the pith to translucent flesh. "*Why* are you being so mean?"

"Agoraphobia is such an ugly word."

"Don't hyperventilate, *sweetie.*"

"I hate thinking of myself as agoraphobic." Nevada starts cracking walnuts on the zinc countertop.

"Maybe we *should* found Agoraphobics Anonymous, if it doesn't already exist.

"A support group for agoraphobics seems like an oxymoron."

"Why? We're out."

"People would probably call us to jump-start their cars."

"That would get us out of the house."

Nevada acknowledges my joke with a grudging nod. She plunks down a bunch of very ripe bananas in my work space.

"So what's sacred space for you?" I ask, slipping a rotten-ripe banana out of its skin.

"I bet you can guess."

"Inside your Thing?"

"Give the lady a Kewpie doll."

"You're lucky."

"Only if I ever get back there."

I don't say anything.

Nevada throws a bunch of black banana skins in the trash. "These bananas are black gold. What could they possibly be saving them for in a French kitchen?"

"Banana soup?"

"That's a truly disgusting idea."

"Isn't it?"

"Well don't sound so proud."

"Disgusting is Us." I mash bananas with a tool that looks like a miniature farm implement.

"Did I ever tell you about the time I out-mothered my mother?"

"No. It sounds fascinating." I sit down and give Nevada my full attention.

"While it's flattering to be the center of such rapt attention," Nevada says, pointing a half-peeled banana at me, "I would enjoy it more if I didn't suspect you of ulterior motives."

"And what would those be?"

"You think it's easier to listen than to make me up."

"That's not fair, Nevada. I find you fascinating. Anyway, if I just make it all up, I might get it wrong. Is that what you want?"

"You've been doing OK so far."

"Thanks."

"You're welcome."

"*Please* tell me the story about out-mothering your mother."

"Hand me that glass measure?" Carefully Nevada pours out a cup of honey. "Well, you know how mothers always cook like crazy when their kids come home and force food on them and ignore their diets and send them home with doggie bags?"

"Kids who are lucky, you mean."

"Right. Well my mother came down from Nyack to visit me when Alec was away. She can't stand Alec."

"And right she is."

"Don't interrupt. As I was saying, she can't stand Alec so I usually go to Nyack. Alec drops me off in his truck. I've never really had a chance to mother her, so I ordered tons of food from D'Agostino's and cooked for days. I made boeuf bourguignon and paella and strawberry shortcake and homemade brandy-peach ice cream and all those little salads they make in farm country. I thought she'd love it. I mean I was only trying to do for her what she does for me."

"So what happened?" I ask, studiously sifting flour. I don't want Nevada to think I'm taking notes.

"Well, it's not that she didn't love the food. She did, but she seemed overwhelmed, like there was too much food, like I was being oversolicitous, fussing too much, crowding her space."

"You mean Mother Space?"

"I guess."

"Maybe there's only room for one mother in Mother Space."

"You would think that someone who always takes care of everyone else would love to get taken care of."

"I would."

"It was kind of funny, really. It was as though I was torturing her with her own devices. I guess I learned her lessons too well."

"It must have been deeply satisfying to out-mother your own mother, especially a bread-baking, organic-gardening mother like yours."

"It's not a revenge trip, you know, Claire. It's not a contest. She's my mother. I love her. I wanted to make her happy."

"Trying to *make* someone happy could be seen as an act of aggression."

"Don't get linguisto-political on me."

"Why? Does it feel like an act of aggression?" I beat the eggs and honey together with a wire whisk and ignore Nevada's stuck-out tongue. "Do you ever feel that you'd like to feed the world?"

"All the time. Maybe that was the problem during my mother's visit. I thought she was the world."

"A dangerous assumption," I say, wiping up some spilled honey. "You know, you really could feed the world from a kitchen like this. Look at these soup pots. I bet you could fit a whole pig in them."

"Don't forget the croutons."

I laugh and measure two teaspoons of baking soda into the flour. "I've been feeling lost without my own kitchen. Being in a professional kitchen like this is almost as exciting as having sex."

"I think it's time for you to get out of the house." Nevada adds my grated lemon rind to the eggs and honey. "Celibacy is curdling your brain."

"Are you throwing me out of the house, Mommy? Don't mothers want to keep their daughters at home as long as possible?"

"Don't get carried away with this mommy thing," Nevada says. "I don't feel up to existing in mythic proportions."

"What about in your Thing?"

"That's different. It's limited, self-contained. I can't be a monolithic goddess twenty-four hours a day. I find it hard enough to be a mere mortal."

"Who says mothers have to be monolithic twenty-four-hour-a-day goddesses?"

"Sons and daughters everywhere."

"Sounds like a tough life."

"It is, girlfriend, it is."

"How would you know?" I ask, rinsing the grater. "Do you have a bunch of children I don't know about?"

"No, but I've made a study of this. I find it fascinating. And, of course, monolithic goddesses are of professional interest to me," Nevada says, putting her whisk down.

"How come you never sculpt huge exterior goddesses?" I ask. "All of yours are little and hidden in your Thing."

"Sort of like a clitoris?"

"Sort of, but more hidden."

"So you want me to make huge phallic exterior goddesses? That makes about as much sense as a support group for agoraphobics."

"You said phallic, not me. I just mean big and out there. As though you weren't afraid to claim your own power."

"I'm afraid this banana bread is going to be half-baked if someone doesn't preheat the oven," Nevada says, pouring the honey, egg, and lemon mixture into the mashed bananas.

"Like my theories?" I laugh and turn on the oven.

"Your theories aren't that bad. But you know, Claire, as hard as you try, you can't make the world safe with banana bread."

"But doesn't it feel a little safer? While you're grating the lemon peel and mixing the honey and sifting the flour, you feel as though nothing could ever hurt you."

"The point isn't what you feel. The point is what's true."

"The point is how you hold what's true. While I'm baking, I hold it just fine."

"You're just trying to be safe by being mommy's good girl. You really think that will protect you from what's out there? How much power do you think mommy has, anyway?"

"What is your problem, Nevada? Did I push one of your precious buttons?" I shove a square of buttered brown paper around the pans. "Your lack of compassion astonishes me. I can't say I'm enjoying being around you very much right now."

"Fine. Finish the bread yourself." Nevada wipes her hands on my gown. "I'm going to have dinner with Nicholas."

CHAPTER SEVENTEEN

Eating a slice of banana bread, I sit down at my desk. I take the dust cover off the typewriter and put in a fresh piece of paper.

Nicholas and Nevada. Nevada and Nicholas. Nicholas's apartment. Nicholas and Nevada in bed. Nicholas and Nevada not in bed. Who cares? I blow my nose. That Nevada can be such a bitch. How could I have given birth to such an uncompassionate character? I thought *I* had problems, but Nevada is really something else. It's a good thing she's not a teacher. She'd terrorize the kids. Scorched earth—that would be Nevada's pedagogic policy. She'd destroy years of work the other teachers have put in, trying to build the kid's self-esteem.

You'd think that artists would be caring, compassionate people. They certainly take their own feelings seriously enough. I brush banana bread crumbs off the keyboard. The truth is I don't even feel like going on with this book. Who wants to hang out with a bitch like Nevada for another couple of hundred pages? Who wants to be in bed with Nevada and Nicholas for the next few months? Maybe that's what the rest of the world wants, but not me. The hell with it. I'm going to bed. Tomorrow I'm going to jump-start my own life.

CHAPTER EIGHTEEN

When in blazes is Claire going to get this chapter started, Nevada thinks, pushing against the foggy confines of hyperspace. How long has it been? When your author strands you like this, it's hard to tell whether it's been five minutes or three hundred years. She wonders if Nicholas is stuck in his own hyperspace somewhere and whether it's contiguous with hers.

She just wanted to get on with the story line. Isn't that what Claire wants? Isn't that why Claire ejected her, at great personal cost, from her Thing? Claire's such a coward. There's nothing Claire likes more than hanging out in denial. She thinks she's hot stuff because she isn't *currently* agoraphobic.

Nevada kicks her feet hard, but all she accomplishes is creating a little fog gush. She seems to be sitting on a piece of solidified fog, but pushing against it isn't getting her anywhere. Not that there's anywhere to get.

She wonders if there are other characters wandering around in the fog, waiting for someone to open their books or boot up their files. Claire's too backward to even use a word processor. Why *is* Claire so attracted to the nineteenth century? Who does she think she is—Charlotte Brontë? Nevada bets if she were on hard drive, she could figure out how to get herself somewhere interesting. When you erase things off the hard drive, they still exist in some computer ghost realm, somewhere. An accomplished hacker can return ghosts to flesh.

Nevada drums her heels against her solidified fog perch. It's starting to take on the classical adornments of a garden bench. There's got to be a way out of here. If she can't get back to Nicholas, maybe she can make contact with some fictional artists sitting around drinking absinthe or something. It's really too bad she missed out on the banana bread. Maybe she was a little hasty in her exit, but she just couldn't take hearing Claire go on and on in her denial. Claire could cocoon *forever* in her kitchen haven, in her Orange Cat Bistro, in her fantasies of Mother.

Still, she wonders how the bread came out. Those were primo bananas, at exactly the right stage of rotten-ripe. She can smell that fly-attracting sweetness in this place of no-smell, no-taste, no-touch. She can feel her stomach rubbing against itself like a fly's wings rubbing together in anticipation of a feast. She can feel her body condensing itself down into a big, black, hairy, winged fly-body. Nevada tries a few experimental wing flaps and finds herself rising through the fog. Down below she can just glimpse a river winding through lush green lowlands. It looks as if she's launched herself into the world of the English country novel, the *old* English country novel, although why, she can't imagine. Maybe it's punishment for making fun of Claire's beloved old technologies.

She just hopes she doesn't get stuck in a Jane Austen novel. Even letting Claire write the story of her life has got to be more exciting than that. Nevada flaps onward. All she can see through the wisps of grey fog are trees and an occasional cart horse or cow. She's really got to get back to the city. There's too much emptiness out here in the country. Especially the old country. There's nothing happening—no Zabar's, no coffeehouses, no pretentious gallery openings to make fun of. She supposes if she were really a fly, she'd go down and feast on cow flops, but she's still too human for that not to turn her stomach. She wants the city with its modern smells and noise; she wants Nicholas's apartment and the dinner he was going to cook. Casting around for the scent of pasta primavera, she thinks she smells it way off toward the east. Buzzing triumphantly, she flies toward the smell. She may be hungry, she may be lost, she may be a fly, but she's finally becoming the author of her own tale.

CHAPTER NINETEEN

Nevada doesn't know how lucky she is, I think, sitting across the table from Barney, my blind date du jour, in a seafood restaurant on the East River. Boats chug by just feet from our table, and the trees outside are strung with lights. Doggedly I sip my wine. I gave her Nicholas, who's probably too good to be true. I gave her Alec, who isn't, but is at least fun to play with, unlike Mr. Misery across the table. Nevada's never had to be out here on the frozen tundras of dating, dealing with the real life men of the nineties.

I smile dutifully at Barney, who's been talking for two hours straight about his considerable psychological problems, and take a bite of shark steak. I hope there's a bone in it. If I choke, I'd have a great excuse to get out of here. It would even be worth having to go to the emergency room. Maybe I'd meet a cute EMT. It would even be worth dying to get out of this date. I might meet a lonely mortician or some other woman's dear departed. Once they're dead, they're fair game. After all the wedding vows do say, "till death do us part." Although in some religions, you are supposed to be your husband's heavenly footstool. If I get to heaven with some other woman's husband, I can negotiate for property rights later. But who wants to be a footstool, anyway? I'll just be a pirate, a predator, looking for newly deceased men, like those Manhattan apartment hunters who scour the obituary columns for recently vacated properties. I'll focus on men who lived fast, died young, and left good-looking corpses.

"My therapist said I wasn't ready for dating so soon after my breakdown," Barney says, staring intensely at me without seeming to see me.

"Maybe your therapist was right. It sounds like you have a lot to work out before you're ready to relate to another woman." He's blond and beefy, not my type but not out of the question. I could even deal with the nervous breakdown, if he would just acknowledge my presence.

"But I feel desperate," he says, not looking at me. "I've got to have some relief." He downs his beer in three gulps.

"That's not a good place to start a relationship from." I put myself on auto-therapist. There's no way I'm going to be his relief. He'd down *me* in three gulps. There's no way I'm going to succeed at turning this Date from Hell into a celebratory event, but maybe I can help a soul in torment. Although it's doubtful Barney can even hear me. He doesn't seem to have noticed my existence except as a giant ear. Why did I spend all that money on a dating service, and why did I believe them when they said they carefully screened and matched their clients?

At least I didn't meet him at The Orange Cat Bistro. I would hate to be seen with this loser. What an idiot I am! I should have met him for coffee and not stuck myself with three hours of being a giant ear. If I *were* his therapist, I'd be getting at least three hundred dollars for listening to him go on and on about his dead father and his ex-wife's betrayals. All I'm getting is dinner. It's not often that a teacher gets to eat in restaurants this elegant, but I'd rather be eating Madame's peasant cooking. I could be reading *The Stories of Eva Luna*, right now. I'd even rather be arguing with Nevada. I'd rather be writing about Nevada and Nicholas in bed.

We don't even look as though we're on the same date. I have on a rose-covered dress, lent to me by Madame's granddaughter, and he's wearing faded pink jeans and an old tee shirt. We must look like those Steinberg cartoons where the man and woman are drawn in different mediums, the man in crude pencil shadings, the woman in elaborate pen-and-ink curlicues.

The only thing that could make this date any worse is *actually* about to happen. My ex-husband and his girlfriend are walking into the restaurant. Who writes this stuff? If I did this to Nevada, she'd kill me. Nevada would say it was too unbelievable for words, but here it is happening and who can I complain to? The Goddess? Surely the Goddess has more important things to do than worry about my life turning into a bad novel.

I try to hide behind my napkin. I'd hoped Aaron and his little homewrecker were history, but they seem cozier than ever. Aaron, whose bald spot has grown since I last saw him, kisses Vivian's neck as he seats her. Vivian shakes her mousy hair and simpers. Vivian's hair is a lot shorter than I remember. Aaron is probably the only heterosexual man in the history of the world who doesn't like long-haired women. He always said my hair looked messy when it got to be a decent writerly length.

I take a sip of white wine. Nevada would have a good laugh at me, sitting here with the Date from Hell while my ex-husband gets romantic with the slut who broke up our marriage. He's so engrossed in Vivian, he hasn't even noticed me and my clown.

Everybody has somebody but me. Aaron has his slut and his slut has him. Nevada has Nicholas and maybe Alec, too. Everyone else in this restaurant is part of a festive group. I focus in on Barney, who hasn't noticed my distraction or despair.

"I know just how you feel," I tell him when he says lonely and desperate again. Tears start to trickle down my cheeks and still he doesn't notice. Nobody notices, my ex doesn't notice, the waiter, who's cute, doesn't notice; I might as well be an *invisible* giant ear as a flesh-and-blood woman dying of sadness. I should have stayed home with my books.

Nevada doesn't need Alec. She's got Nicholas. And Nicholas is too good to be true. Alec's got a tang of tainted nineties reality about him. And if I remember correctly, he's not bad in bed, if you don't care about phallic completion. Maybe if I ever escape from Date Hell, if the Goddess will let me out of this badly written excuse for a story line, I'll borrow Alec for a while. Why should Nevada mind?

CHAPTER TWENTY

Nicholas hands Nevada a glass of red wine. This is much nicer than literary hyperspace, she thinks as she sinks into the deep cushions of a wicker chair. It feels wonderful to be back in the horrible, overwhelming city. Nicholas's wine smells much better than overripe bananas. "Do you need help?" she asks, but he tells her to sit and relax. How much help could she be to him with her eyes closed anyway? Is she going to keep that up without Claire making her? It's like an old friend by now, a shaggy, mangy old sheepdog you could never have put to sleep, the kind of dog that licks your face when you're crying over something your stupid boyfriend did.

She can't believe she's wrested control of her story line from Claire. There's no tugging at the other end of the string, no subtle tension, that awareness of Claire's presence, Claire's agenda. A little smile pulls at the corners of Nevada's mouth, but she tries to keep it from bursting into a full-fledged smirk. If Claire sneaks back to the typewriter in the middle of the night, she doesn't want her to see a triumphant grin smeared all over the page. If Claire doesn't think it's a contest, she might not try to wrest back control of the story line.

Nicholas walks in and out of the room doing dinner-related things. She can hear the clatter of dishes and smell garlic sautéing. She has to admit Claire did well by her with Nicholas. Men who cook are better in bed. Plus you get dinner. However, even if Claire *is* good at this, she's tired of being Claire's guinea pig. Who knows if her healing path is through the same forest as Claire's?

This wine is going right to her head. When did she last eat? Through the winey fog, Nevada wonders if she can find a way to hide herself and Nicholas from Claire's prying gaze, a device that would jam Claire's radar. Claire's sure to show up sooner or later. She herself could never stay away from the Thing if Alec hadn't forced her hand.

If only she could be here and in her Thing at the same time! Or with Nicholas inside her Thing, drinking the goddesses' red wine, making love in their sacred meadows. She's never taken anyone with her into her Thing. Even Alec has only been inside on public occasions, like that Thing-finishing party he threw. At times like that, the goddesses hide deep, deep in, much deeper than anyone but she would be willing to go. Even if she gave people aerial reconnaissance maps to the most remote regions, who but she has the courage to walk the rope bridges strung precariously over bottomless chasms? She doesn't know why she's fantasizing about taking Nicholas in with her. She barely knows the man. How does she know he won't try to rape the little goddesses? She really shouldn't fantasize about the Thing, unless she wants her heart broken again and again.

Nicholas walks in from the kitchen. "Usually I put music on as soon as I walk in the door. Before I put down the mail or take off my coat." Putting *Madama Butterfly* on the CD player, he shakes his head. "I don't know what you're doing to me."

"That's as it should be." Nevada smiles and stretches. "You shouldn't know what I'm doing to you."

"Am I in danger?"

"I haven't decided yet."

"Are you a witch?"

"If I were, do you think I would tell you?"

"If you were a witch, would you be a good witch?"

"Of course. I'd be a mistress of herbal healing, a nature worshiper, the best midwife in the county. Really, Nicholas. Where have you been all afternoon? I mean would I even be in your apartment if I were Snow White's evil stepmother?"

"I'm surprised that you're here at all. You're the first woman who has been since . . ." Nicholas's voice trails off. "Well, for a very long time. Have you cast a spell on me?"

"Of course I've cast a spell on you," Nevada says. "But you have absolutely nothing to worry about. You're in the best possible hands."

"Are you going to heal me?"

"Of *course* I'm going to heal you. What do you think women do?"

"Not all women," Nicholas says, his words trailing off as he disappears into the kitchen.

"What did she do to you?" Nevada asks, but her only answer is the sound of water running. She slips her canvas espadrilles off. Her manicured toes feel shiny and strange, and she wiggles them against what feels to be a sisal rug. It's itchy, rough, and feels like outdoors. She wonders what the little goddesses are up to. Probably stirring up a witches' brew in their iron pots or planning how to introduce agriculture to the human race. She doesn't care what Claire says. The goddesses are happy where they are. They don't want to be exposed to the indignities of weather and graffiti artists. America is not a friendly home to goddesses. If she puts them in public space, they'd probably be disarmed, even raped. It's always open season on goddesses, not that hunting restrictions have ever stopped a bunch of hairy jerks with rifles. Nevada shivers as the smell of sweat and beer assaults her nose. Although the goddesses might be better off in public than hidden away in Hassiloff's museum. Who knows what he's capable of?

"Would you like to read the paper while I finish dinner?" Nicholas calls from the kitchen. "I've got the *Times*, *Variety* and the *Village Voice*."

"*Three* newspapers." Just imagining reading the *New York Times* makes her heart pound. Her mouth feels as dry as if someone had stuffed it full of newspapers, then sealed it with duct tape. "Do you want me to have a nervous breakdown?" she says weakly. It's amazing how brave she can be in the treacherous inner regions of her Thing, where almost everyone she knows would refuse to go, and how cowardly she is in the world they negotiate with such ease.

"I'd rather you had a good time," Nicholas's voice cuts through her escalating panic.

"Why do you have three newspapers?" Could Nicholas be the one responsible for all the bad news? Someone has to be. Pride could explain his newspaper mania.

"To find out what's happening," Nicholas says as he wipes the dining room table with Murphy's Oil Soap.

"I hope you have a *big* bottle of Valium," Nevada says. The soap smells like her mother's clean pine floors.

"Never touch the stuff."

"Neither do I, but there's no way someone who's reading three newspapers is going to be able to self-soothe."

"You take it too seriously, Nevada. It's just the world," Nicholas says, folding yellow cotton napkins into fans.

"I hate being told I take things too seriously. It's like being told I'm cute when I'm mad. And how do you think the world feels about being called 'just the world'?"

"I think the world's too busy to listen in on my private conversations."

"Maybe in your apartment, but what about outside? When we were in the park, the world was listening. I could hear it breathing around us. You have to be careful, Nicholas. There are gods and goddesses everywhere, in the trees, the rocks, the earth. You don't want to offend them."

"I don't think I said anything to offend the world when we were in the park." He takes a few CDs out of their rack. *The Magic Flute* might soothe his flighty visitor.

"I hope not. The spirits of tree and rock and sky are not honored in this city. You can imagine how they feel."

"The spirits of music are honored in my house." Nicholas rubs his hand lovingly over the spines of his CDs.

"That's a good start," Nevada says. She loves the way Nicholas loves music. She loved the way Alec loved painting, but it was his canvas he gave himself to. In Alec's bed, she was always a second-class citizen. Could Nicholas love *her* in the way he loves music?

As the opening notes of *The Magic Flute* make the small room large, Nicholas sets bowls on the mahogany table. "I'm not surprised to find you're a pagan but, being such a passionate sculptor, aren't wood and stone alive for you, too?"

"If you're talking about furniture, that depends on how it was made." Nevada strokes the wicker arm of Nicholas's chair. "If it was made by an artisan, it's definitely alive. If it was made on the assembly line, it's a thing. This chair, for instance, is a thing."

"Who can afford to furnish with only whole-souled furniture?" Nicholas pats the armchair, which Eileen chose, apologetically. "My wife liked cozy things. She chose everything in this apartment."

"Your wife?"

"My dead wife," Nicholas says, retreating to the kitchen.

"Is that all you're going to tell me? I've told you practically the whole story of my life."

"Hardly."

So Nicholas has a dead wife. Nevada shifts uneasily in her soulless chair. Is he a Bluebeard with dead wives behind every door? It's a little late to worry about now, but she wonders if Claire's guarantee of safety still applies. She would hate to ask Claire to take over the story line. She tries to open her eyes, but the lids won't budge. Have her eye muscles atrophied? That would be embarrassing to explain at the emergency room, though she *could* blame it on Claire.

Nicholas sets out Eileen's good silver and lights the candles. Nevada could have taught Eileen a lot about loving life enough to stick around to live it. Eileen never learned to be passionate about anything other than her unrelenting quest for bodily perfection. "Dinner's ready," he calls, bringing out a huge platter of pasta primavera.

Nevada gropes her way to the table. Maybe he's drugged the food, preparatory to introducing her to his dead wives. But how much room could there be in a Manhattan apartment for dead wives? Maybe since Claire set the context for this universe, the basic rules still apply and safety, if not guaranteed, is at least possible. Nevada decides to embrace that possibility. She takes a forkful of the pasta Nicholas serves her.

"Mmm. Delicious." It doesn't taste drugged. Though Nicholas, courtly and robust as he is, would make a perfect Bluebeard. It's too bad he's so nineties about sex. Not only is sex more fun than Valium, it's one hundred percent natural, though it *can* have unpleasant side effects. Well she's not going to think about *those*. Let her hallucination worry about AIDS. "Do you do everything as well as you cook?"

"What did you have in mind?"

Nevada smirks at him. Pretty soon she'll be engaging in promiscuous winking. Blame it on non–goddess-blessed wine.

"Don't be a bad girl, Nevada." Nicholas gives her a stern look.

She cannot get this man to laugh. "Have some more wine, Nicholas."

"If you're implying that I'm uptight"—Nicholas puts his fork down—"I won't argue with you. But don't expect me to be ashamed of it. If more people were as uptight as I am, you might not find the world such a terrifying place."

"But you have to acknowledge your dark side. You have to play with it." After two years with Alec, she could get a dark side Ph.D. And she won't say it hasn't been fun. How could she have carved all the bright things in her goddess habitat without full working knowledge of her depths?

"I don't have time to play."

"If rescuing me is what's crowding your schedule, I'm letting you off the hook." Nevada winds pasta around her fork. She wonders how much of a mess she's making. This is hard enough to do with your eyes open. "From now on I'm going to rescue myself.

You're long overdue for a vacation—why don't you try to have some fun for a change?"

"Trying to have fun." Roughly Nicholas tears off a piece of bread. "The great American ideal."

"What are you afraid of?"

"You really don't want to know."

"Try me."

"I really don't want to talk about it."

"Far be it from me to pry," Nevada says. "But I'm a good rescuer, too."

"I don't need rescuing."

"Fine," Nevada says. "If you want to take care of my needs so badly, what I *really* could use is some sexual healing."

"You're on your own there, my dear."

She can*not* get this man to laugh. "Are you implying what I think?" Nevada tries one last time. If that doesn't work, she's giving up.

"I have no idea what you mean."

"I give up."

"I'm glad to hear you say that."

This guy is one tough audience. She wonders if Claire would have done any better with this material. Would Claire have gotten them into bed by now? Would Claire have made him laugh? Although she is working with the tenets that Claire set up. This is Claire's Nicholas. He was like this from the beginning. Nevada gulps down half a glass of wine. Is everything preordained? Is there nothing she can do to influence the outcome? Writers. It figures that if Claire wants to play God, it would have to be in a Calvinist universe. Nicholas fits right in there.

CHAPTER TWENTY-ONE

I walk up to the western wall of Westbeth and pause. The late sunlight bounces fiercely off the upper windows. If I enter Nevada's life, will I be able to get out? With the sun glare in my eyes, I push through the big glass doors. The doorman likes my smile and lets me in without calling up. Just because I've got English teacher written all over me, doesn't mean I'm not an ax murderer. No wonder Nevada never feels safe.

The elevator button really does feel like licorice. At least I got that right. It's been a long time since I've been in an elevator. I glance around the lobby nervously. An elevator seems like a good place to get raped. A bad place, I amend as I step into the silver box. No one is on board, but a man could get in on any floor. Would I remember my aikido? Would it be effective against a gang or a gun? Elevators were not invented by a woman, that's for sure. I must have been nuts to let Nevada walk in here with her eyes closed.

Clinging to the wall of the elevator, I try not to hyperventilate. Why hadn't I realized that Nevada lives on the thirteenth floor? In some buildings there is no thirteenth floor; the elevator buttons go directly from twelve to fourteen. Thirteen would be the imaginary floor, the floor of the imagination. Would Nevada's Thing still open onto infinite space in a street level gallery?

The elevator doors open. I breathe a sigh of relief, but the hallway tilts ominously. Why is this happening? My agoraphobia is ancient history, isn't it? Writing about Nevada was supposed to protect me from a reccurrence, not deposit me directly in the blast furnace. Nevada's the one who's supposed to be taking the heat.

I lean against Nevada's door and push the bell with a red-tipped finger. I don't remember painting my nails! I don't even know how. Is Nevada's red seeping through from the inside?

As Nevada's door opens, I stumble and grab onto Nevada's boyfriend. I never realized how much Alec resembles my old boyfriend Paul. The long stringy blond hair, the Zen hippie patriarch beard, the tiny, babyish teeth set in long gums that his slightly goofy smile reveals. A long string bean in paint-stained jeans and prayer beads. Seeing him makes me feel nineteen again, hair brushing the waist of my long, Indian print skirt.

Alec seems to recognize me too, although he can't quite figure out who I am. "You're Nevada's sister? Cousin? Best friend from childhood?"

"Hardly," I say. "Don't you recognize me?"

"I can't put my finger on it."

"You used to be able to put your finger on it quite well." I haven't said anything that bold for years. That was one of the things I liked about Paul. With him I could say or do anything. He really helped me get the suburbs out of my system.

"Oh, you're one of my old girlfriends." Alec grins. "Come on in. I didn't think my memory was that bad. I mean I've had a lot of ladies, but I never thought I could forget someone so lovely."

"Thanks. You always were a gallant fibber. It's Claire." I step into Nevada's light-flooded loft. "But you never exactly had me, although I had you."

"A riddle. I like riddles. And it wasn't a fib, Claire."

"Don't overdo the charm. I look like a middle-aged English teacher. The doorman let me in without even calling up. That's how dangerous I look."

"That glint in your eyes looks dangerous to me." Alec leads me to the living area of the loft. "But you know, I'm living with someone now."

"That's why I'm here. Did you know that Nevada's run off with another man?"

"So that's what happened to her. It's not like her to go out without me."

"Was she agoraphobic before she met you?" I ask.

"I prefer to think of her as eccentric."

"Was she eccentric before she met you?"

"Not in that way."

"Do you blame yourself?"

"I never blame myself for anything." Alec flops into a ragged armchair. "You want a beer? I think there's a couple in the fridge."

"Sure." I sink into a pile of velvet pillows. Inside Nevada's loft, I feel safe. The high ceiling is sky-colored and painted clouds drift toward the open windows.

"Could you get one for me while you're up?" Alec says.

I look at him. Paul would have gotten me the beer. Paul would have made me tea in a cup with leaf fossils pressed into the bottom.

"Be *happy* to." Alec is probably used to being waited on hand and foot by an agoraphobic slave. Do I really look that much like Nevada? Maybe I'm prettier than I thought. I get up from my pillow nest and go into the open kitchen, which is already suffering from Nevada's absence. Still it's an inspiring room with glass-fronted cabinets and pedestal oak table. It makes me want to throw a dinner party for everyone I've ever known.

"Aren't you upset that your girlfriend's run off?" I ask as I hand Alec a Rolling Rock.

He pops the top and takes a swig. "I never let myself get upset by anything."

I sit back down on the pillows and sip my beer. That's exactly what Paul would have said. There's nothing more exasperating than a boyfriend who refuses to get upset about anything. Unless it's one who refuses to feel happy about anything, including your presence in his life. Maybe it's Nicholas I should be after.

"You want something to eat?" Alec asks.

"Not if I have to cook it."

"Hey, I invited you. I can make dinner. Nevada left some lasagna. There's Italian bread, peanut butter, matzos. I could fry up some hamburgers. That's about it, I think."

"How about hamburgers on matzos, or lasagna with bread and peanut butter on the side?"

"How about both?"

"I was kidding."

"Why? Peanut butter goes with everything."

"Even shrimp scampi?"

"Why not?"

"Ugh." Paul would have stir-fried tofu, brilliantly. "There's no way you can claim peanut butter goes with veal parmigiana."

"I can claim anything I want."

"I suppose you can. Would you really eat your hamburger on matzos?"

"Woman, don't be so narrow-minded. Matzos have been around for thousands of years. How long do you think hamburger rolls have been around?"

"What goes around comes around."

"True enough. Well, if you want to be conventional, how about I nuke some lasagna and make garlic bread?"

"Sounds great. Do you have any salad?"

"I think it went bad in the bottom of the refrigerator. Do you want to look?"

"I'll pass." I can't wait to see if Nevada's lasagna is better than mine. Since I lost my husband and kitchen, I haven't done much cooking. Nevada's more recently agoraphobic. That's enough to turn any woman into a gourmet cook and household slave, especially if she's got a protector she's trying to placate.

"You're as familiar as my own reflection," Alec says, heading toward the kitchen. "But I just can't remember when we were together. Or where. Or how it was."

"It was good," I say, grinning. "It was a lot of fun."

"It must have been a long time ago," Alec says, taking a head of garlic out of a hanging basket.

"That's one way of thinking about it. One thing I can tell you is we definitely had good chemistry. Weird but good."

"You aren't going to tell me what we did, or when we did it, or for how long?"

"Don't push your luck. When a woman gives her all, she expects at least a couple of pages in a man's memory scrapbook."

"OK. OK. I was just asking." Alec turns on the oven. "There's more beer if you want one."

"I know." I open the refrigerator and take one out for myself. "Want one?"

"Yeah." Alec catches the beer I throw him. "Thanks." He starts mincing garlic.

"Can I do anything?"

"Sit down and tell me your life story."

"You think you can trick me into telling you how we met?"

"Maybe." Alec slices a loaf of Italian bread and puts butter and garlic between the slices.

"I'm not going to make it that easy for you." I sit down at the round oak table and open my second beer. I'd forgotten how much fun it is to flirt.

"You want to make it hard for me?" Alec shoots me a pirate grin as he sticks the garlic bread in the oven.

"If it doesn't happen from just being in my presence, it's not even worth talking about."

"Give it time, woman, give it time." Alec puts Nevada's lasagna in the microwave and sits across from me. He drinks his beer and looks at me out of pale blue eyes. There's a funny kind of light in them that I remember from Paul.

"What?" I ask.

"What what?"

"What are you looking at?"

"Hasn't anyone ever looked at you before?"

"Of course. All the time." But I can't remember anyone looking at me in a long time. Aaron must have when we were first together. But in the last few years of our marriage, if I'd needed to see myself in his eyes, I would have shriveled up and blown away.

Alec's gaze is giving me sunburn. Or maybe it's just the hot garlicky breath of the oven.

"You have an evanescent kind of beauty," Alec says. "It comes and goes like the light on the river."

"Maybe if I smiled more when I look in the mirror, I wouldn't feel like such a plain Jane," I say, trying to hide my pleasure. I don't want him to think I haven't heard a compliment since way before the advent of Vivian. I don't want him to think I buy his line, if it is a line. And what if it is? No one's been motivated enough to feed me a line for years.

"When you smile, it looks like there are votive candles behind your eyes."

"Aren't you laying it on a little thick?" I press a hand to my hot cheek.

"Not thick enough to spread with a shovel. Anyway it's true." The microwave emits its triple beep. Alec unfolds his long body and gets the lasagna.

"It's too bad we started with beer," I say, taking a slice of garlic bread. I nibble at the charred crust. "Red wine would be perfect with this meal."

"Beer goes with everything," Alec says, serving me a big chunk of lasagna.

"Like peanut butter?"

"More so. Beer is the universal solvent."

"What does it solve?"

"All manner of human ills, baby. All manner of human ills."

"You sound like a real drinker."

"Just a realist."

"You didn't used to drink that much."

"I didn't used to be a realist."

"That's a strange definition of the word."

"No, just a realistic one."

"If you say so." I take a breath and stop myself from saying more. I'm not here to reform Alec. I put in enough time trying to turn my husband into a mensch. My time would have been better spent working on my own life. I'm already ten years behind where I'd like to be, personally *and* professionally. "Does beer go with strawberry shortcake?"

"You've hit on the one and only real exception," Alec says. "But if you want wine, there's a jug under the sink."

"Not after a beer and a half."

"Beer really does go with everything, other than cream cake."

"You must be Irish."

"Don't you know?"

"I haven't decided yet."

"What?"

"I mean I don't remember."

"You don't have to be Irish to like beer."

"True. You could be German."

"Or Chinese."

"So which is it?" I ask.

"I'll tell you when you tell me where we met."

"I'll just think of you as Chinese for now."

"If that's what turns you on."

"I'm not a faucet," I say crossly.

"I never said you were."

"Good. Don't forget it."

"Do you want me to turn you on?"

"Just being here turns me on," I say, my face getting hot. Alec-burn again.

"You don't mince words."

"No, just garlic."

Alec laughs and takes a swig of beer.

"Do you prefer minced words?" I take a bite of lasagna, but it burns my tongue.

"Would it make any difference if I did?"

"Not really. I minced enough words when I was married to make soup for the army, the navy, *and* the air force."

"Interesting analogy." Alec leans back in his chair and gets himself another beer from the fridge.

"When you're married words are clams," I say, "slippery and dangerous when raw. You have to mince and cook them so thoroughly, they don't have any mmmph left."

"Where did you get that recipe?"

"My mother-in-law's cookbook."

Alec laughs. "That's why I'm never getting married."

"Wise man."

The lasagna's cooling down. I take a bite and smile. It's full of fresh garlic and tomato chunks. I'll bet Nevada made the sauce from scratch. Well, there's not much else to do when you're agoraphobic. Make sauce and scratch. I used to make great stews and other pre–Industrial Revolution all-day projects like bread and yogurt. I'm a little out of practice now, but if I worked on fattening up Alec, I'd soon be ready to challenge Nevada to a cook-off.

I take another slice of garlic bread and smile at Alec. Nevada might beat me in the kitchen department, but she's not the only one with a man to feed and flatter her. Although it would be impossible to entertain the usual illusions about this relationship, it's a big improvement over playing the ugly duckling to Nevada's swan. And it's a vast improvement over feeling I inhabit a visual spectrum men just can't see. And it is, without a doubt, a humongous improvement over Date Hell.

"I never thought Nevada appreciated you enough," I say to Alec. "Pass the lasagna."

CHAPTER TWENTY-TWO

Nevada and I perch on opposite ends of Nicholas's old sofa. I'm knitting and Nevada's quilting. The apartment is cozy in a poky, too-small East Village sort of way. I can see the clawfoot bathtub through the archway that opens into the kitchen. It's obvious that Eileen made the chintz curtains and slipcovers, which are starting to fray, and that Nicholas hasn't had the heart to redecorate. Nevada's particularly interested in a little shrine Nicholas has set up to Eileen, complete with pink satin toe shoes and performance photos.

"So that's the dead wife," Nevada says. "She's pretty."

"So are you," I say, pouring tea from an indigo pot.

"But I'm not dead."

"It *is* hard to compete with a dead ballerina. But you have your resources."

"I do." Nevada's needle flashes in and out of her quilting square, precise and delicate as a hummingbird.

"I suppose congratulations are in order." My needles feel like oars but, I tell myself, I've only been knitting a week. "You probably think you're doing a better job on your story line than I would have."

"Well at least I'm doing things my way," Nevada says. Nicholas's grandfather clock chimes 3:00 A.M. If that doesn't wake him, neither will they. "You're so hung up on being touched. I don't see why you're in love with being an object. Isn't it time for women to become subjects? It's exhilarating taking control of your life. You really ought to try it."

"Ahh. So this is a feminist revolution." I shake out more wool. What would Nevada say if she knew just *what* I've been taking control of? "Since when did you become such a feminist?"

"I came out of my mother's womb a feminist."

"How politically correct of you."

"Thank you." Nevada pulls a green and tan afghan over her legs. "What's with the knitting? I didn't know you enjoyed working with your hands."

"Why does a woman have to apologize for enjoying womanly endeavors? Isn't knitting politically correct enough for you?"

"Don't be so touchy, Claire. I'm quilting." Nevada rummages around in her crewelwork bag for a pair of scissors. "I've been thinking of doing a series of textile wall hangings, you know the kind, with wildly contrasting textures and frayed ends of hemp emerging like expletives. At least until I can get back to my loft. There's no danger of cocooning in a wall hanging. Anyway, I think it's great that you're working with your hands."

"You think I'm wasting my time working with my brain?"

"Are you feeling guilty about something?"

"What should I be feeling guilty about?" I say, not looking at her.

"You tell me." Nevada looks at the huge blue shapeless thing in my lap. "What are you knitting, anyway?"

"I don't know." Since Madame's granddaughter gave me a lesson last week, I haven't been able to stop. I finish a row of purl and start a row of knit, ignoring the stitch I dropped half a row back. "Knitting *is* relaxing. I see why you like to live in your hands."

"I don't know how you can sit and write all day. I'd go out of my mind."

"Being in your mind is being out of your mind."

"You seem to be holding it together pretty well."

"I try to keep myself knitted together." My knitting is getting bigger and lumpier and more shapeless by the minute. Trusting my instincts doesn't seem to be working as far as knitting goes, but somehow I can't stop. It's like potato chips; one stitch leads inexorably to the next. I hope I'm not going to have to join Knitters Anonymous. Being agoraphobic was enough for one lifetime.

I take a sip of tea and a deep breath. I have to tell Nevada about Alec. I would expect at least that much from her. But I hate to align myself with Vivian the homewrecker. Well, there's no way around it. If Nevada hates me, she hates me. I take another deep breath and plunge in. "You'll never guess what I've been up to."

"What besides knitting?" Nevada tucks her legs up under her and smiles.

"Guess."

"You've started a new book."

"Nope."

"You're volunteering at a homeless shelter."

"Nope."

"You're going back to school to become a TV anchor-woman."

"Nope."

"So what did you do?"

"Do you want me to start a new book?"

"That's up to you." Nevada rethreads her needle.

"Don't you want me to finish your book?"

"Not if you're going to abandon me for weeks at a time."

"You've been doing OK."

"No thanks to you."

"Well, that's the point. Do you want to always have to be thanking me?"

"I don't have a problem thanking people." Nevada appliqués a chintz nautilus shell onto a quilting square. "So what do you want to tell me?"

I feel as if I'm about to tell my five-year-old the truth about Santa Claus and the Easter Bunny. "I've been seeing Alec," I say in a low voice. All I'm responsible for is saying it. If she doesn't hear it, it's not my problem.

"You have got to be kidding."

"Nope." I have to grin. I've never produced exactly that expression on anyone's face before. Apparently there's nothing wrong with Nevada's hearing.

"Why, in heaven's name, would you want to do that?"

"He reminds me of my old boyfriend, Paul."

Nevada's still looking at me with an indecipherable expression on her face. "Paul was always fun to play with," I go on. "And you would not believe what the guys out there are like. Poor dear. You've been missing out on the joys of Date Hell."

"I've had plenty of opportunities to be in hell in my lifetime." Nevada picks up the needle she dropped. Her thread's tangled and carefully she pulls at the knots.

"So you don't mind?" I look at her sideways.

"Why should I mind?"

"Well, Alec is your boyfriend."

"Alec isn't anybody's boyfriend," Nevada says. "If you want to make yourself really unhappy, try to own Alec."

"Thanks for the advice."

"Anytime." Nevada resumes her appliqué work, taking tiny perfect stitches. Who would guess that a woman who sculpts stone would have the patience to make such delicate stitches? Nevada is a truly amazing woman. I guess I won't be reincarnated as a snake in the grass after all. I would have hated to coil around Vivian for all eternity.

"You're a saint," I say.

"I just can't understand why anyone would want to waste her time with a loser like Alec."

"One woman's trash is another woman's treasure," I say. "You know—the thrift shop concept of dating—so nineties. But tell me, would you be as unpossessive about Nicholas?"

"You wouldn't dare."

"Daring isn't the issue. I would never do that to a friend. I was just wondering, in a hypothetical kind of way."

"Don't you *ever* get tired of manifesting girlfriend?" Nevada sips the last cold, bitter dregs of the tea and makes a face.

"Are you trying to stop me from dating Alec?"

"Are you accusing me of harboring unconscious motives?" Nevada heads into Nicholas's tiny kitchen to make a fresh pot of tea.

Reluctantly I put my knitting down and join her. "Who said

anything about unconscious? You could be trying to psych me out."

"I could be, but I'm not. I'm talking about a very common phenomenon," Nevada says as she fills the copper kettle.

"You mean feeling like a giant ear with a pasted-on smile?"

"That's exactly what I mean."

"You mean like rushing to get dinner ready and making sure your legs are shaved and the house is clean and forgetting who you are because it's too complicated to say what you feel?"

"Go with it, girlfriend." Nevada lights the burner with a wooden match from a tiny pottery pitcher.

"No, I don't have the faintest idea what you mean."

"Don't stop now."

"You mean like trying to maintain your cheerful demeanor while listening to him bad-mouth the whole universe?"

"Why is it that men feel they can mouth off about everything in the world?" Nevada asks as she rinses out Nicholas's teapot.

"And we feel we have to smile and be cheerful."

"You know what I really hate?" she says. "The way they make you feel guilty and inadequate every second they're helping you. They grouse and curse until you wish you had never asked them to help you put up your shelves in the first place."

"Why do we let it get to us?" I run my finger over the top of Nicholas's olive oil can, which is coated with a faint sheen. "Why can't we just let them be unpleasant and ignore them?"

"Maybe because they seem to have the license on that kind of behavior. We feel we have to keep smiling."

"What do you suppose would happen if we gave ourselves license to be equally unpleasant?" I wipe the top of the olive oil can with a paper towel.

"The world would fall apart."

"Manifesting girlfriend is causing the hole in the ozone layer?" Idly I pump the foot pedal on Nicholas's garbage can. The smell of stale garlic wafts into the room.

Nevada frowns at me and I let the garbage lid close. "Manifesting girlfriend gives them license to manifest whatever asshole behavior they want," she says.

"It takes so much energy and what do you get for it?"

"What do you get for anything?" Nevada arranges some biscotti on a glass plate embossed with grapes.

"A door prize?"

"You want a set of cheap china?"

"At least it's something."

"The reason to do things is to do them."

"How spiritual of you."

Nevada tosses me a saintly smile. She throws two tablespoons of jasmine tea into the indigo pot and pours boiling water over them.

I watch the little flowers float to the top like water lilies. "So why do we do it?"

"We can't figure out what else to do?"

"That's not very resourceful of us."

"What do you suggest?"

"I'm not going to do it anymore," I say.

"What if that means you lose your boyfriend?"

"Then he wasn't worth having, was he?"

"Hard to say. How did you feel about losing your husband?"

"I didn't lose him because I wasn't manifesting wife. I lost him because I manifested it too strenuously. I stopped being anything interesting at all." I start taking the dinner dishes out of the drainer and putting them away. "Aaron was a knight in rusty armor. I tried to polish his armor, but the more I scrubbed, the more the rust seeped through from the inside, kind of like desiccated blood."

Nevada wrinkles her nose. "Do you think all knights have rusty armor?"

"I haven't taken a representative sampling. Are you wondering about Nicholas?"

"He does that courtly thing so well. It does make you wonder what's underneath."

"That remains to be seen." Taking the tea Nevada hands me, I head back to the couch.

"You mean you really don't know?"

"I really don't know."

"Whatever happened to your guarantee of safety?"

"It passed its expiration date the day you declared your independence."

"The price of safety in your world is slavery? How can you align yourself with the patriarch oppressors? That's as bad as manifesting girlfriend."

"It is manifesting girlfriend. And after you've paid the price, you discover the safety you sacrificed your freedom to obtain is an illusion."

Nevada nods. "It's terrifying how easy it is to fall into that old trap."

"I know what you mean. It just opens up in front of you, and you can't keep yourself from sliding in. The only way to escape is to gnaw off your own foot."

"Do you think the only way to be a free woman is to be a wild creature?"

"Maybe we should just have fleeting encounters with men in

the wilderness, then go back to our lairs, where we can crunch bones and howl at the moon in peace."

"I can think of worse ways to live." She ties Nicholas's royal blue silk robe more tightly around her. There's enough room for both of us in there. "Well, now that we've got that settled, and I'm sure women everywhere will be thanking us, what I really want to know is—doesn't anyone want to get laid anymore?"

"You're asking the wrong person. You've at least had sex in this decade."

"If you can call it sex."

"It's more than I've had," I say, swirling the water lilies in my cup.

"Are you telling me you didn't have what passes for sex with Alec?"

"I certainly did not. Not on a first date."

"I don't know if I'd exactly call it a first date. You did write the man into existence." Nevada takes a biscotti and nibbles at it. "If you think about it, you've been more intimate with him than I have."

"I don't think that's where characters are born from. It is an intriguing idea, though." I get down on the floor and start stretching.

"Well I don't think you should be shy about sleeping with Alec," Nevada says. "You can do whatever you want. You're in charge of the story line. You can make him feel about you any way you want."

"Things happen. They take on a life of their own. You have less control than you would think."

"I've been noticing that," Nevada says. "But I thought that was because it's your book."

"I don't think that's it, but I can't be sure."

Nevada joins me on the floor and throws her feet over her head. "So you really didn't go to bed with him?"

"I wouldn't want to give Alec the wrong idea." I try to do what Nevada's doing but come up a foot short. Oh well. When I start having sex, my back will loosen up. It's got to happen soon! "All we did was engage in a little innocent flirtation. And I did have to go to work. Do you think I would go in wrinkled clothes with three hours of sleep?"

"You could have borrowed something of mine."

"There's nothing in your closet boring enough to teach in, or huge enough to pull over my hips."

"I forgot about people having to go to work," Nevada says, pushing herself up into a perfectly straight shoulder stand. "Is Nicholas going to have to go on tour soon?"

"Would that bother you?"

"I wouldn't mind too much if you let me get back to my Thing. There is a lot of unfinished work in the meadows."

"I thought you promised Alec you'd stay away from the Thing."

"Do you really think I owe Alec anything?"

"Wouldn't it be nice to start something new?"

"How can I?" Nevada says. "I can't go back to the loft if you're there with Alec."

"I don't know," I say, chewing a jasmine blossom. "It might be interesting."

Nevada makes a face at me. "This apartment's too small and so is The Orange Cat Bistro."

"So you want to work on something big!" I decide to give her the benefit of the doubt. "That's great! I could meet Alec at The Orange Cat Bistro, and you could go back to the loft to work. We could work out a system of signals."

"That's not a bad idea," Nevada says. "If he's going to sleep at your place, I can work all night. I love working at three, four, five in the morning. The air is free of all the daytime pressures then, and you can really go out on a creative limb."

"I'm proud of you."

Nevada blushes. "Did I tell you I've been fantasizing about taking Nicholas into my Thing?"

"Wow. Really?"

"Really. I really like him. Wouldn't that be a great place to make love for the first time?"

"What an idea!" I pop a biscotti into my mouth. "You know you're getting really good at this, Nevada."

"Well, I have a good teacher."

"You're leaving me in the dust."

CHAPTER TWENTY-THREE

"Are you sure it's OK to be here?" Nicholas asks as Nevada, eyes still closed, leads him into her loft. The scent of lasagna lingers in the air.

"Yes," she says impatiently. "I explained all that to you already. There's nothing to worry about. Everything's taken care of." She wonders how Claire liked the lasagna.

"I know you explained it, but I can't say it made a lot of sense to me." Nicholas takes off his navy blazer and throws it over the back of the sofa.

"It doesn't have to make sense to you. Just know that it's OK."

"I prefer for things to make sense."

"What happened to your plea for faith?"

"What happened to your memory, my dear? My plea was for faith, not foolishness."

"Well, if you haven't figured it out already, being involved with me is a plunge into inspired foolishness."

Nicholas laughs. "Thank you for explaining that to me. I feel better already."

"That's why I'm here," Nevada says. "To make you feel better already."

Nicholas studies the luminous shifting shapes in Alec's paintings. He could swear things, creatures, are moving behind the paint, just out of the range of his vision. But when he turns to catch them, he sees nothing but swirling shapes.

It feels strange enough to be intruding on another man's turf, but to have that man be such a fine artist is giving him second and third thoughts about what he's doing with Nevada. How would he have felt if Eileen had brought a strange man to their apartment? Although truthfully, he would rather have lost her to another man than to anorexia. Even to another woman. At least she would be in the world somewhere, her beauty shining in more than his memory.

"These are really good," he says, turning to Nevada.

"Yes, one thing you have to say about Alec—he is a terrific painter." Nevada moves across the room to join Nicholas and bumps into a table. "Ouch!" she says, rubbing her leg. You'd think she would know her way around her own loft with her eyes closed. Has Claire been moving furniture?

"It sounds like you have a lot of respect for him."

"As an artist I always did."

"And as a man?"

"I wouldn't exactly call Alec a man."

"That's rather harsh, isn't it?"

"You don't know Alec."

"Was he cruel to you?"

"Yes."

"Well, that is different." Nicholas settles on the couch. "Why did you stay with him?"

"Do you want the short answer or the essay?" Nevada perches next to him.

"Which do you want to give me?"

"The essay will take all day."

"How about the short answer, then."

"It's impossible to explain in a few words."

"Then why did you offer?"

"I was stalling for time." Nevada takes a sip of something someone left on the coffee table. Red wine. Claire. "How about multiple choice?"

"I don't want to play games, Nevada."

"That's too bad, Nicholas. Because that's exactly what I want to do."

"Because you want to run away from your pain?"

"Don't you?"

Nicholas thinks about that. Is it really such a bad idea? Mourning hasn't lightened the pain any. He could mourn for the rest of his life and still have a heart as heavy as Eileen's gravestone. "Maybe."

"Then run away with me."

"Where to?"

Nevada stands up and holds out her hand. "Into my Thing."

Nicholas lets Nevada take his hand. She leads him to a large draped object in the center of the loft and pulls off the drop cloth. Getting down on her hands and knees, she crawls into the opening of what looks to be an ancient cave.

Nevada pauses inside the entrance, surprised to find herself trembling. She's gotten so used to thinking of the Thing as Hassiloff's, she forgot it was still available to her. And after what Alec's been up to with Claire, she doesn't feel the slightest bit guilty about breaking her promise. But if she lets Nicholas come in with her, will the goddesses take their iron pots and magic fires and disappear? Slowly she unlaces her hiking boots. What if he feels trapped by the rock walls? The best of her is in the Thing. If he can't love it, can he love her? Nevada pulls off her left boot. But she's already offered Nicholas medicine for his pain. She lets her right boot drop. And he's been so kind. The goddesses might like him as much as she does. She pushes some fire-blackened bones out of her way and crawls into the entry tunnel.

Nicholas gets down on his hands and knees. The closer he gets, the more the entry hole looks like a giant vulva. Rainwater runs in the crevices between the rocks. How did Nevada get stone to look so soft and giving? Could she sprinkle magic dust on his company's dusty old sets?

Nicholas runs his hand over the creases in the rock. Is he really ready to crawl into a giant vulva? He's been comfortably immersed in his suffering and loneliness for so long. He's been immune to the Virus by virtue of keeping his love life limited to ghosts. Ghost women are dangerous enough. What will a real woman do to his equilibrium?

Maybe it's time to start believing in Nevada's guarantee of protection, Nicholas thinks as he slips out of his loafers. Some of his favorite operas are based on stranger premises. But what if it turns out to be like Eileen's promise that she had everything under control, she knew what she was doing, she could handle it?

Nicholas pulls off his socks. All he wanted was to rescue a few wounded birds. All he wants is to stop feeling this pain for a little while, to know that it's possible, that there is balm for his pain, other than work, which try as he might, he can't do twenty-four hours a day. All he wants is to feel Nevada touch him, to feel the solid presence of another human being beside him, not dead, not a ghost, not a thin-as-death memory. He crawls through the opening and follows Nevada's rapidly disappearing behind down a long twisty tunnel.

Now that she's safely ensconced in her Thing, Nevada confidently flexes her eyebrows. She wants to bathe her eyes in the pearly light whose source even she has never been able to locate. Surely in here her eyes will open! But her eyelashes still feel stuck together with Krazy Glue. Has her refusal to look reality in the face blinded her? She hopes the goddesses are cooking up a sight-restoring balm for her in their mysterious pots, a soothing lotion that smells of cucumbers and eyebright.

Nevada pulls her denim jacket free from a crevice. She's never been in the Thing with clothes on before. It feels as though she's entered a Japanese home with shoes on, her soles contaminating the immaculate mats. But she didn't want to scare Nicholas by disrobing in full daylight.

"Nicholas." She pauses in the first chamber where water trickles over stone. "I'm not doing this to seduce you. The last thing I want to do is make you uncomfortable. But this is not a place to wear clothes." She takes off her jacket. "If I were you, I would get naked. You're completely safe from me. I couldn't open my eyes if I wanted to."

Nevada wasn't joking about her stone-cutting muscles, Nicholas thinks as he slowly unbuttons his shirt. Well, he's always liked lean women. An unfortunate taste, perhaps. But Nevada doesn't have that Biafra look that Eileen developed toward the end. Nevada has flesh on her bones—not enough to please his grandmother, but she looks full of life.

Nevada breathes a sigh of relief as her clothing comes off.

Her body feels fluid, of a piece, without the artificial restrictions of this can be shown and that must be covered. One thing you have to say about artists—a little nudity never throws them.

Nicholas sits on a rock and pulls his trousers off. The walls of the Thing are cool and smooth against his bare skin. It's almost like touching flesh, almost like being touched, surrounded, by flesh. He can sense eyes all around. But it doesn't make him self-conscious—he feels watched over, mothered.

Nevada gropes her way over to Nicholas. "Doesn't it feel better to be naked in here?" she asks him.

"Yes," he admits, "but I'm glad you can't see me."

"I can touch you, if you'll let me."

Nicholas thinks about that, about how one thing leads inevitably to another and about how he doesn't have protection. He doubts Nevada does, either. He thinks about Eileen's emaciated body at the wake and how much pain you open yourself up to when you agree to love someone. People just won't take care of themselves for you, even when you love them. They won't stop starving themselves, they won't stop doing coke, they won't open their eyes, they won't stop going home with strangers they can't see. But he wants so much to be touched. He wants so much to touch Nevada.

"Let me touch you," Nevada says softly. "I want to sculpt you with my hands."

"Don't think I don't want to touch you."

"Later."

"You're so beautiful. I want to get my hands all over you," he groans. "I don't have enough hands."

"Then borrow mine," Nevada says, nimbly eluding him despite her blindness. She doesn't want him to get her in the position Alec always got her in. She wants to be the subject, not the object, for a change. Does she have the courage to love a man who's not crippled, not impotent, she wonders and shudders even thinking the I-word. She never dared to use it around Alec, though he probably would have laughed. Actually, he got a kick out of his impotence, as if he were purposely withholding something from her, refusing to make a bowel movement for mommy.

Nevada lets her hands roam over Nicholas's body, as though feeling out a new block of stone for possibilities. Nicholas is not a modern man, not the Nautilus-sculpted hunk from the latest video hit. She can imagine him as a Victorian explorer with muttonchop whiskers, big-bellied, thick-limbed, muscular, wearing a shooting jacket and high boots. She would sculpt him on a mountain peak in some strange, wild place, practicing manifest destiny. But compassionately. She can't wait to see if her vision is true. But her hands are so well coordinated with her eyes, she sees his lines as clear as the connections that turn stars into constellations.

Nicholas relaxes into Nevada's touch. Eileen's ideal was to perfect her body to the point of nonexistence, and she really didn't care for the solidity of his body, his largeness. She liked his worship of her almost nonexistent body, she liked him to come to her as a supplicant. But she never liked the physicalness of it, the smells, the things that would never be implied in classical ballet. And while he loved her delicacy, her art, he could love Nevada's love of his man's body much, much more.

Nevada lets her hands circle down Nicholas's massive back. Nicholas she'd sculpt in granite, as Atlas holding up the world. Can someone like Nicholas, who's not weird, not crippled, love someone like her? She wants him to love her for *everything* she is, her art, her fear, her sadness, her beauty, the walls surrounding her heart. She's tired of her shame, tired of letting her hands be tied behind her back, tired of letting fear make her choices.

Nicholas relaxes under Nevada's touch, lets himself be pampered, cared for. His skin grows soft and silken. In the distance he thinks he hears the motif from *The Magic Flute*, the flute that tames wild beasts and offers magical protection to its owner. Is that where Nevada gets her guarantee of protection? If the music keeps playing and Nevada keeps stroking his skin, his memories of Eileen might just disappear like the lingering notes of the flute's refrain.

The goddesses must be brewing up love spells. Nevada thinks she can smell red things in the air: roses and love apples, as well as hearts of palm, rosemary, thyme, chocolate, champagne. She's very glad to have the goddesses' blessing. The goddesses, like her mother, never thought much of Alec. What was she thinking to ignore the goddesses and her mother?

When Nicholas reaches for her, she doesn't push him away. He holds her, and she lets her hands rest, lets her heart beat in harmony with his. She can feel his chest hair against her face, soft and curly, matting under the damp pressure of her cheek. Are his eyes filled with lust? longing? tenderness? She can feel them all in his embrace, but which is strongest? If only she could see his eyes. Or is it as the song says, in his kiss?

If the song is right, it is love. Nevada's heart floods with happiness, but her mind asks, *How could he love someone as damaged as me?*

So, what's not to love? It's high time she started talking back to her negative voices. *I'm smart, funny, talented, pretty. My only problem is I can't open my eyes. And I used to have a weird boyfriend. But he's history.*

There's a shift in the air and the electric charge that signals the approach of a goddess. A glass of champagne finds its way into Nevada's hand.

"Where did this come from?" Nicholas holds his glass aloft.

"Our union is being blessed."

"I've been learning that down here, it's better not to ask too many questions." Where the lines of perspective meet, Nicholas thinks he can see goddesses laying Eileen to rest. They cover her grave with white lilacs. "To the goddesses and their blessings," he proposes.

Nevada links her arm through his and they drink the pure sparkling stuff, cold as river's source, so cold it makes Nevada's teeth ache. Light is beginning to creep under her lashes. She feels more awake than she's ever been. Who could have guessed that the goddesses' sight-restoring balm would be champagne?

She could still, in these last minutes before regaining her sight, imagine anything she wants about Nicholas—that he's a city god, a glowing prince, a fascinating monster. But despite the kaleidoscope of fictional possibilities, she wants nothing more than to stay in this moment, to finally align herself with reality.

Nicholas touches her and she softens. Guarantee of safety or not, she would have to trust a man who touches her like this, who kisses her so tenderly.

Is that a backup chorus of goddesses singing Motown? Did she forget to put the safety catch on her imagination? The goddesses have never sung rock 'n' roll before, not when she's been around. But even goddesses grow and change. If they can overcome millennia of habit and conditioning, why couldn't she?

Nicholas kisses her gently and enters her, filling her with presentness. The moment's inside of her, she's pregnant with the moment. He kisses her eyes, soft, sweet kisses, and she opens them, she opens to him. His face is so familiar, something about the soft golden light on it, the almost feminine softness of his brown eyes, the velvety, slightly smudged intimacy of his skin, but she's sure she's seeing it for the first time. His face is like the sun, like an archaic portrait of the sun. He's a sun god with his gold hair licking around his face like sun fire. She can see his fat cheeks and wide curving mouth done in the fine sharp line of an old engraving as he rocks her in the archaic rhythms of love, his face flushed with love, her sun god.

CHAPTER TWENTY-FOUR

I peek curiously under the drop cloth Nevada has thrown over the Thing. Alec has gone out for beer, so I have at least twenty minutes to see if the Thing is as fabulous as I'd always imagined. I wriggle inside. This is definitely a place to be naked in, to feel smooth stone against bare skin. Slipping out of my dress and panty hose, I go farther in. Nevada must have drained the Thing before she covered it. It's cool and dry and clean as a well-endowed museum.

If this were my Thing, I would never come out, if I could get someone, Alec for example, to bring me food. I wriggle farther in and greet a gathering of tiny goddesses engaged in womanly labors. One is growing flowers and vegetables. Another is cooking something in a big iron pot. Others are weaving and knitting.

As I head farther in, I hear Alec open the loft door and call my name. My feet keep walking inward. Why should I come out for him? He's not even real. And if he were, would he be worth leaving the shelter of the goddesses' world? Maybe they'll teach me about magic and herbal healing. If I stay in here for ten or twenty years, I might become a wisewoman. The goddesses whisper to me of the pleasures of solitude. They tell me everything in life is ashes without enlightenment. How can I get enlightened amid the noise and confusion of New York? They show me their gold masks of serenity and promise to make me an even more beautiful one.

"Claire," I hear Alec calling from a great distance. "Claire, I'm not sure it's OK for you to be in there." I wouldn't have expected Alec to show so much respect for Nevada's privacy. Still he doesn't fully understand the situation. I move farther in, and catch a glimpse of snowcapped mountains. Funny, I don't remember putting the Himalayas in here.

"Claire," I think I hear. "I bought you a present. Come and get it."

I start walking toward the mountains. The thought of snow on my bare skin makes me shiver. It would be so pure, so white, so all-consuming.

"I bought you a teddy bear."

I've got to be making this up. Alec would never buy anybody a teddy bear.

"Please don't turn into Nevada." Alec's voice comes out of the sky. "I never could get her out of that damned Thing."

My resolute mountainward steps falter. I never would have dreamed Nevada's behavior would hurt Alec. He's a man who likes his space and plenty of it. Doesn't he? Then I hear the faint strains of a flute. "Alas, my love, you do me wrong / to treat me with such discourtesy," I sing along with Alec's thin, silvery rendition of "Greensleeves." I never meant to hurt Alec.

My bare skin is so cold. It needs the caress of warm hands, not icy crystals. Alec's hands would trace delicate patterns, lighting my skin with pale fire. I start walking in the direction of Alec's voice. If I stay in here, there's no telling what will show up next: the northern lights, the Red Sea parting before my eager feet. But how can I resist a man who buys me stuffed animals? I can come back in and get enlightened some other time.

I wave to the goddesses, who wave sadly back, and pick up my dress. There's no point in making things *too* easy for him. Slipping it over my head, I wriggle out the entrance.

"Hullo," I say. I was gone just half an hour. Why is he so white and shaky? He holds out a pink teddy bear.

"You really did buy me a teddy bear. I thought I was hallucinating." The heart-shaped pillow it holds says, "Captive Heart." "No one's bought me a stuffed animal since I was a kid. I never got to be a sweet young thing with a boyfriend who bought me ankle bracelets and took me to amusement parks. I was always the lonely, strange girl carrying a huge pile of books."

"I'll have to remember that," Alec says in a husky voice. He grabs me and hugs me hard. Something's melting deep inside me, and my mouth floods. I swallow hard. It's not cool to be this needy. I'm actually salivating. I can't let Alec see how much I want it. Although the truth is, I never thought I'd see him so needy and uncool either. I don't feel in control of this material at all. Could Nevada be writing this chapter? It certainly doesn't feel like my style. But who would have guessed Nevada, the lady of granite, had a sentimental streak? Maybe she just wants me out of her Thing.

Alec leans his face down toward me and the rest of the world disappears. I could stay stranded inside this kiss forever. Why move relentlessly forward?

When we come up for air, he lets the space between us in-crease and leads me over to the couch. He puts his arm around me and pulls me close.

"Is your heart really my captive?" I ask.

"If you can find my heart, doll, it's yours," Alec says, stroking my hair. I've never thought of my hair as an erogenous zone before. Foolish me.

"I don't think the whereabouts of your heart are such a mys-tery. It's here." I touch the teddy bear's heart. "And you gave it to me. It's here." I touch Alec's chest. "And it's here." Lightly I brush my fingers across his lap. "And this one's mine, too."

"That's my heart-on, dollface."

"It's mine, tough guy."

"Yeah, I'm real tough." Alec's fingers brush the neckline of my dress. "And don't you forget it."

How could I forget it? I wrote him that way. But I never real-ized he had such talented hands. "Hard as nails, too."

"I have you to thank for that."

"My pleasure."

"I hope so."

His mouth tastes like beer and cigarettes—an oddly pleasant bitterness. His lips feel both firm and soft. I like the way he nuzzles me. Paul was never this good a kisser. Aaron was never this good a kisser. I'll bet Nicholas isn't this good a kisser. Why would Nevada have given this up? Nevada doesn't appreciate anything I do for her.

When Alec lets me up for air, I ask him, "If you're so tough, how come you're shaking?"

"How come you ask so many questions, dollface?"

I laugh. "I don't know. It drives my students crazy. I'm always trying to get them to think. But I'll tell you one thing without a question mark on the end of it—I like it when you call me doll-face." I cuddle into him. "It makes me feel like a gangster's moll."

"Whatever turns you on."

"It sure beats feeling like an English teacher."

"Nothing wrong with English teachers," Alec says, caressing the curve of my calf. "Do you know how many boys fantasize about what their English teacher has under her skirt?"

"Oh, the usual equipment."

"Yeah, but those proper clothes make it all the more excit-ing. It's such a challenge getting to it." Alec's hand creeps be-neath my skirt.

"I'll have to remember that," I say, laughing. "I always thought sexy was black lace lingerie with embarrassing cutouts." It's been a long time since anyone's hand has attempted the long climb.

"You're sexy," Alec says, unbuttoning the bodice of my shirt-waist. He caresses each bit of flesh as it comes undone.

"Me?" I say wonderingly. I long for him to stay forever on each spot, while each untouched part longs for him to continue his slow ramble.

"I love the way you love to be touched. That's much sexier than some hard-as-nails bitch in a stripper's costume."

"Who wouldn't want to be touched like this?" I say without thinking. I arch back, so he can get at more of me.

"Not everyone appreciates the hands of a master."

"Oh you mean *her*. Let's not talk about her."

"Fine with me."

"Does she wear stripper's costumes for you?" I sit up. I never wrote that in. And I wouldn't call Nevada a hard-as-nails bitch either.

"I thought you didn't want to talk about her," Alec says, pushing me back down.

"I don't. Just tell me if she wears stripper's clothes for you."

"Claire."

"I could be a bitch in a stripper's costume if you want me to be."

"Claire. I just told you I find you incredibly sexy the way you are—prim and repressed on the outside, soft and melting on the inside."

"Oh yeah. You did. Sorry." I let him lick me where I'm all soft and melting. I banish all thoughts of Nevada from my mind. I banish all thoughts of everything I'm not—blond, eighteen, a Victoria's Secret's model. Alec makes me feel he desires me for everything I am—plain Jane, thirty-something teacher hiding a crazed bacchante. I thought that part of me was lost forever in the wreckage of my marriage. Einstein was right. Nothing is ever destroyed. It just resurfaces years later in a different form. And I definitely like the form it's taking.

Shamefaced, Alec lifts his head from my body. He looks like a tousle-headed little boy who's just been caught with his hand in the cookie jar. As far as I'm concerned, he can stick his hand in my cookie jar anytime. "You know that little problem I used to have?"

I nod, but actually I'd forgotten all about it. Orgasm always turns my brain to mush.

"Well, I still have it."

"That's OK. I don't think I'm ready for the real thing." I stroke his hair.

"I thought women always wanted the real thing."

"Well, I am still convalescing from my divorce. And this *is* only our second date. English teachers never do it on a second date."

"I'll have to remember that. In case I ever get my act together."

"I'm sure you will. Maybe I can help."

"You're sweet, doll. But a lot of women have tried. A lot of women. I'm very intractable."

"I have resources you couldn't even begin to dream of."

"She was never able to."

"Did she try?"

"She's young. She doesn't have your experience or compassion. And she was very involved in her work."

Should I feel pleased that Alec prefers my age to Nevada's youth or upset that he finds my character shallow? And who isn't very involved in her work?

"You're a very sweet woman." He rests his head on my breast, and I lie back and stroke his hair. "There's no reason we can't have fun, Claire. I know how to please a woman."

"You don't have to tell me that, Alec."

"Really?"

"Couldn't you tell?"

"I thought so, but I wasn't sure. You don't make much noise."

"English teachers are more subtle in their orgasmic style," I say primly. "More ethereal. Not everyone has to act like an animal. But before you dislocate your shoulder patting yourself on the back, you should realize that one orgasm only counts as a minus six for me."

"Come again?"

"About seven times, I hope. The score stands at minus six. In case you're counting."

"Mmm, an insatiable woman." Alec nibbles my ear.

"Is that another item on men's fantasy lists?"

"You better believe it, doll. Especially insatiable English teachers."

"What about insatiable algebra teachers?"

"Nope. Only English teachers do the trick."

"And what trick is that?"

"Making the soldier stand at attention." Alec jumps off the couch and gives me a snappy salute. I can't remember when he got completely nude or when he was in the service.

"A private, I presume."

"Four-star general." Alec gives me a hurt look.

"Of course," I say. "But watch where you point that thing."

"That's right, doll. It's loaded."

"I've always hated the image of penis as weapon," I shudder.

"I'm just trying to make you laugh."

"You men certainly like to strut your stuff."

"You don't find me unique?" Alec says, starting to do calisthenics.

"Of course you're unique. You're the only man on the face of this planet with an erection."

"It's nothing to take for granted, dollface."

I never thought I'd get to know Alec *this* well when I wrote him into Nevada's story line. I never thought he'd show up in the present tense at all, and here he is squat-thrusting in my direction. "I find it hard to imagine you in the service."

"Do you find it hard to imagine me in you?" Alec asks, bounding back to the couch.

"No."

"Do you find it hard?"

"Oh yes."

Alec caresses my waist. "Isn't that belt bothering you?"

"No, is it bothering you?" If he wants me naked, let him work for it.

"It certainly is, doll."

"I didn't think you of all people would need a map to find your way under a woman's skirt."

"I'll have to perform a skirtectomy."

I lie totally still while Alec works on my fastenings. How long has it been since anyone's thought getting my clothes off was worth the struggle? And these lady dresses with their mysterious closures do make it a struggle.

Alec's right about one thing. I have to remember never to take anything for granted. Maybe no one ever stops being eighteen. All it needs is the right lover to wash away the wasted years, the awkwardness of unloved limbs. My skin feels rosy and youthful, like Gustav Klimt girls lying in pools of gold. Alec's turning me from a dried up old withered Klimt witch to a rosy well-beloved young girl lying in her young man's arms. The faint wrinkles etching Alec's face, the strands of grey in his yellow hair make the renaissance all the sweeter. I thank Nevada's goddesses, who have obviously been cooking this up for me in their iron pots for months.

CHAPTER TWENTY-FIVE

"Ahh, zee banana bread elvz." Madame, huge in a chenille bathrobe, walks into the kitchen of The Orange Cat Bistro. It's 3:00 A.M., and Nevada and I are starting some buttermilk-oatmeal bread. Just as I thought, Madame never sleeps.

"We would have left you a bowl of French pastries, but that's a little beyond our culinary ability," I say.

"Speak for yourself," Nevada says as she pours oatmeal and whole wheat flour into a white-and-blue bowl.

Madame, her broad face shiny with cold cream, looks at Nevada appraisingly. "Your friend, she eez French?"

Nevada flashes her dimple at Madame and makes a well in the flour.

"She's as American as I am." Nobody ever asks me if I'm French. I should have made Nevada ugly but with a good heart.

Readers like that. Well, it's too late now. We'll all just have to keep putting up with how beautiful she is.

"My Marie, she weel make you dresses that make you look like a true Frenchwoman," Madame says to Nevada.

Madame never offered her daughter's couturier services to me, I think grumpily, and sprinkle two packets of yeast granules into a bowl of lukewarm water.

"I never wear anything but jeans," Nevada is saying when Madame's son-in-law, nightshirt covering a big belly, peers into the kitchen. Doesn't anybody sleep at The Orange Cat Bistro? It's no fun staying up all night if everybody does. He eyes Nevada and me in our nightgowns and sticks a toothpick under his mustache. I don't get it. Our granny gowns are less revealing than anything we would wear during the day. I guess it's the idea of clothes you wear to bed.

He and Madame start quarreling in French, something about food, I think. They get very passionate, gesticulating and talking so loudly, I'm worried that they'll shock the yeast. Yeast needs tranquillity to perform its miracles. Yeast needs hope and harmony to make things rise. I wrap a blue-and-white-striped towel around the yeast and cradle it to my chest, sending it images of perfect loaves with brown, shiny egg-washed crusts, enough to feed a multitude.

The noise is subsiding. Madame seems to have won the argument. I murmur encouragingly to the yeast and put it back on the counter. Madame's son-in-law gives Nevada and me a subdued leer out of hooded eyes and slinks out, making sure we can see as much of his manhood as possible. It's hard to believe such inspiring food comes from such a source. I guess chefs are like writers— it's better not to meet the ones whose work you most admire.

"Don't stay up too late, girlz. It eez a school night." Madame takes a brown-flecked golden pear from a blue bowl. I want to ask her where she finds fruit from that looks hand-plucked from ancient Provence orchards, but she's gone.

As soon as her broad rump disappears down the hall, I start to giggle. "There's no one who can make me feel fifteen faster than Madame. When was the last time someone told you not to stay up late?"

"You do have to work tomorrow, Claire," Nevada says, rolling up her sleeves. "Are you going to be OK?"

"I'll be fine. I need a lot less sleep since I've become fictional."

"That's ridiculous," Nevada says. "I can work all night, but then I have to sleep till at least four in the afternoon if I don't want to be a *total* zombie."

"I'll give the kids quizzes and take catnaps at my desk. I love staying up late. It's such a quiet, mysterious, forbidden time. You never know what's going to happen at three in the morning. That's when Alec and I are at our best."

Nevada stirs honey and oil into the yeast. "I think you're writing Alec better for yourself than you did for me."

"That may be true," I say, pouring buttermilk into a glass measuring cup, "but isn't Nicholas terrific?"

"He's fat."

"You want me to put him on a diet?"

"No. It's right for him to be fat."

"Thank you."

"Don't you think it's time to date someone you didn't make up?"

I pour the buttermilk into the yeast mixture. "Have you seen what's out there?"

"Obviously not."

"Well, let me tell you what it's like. It may make you appreci-ate what I do for you. Did I ever tell you about the guy before the Date from Hell?"

"I don't think so," Nevada says. She pours the liquid ingredi-ents into the well in the flour.

"He was my first dating service gem. I never actually met him in person. We talked on the phone quite a few times, though. He always wanted to talk about sex. Exactly what I liked."

"So what did you tell him?" Nevada asks with my avidly curi-ous expression on her face. You'd think she was writing this book.

"Oh I told him I liked the usual stuff," I say. "And when he pressed me for details, I said I liked it the regular way. He made me feel very maidenly. It's embarrassing to tell a total stranger about who does what to whom in your fantasies."

"To whom?" Nevada grins.

"Excuse me," I say. "Being an English teacher is not a termi-nal disease. And not everybody finds it a turn-off."

"Yeah, yeah," Nevada says. "I know all that. But don't you get time off for good behavior?"

"An English teacher is never off-duty," I say primly. "There are always dangling modifiers to be knitted back into the fabric of the sentence, split infinitives to be tenderly glued back together."

"Since when did you join the grammar police?" Nevada sprinkles flour on the marble pastry board.

"My badge came pinned to my diploma," I say proudly.

"It's nice to have a purpose in life," Nevada says as she starts to mix the dough. "But why did you keep talking to this guy?"

"Loneliness, I guess. Naïveté. It was so long since a man showed interest in me."

"You're worth a lot more than these losers, Claire."

I push her out of the way and start mixing the dough with my hands. This is my favorite part. How many opportunities do grown-ups get to make mud pies? "If you're talking about Alec, I think he's sweet."

"So did I. Don't forget I lived with him for two years."

"Alec's a changed man."

"Really."

"In fact I've been wondering if you had anything to do with the changes." The dough's stiffening up under my fingers, starting to feel like flesh.

"Me?"

"Well, I can't believe how sweet he's become."

"I thought I could change Alec, too," Nevada says, putting the buttermilk and the honey away. "I think he likes having women pump out tremendous amounts of energy trying to fix him, while he gets his jollies being intractable."

"This is different. Did he ever buy you a teddy bear?"

"A teddy bear? Alec?"

"I couldn't believe it either."

"*Alec* bought you a teddy bear?"

"Yup."

"So I guess you've healed his little problem."

"I'm not a miracle worker."

"You must be," Nevada says, wrist-deep in dough.

"So *you're* not behind Alec's changes?"

"Only through my absence from his life."

"You haven't been sneaking into my room when I'm with Alec and subtly influencing the story line?"

"Why would I want to do that?" Nevada turns the dough onto the floured board.

"You're sure you haven't been fooling around with my type-writer?" I start washing the mixing bowl and measuring cups. The remnants of dough are as tenacious as thought. I hope we don't clog Madame's pipes.

"Claire, when I'm not with Nicholas, I'm working on my new piece. I don't have time to play games with you and Alec."

"What are you working on?" I turn around, suds dripping down my arms onto the slate floor. "Why didn't you tell me you started something new?"

"I'd really rather not discuss it."

"Was your mother very withholding?"

"Claire. Do you talk about your work when you're in the middle of it?"

"It must be obvious that I don't have an iota of privacy in my creative life."

"If I don't husband my creative energies for my work, nothing gets done," Nevada says, pressing the heels of her hands deep into the dough.

"Is that like athletes having to abstain from sex before the big game?"

"That theory's been discredited."

"Exactly. So tell me what you're up to. You can't imagine how excited I am."

"Can't you respect the way I need to work, Claire? Just because you talk to every dating service jerk about your work in progress, doesn't mean everyone should go prematurely public."

"Prematurely public! It took you *ten years* to finish the Thing. And even then your hand had to be forced." Savagely I wring out the sponge. "Don't condescend to me! Writing this book has been like opening a vein and bleeding on the page."

"How charming." Nevada pummels the dough. "I'm sure everyone will want to read *that.*"

"Nevada, I've been nurturing this book on my body. I created the container. It's taken a lot out of me. I created Nicholas for you."

"So what do you want, a medal?"

"Just a little acknowledgment."

"Fine. I acknowledge you."

"That was gracious."

"Grace is my middle name."

"I didn't know that." I mop up the soapsuds by the sink. The slate shines like river rocks.

"There's a lot you don't know."

"So do you want to tell me some things I don't know?"

"Nice try," Nevada says.

"No?"

"You could tell me some things," Nevada says.

"What do you want to know? I think you'll find I'm more generous with my knowledge than you are. I *am* a teacher, after all."

"It's nice that you don't have a problem with self-esteem." Nevada sprinkles more flour into the dough. "I hear it's a national epidemic."

"So what do you want to know?" I sigh patiently.

"That guy who always wanted to talk about sex on the phone? Why did you keep talking to him?"

"Well, it made sense, sort of. We were trying to find out if we were compatible before we took the plunge, epidemiologically speaking."

"So much for making sense." Nevada stretches a piece of the dough to see if it's ready. It develops little tears in its flecked surface, and she goes back to kneading. "Do you think he was, umm, pleasuring himself during these conversations?"

I shrug.

"You didn't hear any suspicious noises on the other end of the line?"

"No, Nevada. I didn't hear any suspicious noises on the other end of the line." I push my mop under Nevada's feet.

"So, were you sexually compatible?" Nevada shoves my mop aside with her elbow.

"I doubt it. He said he found oral sex disgusting."

"I never *heard* of a guy who doesn't like oral sex."

"This was definitely a first for me."

"He sounds uptight."

"He was finicky. But I could relate to his idea that the lips should be saved for kissing. Don't you think that's sweet?"

"Sweet! We've finally got them doing it to us. This isn't the time, social history wise, to lose ground."

"And not only that, he said it never lasted more than five minutes." I dry my hands and nudge her out of the way. "Let me knead." The dough feels like the upper arms of a pioneer woman who doesn't have the option of running to the store for a loaf of aerated white.

"This sounds like a very interesting conversation." Nevada pulls ribbons of dough off her hands.

"Oh it was, it was. But doesn't five minutes seem awfully short to you?"

"You're asking the wrong person. If penetration is your thing, I don't know why you're wasting your time with Alec."

"Let's time it." I set the timer on my watch and place it on top of the sugar bowl. Perching on two stools, Nevada and I stare at the seconds counting down.

After a while Nevada says, "It's still five minutes."

"Five minutes doesn't seem that short when you sit and stare at the clock." I scrape at some dough clinging to the edge of the counter.

"You wouldn't be staring at the clock if you were doing it."

"Hopefully."

"Let's talk about something that will make time pass more naturally."

"Like what?"

"How about marriage? Do you ever think about getting married again?"

"I don't know," I take a golden pear from the bowl on the counter. "Being married made me cranky. It was sort of like having permanent PMS."

"I know what you mean. I like my space."

"What do you need space for?"

"Eating pomegranates," Nevada says, staring at the watch.

"You can't eat pomegranates if you're married?"

"It's so unladylike."

"What if you do it naked in the bathtub with him?" I can't believe how slowly the seconds are counting down.

"Most men I've known don't have the patience for the pomegranate's subtle rewards."

"Men do tend to think of pomegranates as weird fruit." I bite into the delicate, flowery pear. "If they think of them at all." I look at the watch. "It's still five minutes." I giggle, imagining my legs wrapped around the waist of my gentleman caller.

"Five minutes isn't *that* short," Nevada says. "Maybe he was just being more honest than most."

"I bet most guys would have said they could go all night."

"Maybe you should have met him."

"I think he was turned off by my modern-American-woman

frankness. I should have pretended to be a virgin who couldn't even *imagine* what oral sex could be."

"Where would that have gotten you?"

"Not here, that's for sure."

"So are you happier being with Alec?"

"At least Alec doesn't have any problems with oral sex," I say, wiping pear juice from my mouth.

"That's for sure."

"Oh, he liked licking you down there, did he?" I'm starting to feel jealous despite my current girlfriend status.

"He liked licking me all over, even when I was covered with paint."

"Maybe that accounts for his ghostly pallor."

"I always attributed his pallor to his sexual proclivities."

I stop the watch. "That's it. That's five minutes."

"That doesn't seem so short," Nevada leans back. "I would have come a couple of times by now."

"Me too." I yawn. "If he was any good at all."

"Right." Nevada finishes up the kneading.

"So how many times did you come with Nicholas?"

She doesn't say anything.

"Would you be with Nicholas if you had talked about sex on the phone for three weeks?"

"Can't you respect my privacy?"

"I've been letting my hair down with you. Why can't you let yours down with me?"

"It's too short."

"This feels like a very unequal relationship."

"It is a very unequal relationship." Nevada brushes flour off her granny gown.

"Yeah, but since you emancipated yourself, don't you feel it's all changed?" I ask, rubbing my eyes.

"Why don't we take a nap while the dough's rising? I don't feel up to an all-nighter."

"Sounds good to me." Yawning again, I cover the dough with a towel and put it in the oven where the pilot light will keep it warm. Nevada rolls her sleeves down. Rubbing almond-scented crème into our hands, we trudge upstairs.

"I'll get the first rising," Nevada say sleepily, setting the alarm. "I don't want you to fall asleep on duty. After all you do have a dangerous job. 'Grammar Policewoman'—wouldn't that make a great TV show?"

I smile sleepily and throw her an afghan. "Thanks. I could use some sleep."

"Does Alec tie you up?" Nevada curls up at the foot of my bed.

"No. And he's not painting with his penis, either."

"Amazing. You really have cast your spell on him."

"Jealous?"

"Me?" Nevada says. "Don't be silly. What is he doing with his penis?"

"Not much." I crawl under my quilt.

"You must find that frustrating."

"Not yet."

"Are you planning a great healing?"

"Of course."

"What are you going to do?" Nevada asks, pulling the afghan up to her chin.

"I don't know yet." I'm finding it hard to keep my eyes open. "Do you want to tell me what didn't work for you? That might save me a couple of years."

"You know what didn't work for me." Nevada's voice is fading.

"Not really. I never developed that material."

"It'll be good practice for you."

"Thanks, Nevada. Just what I need. More time-consuming practice that will be good for me."

"If time is an issue, why do you want to take on Alec's problems?"

"Why do you worry about eating pomegranates when a man's around?"

"That's not the same thing at all."

"Isn't it? We're right back to manifesting girlfriend."

"I thought we got that all settled in Nicholas's kitchen."

"Yeah, right. That's like thinking you can master world lit in one term."

"Good night, Claire." Nevada's voice is very faint.

"Wait. Don't go to sleep yet. You haven't told me *anything* about Nicholas. It's not fair."

"Good night, Claire."

CHAPTER TWENTY-SIX

Deep in the belly of the Thing, Nevada takes a bite of butter-milk-oatmeal bread, then washes it down with wine from a goatskin bag. It's too bad the goddesses don't make beer. There's nothing like a six-pack to wash you into a world of sculpting as Dionysian excess. Red wine is good for sex, but it's a little heavy to work on. She and Claire did a good job on the bread, though. It's tender and mellow with a perfect crumb—self-renewing goddess flesh.

Thank the Goddess, Claire has gotten Alec out of the loft for the weekend, though God knows what they're up to. Claire and her famous healing! Well maybe she'll be able to accomplish the impossible. At least it will keep her busy and out of people's hair for a while. How the "new work" is progressing is none of her business!

And it's none of Nicholas's business, either. Although she

misses him, although he begged her to spend the weekend with him, being alone feels as necessary as breathing right now. Her longing to feel his massive body rise over hers will have to wait. It will be there when she has time to give in to it. Longing always is, though men aren't. Well, she'll just have to take that chance. Now what she needs is time to just feel what she's feeling. It seems as though there's always someone in her face, someone she has to talk to, construct a self for. How is she ever going to finish the Thing if she just keeps hanging out, making love, and baking banana bread?

Nevada lifts the goatskin bag over her head and lets a stream of wine flow into her mouth. Claire is too easy to fool. She doesn't even suspect that people might be lying to her. Her students must have her on the ropes. A twinge of guilt tries to get Nevada's attention from beneath the wine-inspired good feelings. She shouldn't have lied about starting a new sculpture. Not that it was a total lie. The new piece is alive in her mind—intermittently. But how can she possibly start it before she's sure the Thing is absolutely, completely, beyond the shadow of a doubt, perfect? Apologetically she strokes the rocky wall which drips rainwater on her bare shoulder. She doesn't mean to imply that the Thing isn't wonderful. It's that and more. What it isn't is perfect.

Who are Claire, Alec, and Hassiloff to decide the Thing is finished? What kind of people would pressure someone to abandon her best friend and shelter? Nevada chews angrily on a heel of bread. At least Nicholas doesn't try to run her life. Not yet, anyway.

Nevada gazes sadly at the old growth forest. How can she allow that self-satisfied prig to plunge naked into her inadequacies and judge her? There's no way she's going to let Hassiloff (and his heirs!) see the gaping holes in the inner reaches. She doesn't know what could fill them. Even herds of goats would be better than letting people see the void there. But even goats take time. It could take her another ten years to get it right. And empty spaces might open up faster than she could fill them. She runs her hand over the tool belt waiting by her side. There's no way Claire, Alec, and Hassiloff will let her alone long enough to get the job done right.

Nevada draws a knife-sharp chisel out of the belt. How do people find the courage to be imperfect? Alec revels in his faults. It's one of the reasons she admires him. If she weren't so obsessed with perfecting her navel, she'd be afloat with Nicholas right now in his kitchen tub. The dull gleam of copper pots would infuse their intimacy with a subtle patina of Old World light—the light that shines off Nicholas—his star quality. Lolling in his clawfoot tub, she'd massage his toes with Vitabath. His strong hands would massage her legs, moving steadily upward. Unlike Alec, Nicholas is easy to please. She doesn't have to fight her way through a thorny thicket of defenses that tear at her flesh.

Nevada tests her chisel on her thumb, jerking her hand when she draws blood. Her quest for perfection could turn deadly! She strokes the whorls of her fingerprints with the scalpel-sharp chisel. If she could slice them delicately off, lifting up a translucent layer of skin, would that be enough to excise the bad parts, the rotten pieces of the past that cling so tenaciously to her innards? Could she sculpt herself into the kind of woman who could enjoy her lover right now? Wreathed in fragrant clouds of steam, they'd be awash and copper-lit in his kitchen spa. His star light, not the rhinestone glitter of Hollywood, but the old-gold luster of the Opera would fill her dark places with subtle radiance.

Nevada winces as the chisel again draws blood. How could a mere demigod like Nicholas have enough light to fill a whirling vortex of neediness, darkness, and negation? If she starts stealing the light she needs to warm her icy white skin, she'll black out the East Coast power grid.

Nevada scrapes red polish off her fingernails, and it drops to the rocks like flakes of dried blood. Nicholas's shine will dim till he's a blacked-out star, and all his fans will know it's Nevada the light vampire's fault because she "let herself be herself." Look at how much damage Alec does by insisting on being his own sweet self!

Strapping on her tool belt, Nevada moves deeper into the Thing. In here no one can see how flawed she is, no one but the goddesses, and they know she's constantly struggling toward perfection. Away from this pine-fragrant shelter, if people see a chink in your armor, they claw you apart!

Nevada caresses the worn wooden handle of her chisel, which fits her hand better than any hand she's ever held. But she doesn't have time to admire the patina of the wood that her hand has turned soft as skin. If she doesn't resume her quest for perfection, that gaping, people-eating hole will rise up from her gut and swallow her. Once inside she'll be forced to reexperience her failed long-ago marriage and her grotesque attempt at loving Alec. Her failures will scroll before her eyes like grainy home movies, full of blips and unraveling splices, the kind sadistic hosts force you to watch for mind-numbing hours as their fried chicken makes insidious inroads on your digestive tract.

Nevada takes a long swallow of wine and pours some on the leafy earth as a libation. Some of her college friends are still married to the men they started out with. Her failures glimmer at her like a string of black add-on pearls. Will Nicholas be the next pearl on the string?

The real trouble with failed relationships, is the pall it casts on neighborhoods. Too much of New York is cursed for her. Fort Hamilton Parkway—her outer borough excursion into marriage. Did she actually live there? It seems like a bad novel now. At the time it had seemed refreshing to get away from the claustrophobic art scene, to breathe air that regular people were breathing, not air that was recycled through the lungs of every Downtown painter. To walk down the street and see the faces of people who were living regular lives—having kids, cooking dinner, sitting on their stoops talking to the neighbors. People actually talked to their neighbors in Bay Ridge! People lived their lives to live them, not to mine them for art.

Now she can't even imagine walking down Eighty-sixth Street. The bricks and concrete are spongy and toxic, having long since absorbed her shame. Her foot would go right through the street, and she'd be stuck there like a fly in aspic for everyone to pity or despise.

No, there's no way she could go back to Bay Ridge and walk her old streets. She just hopes the East Village isn't going to be poisoned for her, too. Nevada gets a hammer out of her tool belt and grasps her chisel lovingly. If she really pushes herself, maybe she can fill in the inner reaches of her Thing with goats before Claire shows up.

CHAPTER TWENTY-SEVEN

"Alec, oh Alec, I have something for you." I'm tucked into the window seat that looks out over Madame's garden, trying to coax Alec into my room. He stands awkwardly in the open doorway, looking too tall. He's so gangly, he makes me feel like a teenager sneaking my boyfriend into my room. "My boyfriend"—what a nice sound that has, so much nicer than "my husband." Though "my boyfriend" in Vivian's mouth, when she was talking about "my husband," never had a sound I liked. Especially in her bossy, bitchy, possessive, triumphant tone of voice. "My boyfriend" like, "Look girls—I stole her husband. Ain't I something?" The way she said "my boyfriend" sounded as if she were doing a war dance in feathers and hair spray over my prostrate body. Why wasn't she hiding in shame over her transgression from sisterhood? But in reference to Alec, I like it—"my boyfriend"—two words I never thought I'd hear myself say again.

"My boyfriend"—it sounds like 1968—hitchhiking down a country road—anything could happen.

Smoothing my striped cotton skirt, I wonder uneasily what Madame thought of Alec with his ZZ Top beard and weird blue eyes. She'd be more impressed with French-looking Nevada's Nicholas, who would, no doubt, kiss her hand. Alec has never, in any of his incarnations, been a hand kisser.

Alec sidles into my room and gives me a little kiss. In his paint-stained work boots and noncool genuine work jeans, he looks incredibly out of context. I bring over the tea tray I prepared downstairs in the lull between lunch and dinner prep. We settle on the bed, Alec leaning against the iron headboard, me sitting cross-legged at the foot.

"This buttermilk-oatmeal bread is very healing," I say boldly. Maybe I should be more subtle, but with Alec, I think a frontal attack is best. "Have a piece."

Alec ignores the bread and sticks his finger in the butter. "Got any beer?"

"Sorry. I was thinking of this as a tea party." I put the plate down and watch Alec lick butter off his none-too-clean finger. "Do you always eat butter?"

"Sometimes I eat jam," Alec says, sticking his finger in the jam jar, the same finger he stuck in my butter, probably the same finger he's planning to stick in me. I tuck my skirt over my knees.

"The bread's really good," I say. "I made it myself." No need to mention Nevada. Who knows what effect she would have on his libido?

"Later," Alec mumbles through a fingerful of peanut butter. Is he trying to sabotage my project or is he always this unhousebroken? I'm surprised at Nevada. Surely she could have done better with him than this.

Alec constructs a peanut butter and jam sandwich between two slices of cheese and downs it in two bites. Do I really want to kiss this man? Where's the Alec who bought me the teddy bear, the Alec who was trembling when I emerged from the Thing? That's the Alec I want to kiss. This greasy Alec sitting on my bed, stuffing my food into his mouth, probably ate that Alec for breakfast.

Maybe I can coax the sweet Alec out of hiding. I pick up my bear and kiss the top of its head. "It was sweet of you to buy me this. I sleep with him every night."

"You smart chicks are such silly bitches," Alec says through a mouthful of peanut butter. "You don't need me to make a fool of you; you do it so well to yourselves. You're not even a challenge."

My mouth drops open and I stare at Alec. I probably look like roadkill. "Why did you come over if you're going to be like that?" I hope he can't hear the tears in my voice.

Alec shrugs. "I never know why I do things. I just do them."

"Like a wolf roaming the forest?"

"Something like that."

I sip my tea and try to think. Alec's a real shape-shifter. After allowing himself to get so intimate with me, a barbed wire fence must have sprung up around his heart. But I thought he wanted this healing. I really shouldn't blame Nevada for his nasty habits. Where would I be if I took the blame for Aaron's departures from humanness? In deep interpersonal doo-doo, that's where. Vivian can just take Aaron's bad habits as my personal wedding gift to her.

Thoughtfully I chew some buttermilk-oatmeal bread. Alec is more of a challenge than I'd anticipated. Do I really want to take him on? I do have a book to finish and a life of my own to get on with. Madame's typewriter gleams at me from across the room. My fingers long to hit the keys running. While it would be incredibly rude to start writing now, rude is something Alec ought to understand. I walk over to my desk. Maybe he'll just go away. Paul was never *this* bad.

"I thought you wanted to do the nasty." Alec comes up behind me. His strong arms around me feel insidiously good. I lean back into his chest and let his warmth and scent surround me like a mini-climate. He may be awful but if I let him go, I won't have anyone to do the nasty with. It'll be back to the, gasp, ugh, dating service and envying Nevada.

"I did want to. In fact I've hardly been able to think of anything else all week," I say, inhaling essence of Alec—cigarettes and linseed oil, with a bottom note of peanut butter. "When I try to grade papers, my mind keeps drifting to wild-thing fantasies. But that was before you started acting like my personal bundle of bad karma." I let my fingers drift across the typewriter keys. "Do you think maybe you could be nice to me for half an hour? Would that be too much of a strain?"

"What's so great about nice?" he asks, stroking lazy circles around my nipples.

"It's nice," I say, or rather purr. His mean streak and the peanut butter under his fingernails dissipate like wisps of smoke in my mind.

"Nasty is even nicer."

"Are you going to tie me up now, do unspeakable things to me, then paint with your penis?"

"Who told you about that?" Alec turns me around to face him. He has a sheepish grin on his face like maybe he's a little bit proud. Isn't anyone ashamed of their bad behavior anymore? First Vivian and Aaron, now Alec. Maybe we went too far in the sixties with anything goes. What the nineties needs is a little conditional love.

"I have my sources," I say, wishing he'd shut up and put his hands back on my breasts. What a woman has to do these days to get a little satisfaction!

"Nevada?"

"Not exactly." I push my breasts back into Alec's hands.

"Are you a seer?" Alec absentmindedly caresses me, but I can tell his focus is elsewhere. His halfhearted attention makes my flesh crawl. Why can't he keep his mind on his work?

"Not exactly," I say, pulling away. "How come you're not doing with me what you do with Nevada?"

"You must have me under an enchantment."

"Great. I've turned the Prince into the Beast." I tap lightly at the typewriter keys, smooth as river stones under my fingers.

Alec laughs. "Don't you find the Beast more interesting?"

"The Prince is a bit of a stiff. But sometimes that's just what a woman needs."

"You know I can't help you with that, doll."

My hand makes a grab for a pad of Post-it notes on the back of the desk. Writing with pen on paper would be less rude than typing. Of course rude does seem to turn Alec on. But I'm not sure I want to be that kind of person.

"This is great material. You don't mind if I take notes?"

"Why should I mind?" Alec licks my face. "I'll be your bulletin board. Slap those Post-its on my chest."

"You want to be of use?" I say, pushing him away. I hate being slobbered on.

"That's right, doll. Use me." Alec kneels in front of me and starts unbuttoning his shirt.

"Maybe I'll immortalize you." I slap a couple of notes on his pale skin.

"I'd rather you tied me up and did unspeakable things to me."

"Really?" I start scribbling again. "Why?" I hope I have enough Post-its.

"It turns me on."

"I've spent my whole life trying to be a nice person, and you're telling me I've been wasting my time?"

"Yes," Alec says in a soft, surrendered voice.

I sit down on the bed. This is getting really interesting. If I get nasty, I might get Alec to give me the sweetness I crave *and* accomplish his healing.

"Be my mistress," Alec begs. I don't think he means girlfriend. He's lying facedown on the floor, licking my shoe.

I can think of places I'd rather have him lick. Still, if I indulge his fantasy, he'll have to do whatever I say. I'd certainly be in more control than I am as his author.

"You want me to get in touch with the Bitch Goddess within?" I pull his head up by his long blond hair.

Alec nods hungrily.

I was a good girl for ten years with Aaron and where did it get me? Horny, unhappy, and left. Why not go out on a limb? I let Alec's head drop to the floor, and press his face into the rug with my foot.

"I like it when you're nasty," Alec says, turning his body to show me the evidence.

A thrill of power rushes through my body. This healing is taking some unexpected back roads, past rotted-out trailers where ragged kids string a cat from a lightning-struck tree. But it's happening! I'm going to have to go shopping for new clothes.

CHAPTER TWENTY-EIGHT

Nevada slumps against a three-hundred-year-old tree. The goddesses have obviously deserted her. She's been in here for forty-eight hours. Her eyes feel like sandpaper. She's out of bread. She's out of wine. Why aren't they renewing her supplies? She thought goddesses supported perfection. The herds of goats roaming the far pastures of the Thing look good, but were they really worth forty-eight sleepless hours and no Nicholas? How long will he wait for her?

Why is she doing this to herself? So she won't be embarrassed in front of Claire? Claire's counting on her to pull it together for them both. Nevada rubs her eyes tiredly. She can't pull it together for herself, even when she pushes way beyond her limits. Alec never abused her *this* badly.

It's not as though she doesn't want to move on. The new sculpture glimmers at her like a distant mirage. But it would be so exposed, so out there. Just the thought of being that daring makes her want to dissolve her shame and her self and become a permanent stain on the innermost wall of the Thing. She has got to stop ruining her life in the service of perfection, a false goddess if she's ever seen one. She wants nothing more than to be able to sculpt a huge goddess that reaches way into blue sky. But she doesn't even have the energy to crawl out of here.

Out of the corner of her eye, Nevada sees a goddess in a Grecian tunic glide up. The goddess silently places a glass of wine, a quill pen and ink, and a long strip of parchment on a flat stone, then disappears behind a herd of goats.

"Thank you," Nevada calls. She takes a sip of wine and feels reconstituted enough to sit up. Claire would love this old technology. It's amazing the woman is even willing to use a typewriter. Nevada dips the quill in the ink and begins writing, too tired to feel any resistance:

I'm so afraid of the agoraphobia returning and claiming me as its creature. It's like my rapist returning and reraping me, or imprisoning me in a permanent rape, my father returning and claiming me as his incompetent little dependent, Alec reclaiming me as his agoraphobic little girl, helpless and miserable. I'm afraid that by looking it in the face, acknowledging that I'm an only partially recovered agoraphobic, it's going to zap me. Like that creature in *Aliens*, it's going to rip itself out of my chest and destroy me. If I focus on these fears, they'll take over my life again. That's what happened in therapy. I just got so focused on my fears, I drowned and became agoraphobic.

Nevada takes a deep breath. The pen is as much an extension of her hand as a chisel. She feels as though she's being sucked from the little stone inkpot, through the quill pen, onto the parchment. This must be what Claire feels when she writes—that she's exactly where she's supposed to be, doing exactly what she's supposed to be doing.

Nevada blots her pen on a leaf and continues:

Hello Agoraphobia, Old Friend, Sister, Tormentor, Mistress:

I've been your slave for too long. I'd prefer to be your friend. I push you away and you own me, I'm your creature like I was Dr. X's, a poor wimpish cowardly thing, like the slobbering hunchback servant, Igor, in *Frankenstein*, drooling, "Yes, Master, can I get you any more living human brains, Master? Can I get you any more human sacrifices, can I lie down and die for you?"

I'm so afraid of going mad, being incapacitated, being a fool, being out of control. When people talk about their fear of going crazy, it triggers my fears and I hyperventilate and get dizzy. I become a dizzy dame.

You're part of me. I feel I'm starting to get free, but you're there under the surface, part of me, potential, that's what scares me, your coming back up and taking over my life again. I'm scared of that part of myself, of my potential to be weak and out of control. I'm scared of you in me like a cancer, a time bomb. I'm scared of anyone who is afraid of losing control and going crazy.

I want you to be my friend. Will you be my friend? I want to be friends with myself, with all parts of myself, my death, my weakness, my potential to be ill, my talents, my potential for failure and success. I want it and you all to be OK with me.

I won't say you've ruined my life because I've managed to do a lot inside your confines: made the Thing, became a gourmet cook, became Claire's friend. But you've made my life a lot harder and lonelier. Maybe, like those who have found their illness a path toward enlightenment, I can take you as my path. Will you be my friend? My sister?

You're like a walled city, a cloister, where I've hidden from the modern world, from the truth of a world where so many women are raped and oppressed, so many people are exploited for the wealth and pleasure of a few, there's so much cruelty and self-ishness. The planet itself is being raped. You've protected me from facing reality, but now I want to face what's real.

What I'm afraid of is that it's a bottomless sink—my emotions, being real with my emotions. That if I open up to them and share them with others, it will be like my time with Dr. X, when I was just drowning in myself. But for me, the deeper I opened up to my fears and dependency needs, the deeper I sank, the worse I got. When I was a good soldier, when I tried to be cheerful and strong, things weren't so totally hopeless.

Looking up, Nevada sees someone crawling through the tunnel toward her.

"I brought you a sandwich," I say, holding out a baguette filled with Madame's green peppercorn-studded pâté. "I thought you'd be hungry."

"Thanks." Nevada grabs the sandwich and tears off the wax paper. Her voice sounds like she hasn't used it for a while and isn't sure it's going to work. "I'm glad it's not on buttermilk-oatmeal bread. I was getting sick of that stuff."

"Alec and I finished it," I say as I build a fire. I put some water up to boil in a beat-up enamel kettle.

"How'd the great healing go?" Nevada asks through a mouthful of pâté.

"Don't ask."

"That good, huh?" Nevada's voice is starting to sound less like a creaky door. "How'd you know I needed food?"

"Chapters Twenty-Six and Twenty-Eight were scrolling out of the typewriter." I hand Nevada a cup of English Breakfast tea and warm my hands over the fire. I wish I hadn't left my prairie skirt and fringed jacket at the entrance.

"So who's writing this stuff?" Nevada crams the last of the sandwich in her mouth and washes it down with my strong, milky brew.

"I thought you were," I say, stirring honey into my tea.

"I thought you were."

"Maybe Madame is."

"What a thought! How would you feel if Madame is behind all this?" Nevada pours herself another cup of tea.

"Well, I've had to unload so much ego already, what with you declaring your independence and Alec acting like a schizophrenic disaster area, what's a little more? Or a little less. Ego that is. Anyway it's just a theory."

"It's a good theory," Nevada says. "It would explain a lot."

"It is her typewriter."

"Maybe she's got it connected to the computer in her office."

"How could you connect an old manual to a computer?"

"Radio waves?"

"Like a cordless phone?"

"Exactly," Nevada says. "But be careful. Don't get her aggravated. If she sends you to Literary Hyperspace, you might not be able to get out."

"It sounds like a rest cure to me." I sigh. "No papers to grade, no meetings, no students pulling at my skirt. Just blissful blissful nothingness. I wish Madame would send me there."

Nevada shivers. "All that nothingness gives me the willies."

I put a log on the fire. "Nevada, I was reading what you were writing . . ."

"That wasn't meant for your eyes!"

"It was scrolling out of my typewriter," I say. "What was I supposed to do?"

Nevada nods grudgingly.

"You shouldn't be ashamed in front of me." I watch the log start to smolder. "It occurred to me there are some things we really need to talk about."

"Oh yeah, like what?" Nevada's studiously licking the crumbs from the wax paper.

"Like getting raped, for starters. That's something neither of us has laid to rest."

"Oh, give me a break, Claire!" Nevada throws the wax paper in the fire and watches it flare. "I've been going through hell down here, trying to fill in the emptiness, and look over there, when those goats move, the holes are starting to come back! I thought I'd have a grace period of at least a few months before bald spots started appearing in the landscape." Nevada scrambles up and grabs her tool belt. She's about to light out for the territories when I grab her leg.

"Nevada. Stop it! You're never going to be able to do it. You're never going to be able to fill in all the empty places. You're never going to be able to get it perfect. Give it up. You're going to drive yourself crazy. You're going to drive me crazy. It's enough. Please, don't drive yourself over the edge. Who will I have to talk to?"

"Alec," Nevada says, trying to shake me off. Usually she's the stronger one, but I've slept in the last forty-eight hours.

"Would you stay put," I say, pulling her down by the fire. "Alec's not you. I'm very happy to have you to talk to. When you brood over stuff in the privacy of your own mind, you start to go nuts."

"So you were raped, too." Nevada's eyes flash at me, then look away.

"Wasn't everybody?" I poke at the fire.

"One in five."

"I've heard one in three. Reported."

"Why do you want to bring up all that old pain?" Nevada asks. Her voice is starting to go again. "It's old hat. Ancient hat. Why go through it again?"

"If that's the way you feel about old pain, why are you bringing me down with this 'relationships like a string of black add-on pearls' crap?"

"I told you, that wasn't for your eyes," Nevada says tightly.

"Do you really think you can keep anything secret from me?" I poke furiously at the fire. "I may have absolutely no control over what's happening in this book, but I am going to find out about it, sooner or later."

"Get out of my mind, Claire," Nevada says in a quiet voice that could easily turn hysterical. "Get out, get out, get out."

"Hey, it's not that bad, Nevada. Think of us as being psychically linked."

"Don't get mystical on me, Claire!"

"Why not?"

"Because I need to keep my feet firmly planted on the ground."

"Otherwise?"

"Otherwise, I'm going to become invisible radioactive dust disappearing into deep space."

"Has it ever occurred to you what an incredible metaphor agoraphobia is for rape?" I say. My mouth is getting dry and I'm starting to think that lighting out for the goat-crowded hills is not such a bad idea. But doggedly I plow on. "You know that feeling that you just can't handle it? Whatever it is, you're going to faint, die, go crazy?"

"My favorite feeling," Nevada says, rubbing her eyes.

"Well, isn't that exactly the way the streets felt after you were raped? Supernaturally menacing. Full of horror. Any man walking down the street could be a rapist. Any car could leap the curb and run you down just for the fun of it. Even the buildings could come loose from their moorings and run amuck. You realize for the first time that the universe isn't your nursemaid."

I take a deep swallow of Nevada's wine. "If you were a Victorian lady, all that fainting, collapsing, dying would have been accepted. What would it say about your modesty if you didn't go crazy, kill yourself or, at the very least, have fainting spells for the rest of your life? Now we're expected to get up, dust off our skirts, and get back to work."

Nevada looks as though she's about to make a break for the hills. I grasp her ankle firmly with one hand and pour her another cup of tea.

"I've been wearing my brain down to a nubbin trying to figure out what the goddesses want me to write in my journal," Nevada says. "I don't have the energy for all this cosmic end to innocence crap."

"Maybe this is what they want you to write about."

"So the goddesses want me to get really depressed, maybe go crazy? I can't believe that."

"That's your agoraphobia talking. If you're serious about starting a new sculpture, this is what you need to deal with."

"You know, Claire, it's not as if I never dealt with this. I was in therapy."

"And?"

"I never felt it when I talked about it with Dr. X," Nevada admits. "I never felt it at all. Not when it happened. Not afterward. Not ever. But, you know, it's bad enough it happened. Why do I have to feel it too? What's the point? It seemed like the more I went into the dark shadows with Dr. X, the more I got stuck in darkness. I started to feel like I was in bondage to him and darkness. Maybe he just wanted me dependent on him. Maybe he needed money for a new Mercedes. Maybe he got his jollies watching me suffer."

I nod, trying to project compassionate detachment.

"Can you explain to me why he advised against marital counseling when my ex and I were in trouble?" Nevada demands. "He said I should work out everything through my relationship with him."

"That is traditional psychoanalytic theory," I say uncomfortably.

"Are you defending him?"

"No. I'm just saying it is traditional."

"People have a life outside of their therapist's office. It's not all about transference. People have marriages and jobs and families and friendships that are going to hell while they work out their transference, not to mention spending enough to buy a small battleship."

"A used battleship." I throw dry leaves on the fire. "But I didn't know you were still hurting over the breakup of your marriage."

"What do you think, Claire?" Nevada says impatiently. "Does anybody ever get over a divorce? Does the pain ever go away? Can you ever start a relationship again without wondering about the next betrayal?"

"No," I say quietly. I know she's right.

"Therapy encourages you to be selfish and stuck. You're just supposed to think about your own feelings, not how your behavior is going to affect your loved ones. And now you want me to go back into that rape crap? You're as sadistic as Dr. X."

"Maybe, but I am cheaper."

Nevada laughs. "You mean I don't have to pay you sixty-five dollars an hour to ruin my life?"

"For you, sixty-three dollars an hour."

"A bargain. But you'll have to wait till we get out of here. My money is in my overalls."

"I'll bill you, sweetie. So," I say, settling into therapist mode, "what are you afraid of?"

"I'm afraid I'm going to have to put my head in your lap and howl."

"That would be OK."

"Most people don't like it if you howl on them. That's one reason I prefer it in my Thing. I can howl without making anyone uncomfortable."

"I know what you mean. I'm much more often the howlee than the howler myself."

"Maybe we should howl in each other's laps."

I start to giggle. "I don't feel like howling right now."

Nevada starts baying, wolflike at the moon. "How's that?" We collapse in each other's laps, giggling, not howling. I guess I'm not much good at maintaining therapeutic distance.

"We're supposed to be howling," I say sternly.

"I did howl," Nevada says. "It's your turn."

"What are your rates?"

"Ninety-five dollars an hour."

"It's a lot cheaper to giggle."

CHAPTER TWENTY-NINE

It's really nice here in literary hyperspace—cool, white, and empty. All the heat of passion is below me in the fog-hidden, distant world—my desires, my frustration with Alec, my fruitless struggles to get my characters to behave, my worries that my book is too weird to get published, that if it does get published, people will either drive me from human society or adore me so much, they'll never allow me a moment's privacy. Of course since I'm not writing it, why worry? In literary hyperspace worry dissipates like fog, becomes nothing. And that's what I like up here—nothing that's pure possibility. Anything could be born out of this fog. I can't imagine why Nevada was so eager to escape.

I stretch out on a solidified fog bench. Through a break in the clouds, I look down on humankind scurrying around like silly ants—so much busyness and desperation about surviving. They're all getting so tired and for what? What are their jobs producing? I feel cool and detached on my perch. Way below me in their little house, Aaron and Vivian squabble about their wedding plans. I laugh, though up here I should be above such pettiness.

My visit to The Dominatrix Shoppe must have been the last straw for Madame. Why else would she have sent me to literary hyperspace? I guess she prefers me as the virgin daughter of her household, though I never thought the French were that big on virginity. Maybe I should have gone two neighborhoods south to Dominatrixes R Us. In New York, that's almost another town. But if Madame really is writing this book, a few miles won't shield me from her shrewd eyes. I'm going to have to find a way to camouflage my next date with Alec—would a lead screen do? I don't want to get kicked out of The Orange Cat Bistro, nor do I want to die of embarrassment. When it's my time to go, I'd rather go as a warrior than as a sex-starved ex-virgin, willing to do anything for a little pleasure.

I wave my hand and watch the fog drift like cigarette smoke in an old movie. Finally I understand what I've put Nevada through. From now on I'll request permission before entering her life, instead of running roughshod over her modesty.

I left my last bit of maidenly modesty in the cash register of The Dominatrix Shoppe. The proprietress, a pockmarked blonde with a cheap dye job and too much makeup, said she personally owned one of every style in the store—her husband liked a little variety. Outside The Dominatrix Shoppe, she would have looked like any secretary hurrying home to Queens to cook chicken cutlets for her family. It was hard to imagine her flabby belly tucked into a red leather corselette, black net stockings digging into her cellulite, almost as hard as it was to imagine me encased in thigh-high lace-up boots with spike heels and a rubber bustier. It made me wonder what all those Wall Streeters wear under their suits.

There was a kind of crowded, overheated coziness about The Dominatrix Shoppe. It reminded me of the old-fashioned corset shoppes your mother took you to for your first AAA bra. Lulled by cozy memories, I browsed through racks of garments strung together with arcane chain configurations.

Looking down through the break in the cumulus clouds, I see that Aaron and Vivian have stopped arguing and have started having sex. Missionary position. Very uninspired. Aaron's not even propped up on his arms, which is the one of the few things that can redeem missionary. He's just lying on top of her, moving in a way she can't possibly feel. She doesn't even have a pillow under her bottom. Should I send them some divine inspiration? I think not.

Turning onto my stomach, I drum my feet against the fog. Wouldn't it be something if I could really make Alec my slave? Not just in play—I want to own him. I want him to be there for me twenty-four hours a day. I'll make sure he wants nothing more than to bring me stuffed animals and tell me unceasingly how much more beautiful I am than Nevada. He'll never cheat on me, or leave me, or make me feel like dirt in any way, whatsoever. How many opportunities like this does a woman get in this lifetime? If it takes a little leather and pain, why should I object?

I thought being Alec's author would do it, but he's the one who's got me over a barrel. I have never worked with a more frustrating character. Even Nevada occasionally does what I want. At least she's consistent. Alec is Mister Multiple Personality Disorder. It's enough to make me give up fiction. Maybe when this book is done, Nevada and I could open a bakery and donate breads and cakes to homeless shelters. Nicholas would know where. Or we could live at Greystone Zen Center in Yonkers and work in their community bakery.

Ideas flow out of the white nothingness. I should insist that Nevada spend more time up here. It might get her unstuck about that new sculpture. If I get any good at this dominatrix stuff, I'll try it out on her.

That thought is so full of ego, I find myself sliding down, down through the white cloud layer, toward the hot, garlic-breathing earth.

CHAPTER THIRTY

Ejected from literary hyperspace, I float toward earth like an umbrellaless Mary Poppins. Through the clouds, I catch a glimpse of Alec trudging up Eighth Avenue. *He* looks like he's just parachuted down from the mountains of the moon and isn't completely sure if human form is what he's supposed to be in.

I shiver as I land on hard, gritty concrete. Have I actually been sharing my bed with this creature? Intelligent perceptions blur at the intimate distance I usually see him. If I were a stranger, walking by on Eighth Avenue, I'd wonder what penitentiary he'd escaped from. Of course, serial killers usually look like the boy next door. Anyone as strange-looking as Alec is probably nothing more serious than a necromancer.

Alec doesn't see me. He keeps walking up Eighth Avenue, looking too tall. He peers hungrily into each pornography shop he passes. Am I really this ravenous for love? I could still return my dominatrix costumes while they're sweat, blood, and whatever-free and invest the refund in a nice cozy pile of books. I'll need something to cuddle up to while Nevada's cuddling up to Nicholas.

I'm about to go back to The Dominatrix Shoppe and see about a refund when Alec notices me. He waves and lumbers over, a sabertoothed mammoth in a fatigue jacket. He makes me feel like a different species, a very short species.

"What are you doing here?" I ask warily.

"Checking out the porno shops," Alec says.

"What do you need that crap for?"

"It's exciting."

"I thought I was exciting."

"What does one thing have to do with the other?"

"How can you find me desirable, make passionate love to me, and then go out on Eighth Avenue and drool over this garbage?"

"Women never understand this kind of stuff," Alec says dismissively.

"Am I just some kind of porno queen for you?"

"Hardly." Alec laughs. "Your boobs aren't big enough."

"I hate that word." I feel a familiar weak sickness in my stomach. "It makes me feel like a cow prancing around on my hind legs."

Alec laughs again, louder this time. He sounds like a hyena.

"How can you laugh like that?" I demand. "When you caressed me, you made me feel beautiful and loved. Now you're looking for the same kind of thrill on Eighth Avenue, just some image to jerk off to."

"I never said I loved you," Alec says, his eyes hungrily following a blond-wigged hooker in five-inch heels.

That's true. He didn't. I must have made up that part, not

that he said it, but that he felt it. That fatal mistake—if a boy touches you, he loves you. How could I still be so naive?

Determinedly I start walking up Eighth Avenue, away from Alec and his pornographic dreams.

"Wait up," he calls, and starts loping after me.

"I don't want your kind of love," I say, walking faster.

"Who said anything about love? You keep using that word, you're going to keep getting confused."

"I'm not confused. I'm repulsed."

"Use that," Alec says, catching up to me and grabbing my elbow. I try to shake his hand off but he's very strong. I'm not angry enough to kick him in the balls, though maybe I should be.

"If you're repulsed, if I make you angry, use that energy. Let's go to your place and you can tie me up and do whatever you want to me. Imagine how good that will feel."

"Has this all just been a setup?" I demand.

"I told you—I never plan anything," Alec says. "But with me you'll get an opportunity to know what men are really like when they're not telling lies about love. I won't lie to you. I'll just be the way men are."

"Mr. Natural," I say, interested in spite of myself. This is an opportunity to penetrate more deeply into the mysteries of male nature. I owe it to myself as a woman and as a writer. Maybe in my next book, I'll be able to do better than this.

"I'm Everyman," Alec says complacently. "After me, you'll really know what men are like when they're not trying to put a pretty face on it."

"If I thought that was true, I'd shoot myself."

"What's wrong with a little stimulation?" Alec waves his hand to include the whole seedy expanse of Eighth Avenue.

"That sweet you who brought me the bear, who was so loving," I say hesitantly. "Was that really you or was that a put-on?"

"I told you, I never fake anything. That's one thing you can count on."

I start crying. "I want that Alec. I want to go back to your loft and have it like it was that night."

"Well you never know when he might show up. A good whipping just might bring him out."

"I don't like this at all," I say, still crying. I grab Alec's wrist and start pulling him in the direction of The Orange Cat Bistro.

CHAPTER THIRTY-ONE

Dabbing a little musk oil behind her ears, Nevada decides she's sick of paint-stained overalls. Nicholas deserves something pretty. She pokes through her closet, hoping that Claire has Alec safely tied to a bedpost or whatever it is they're up to upstairs at The Orange Cat Bistro. Sooner or later she's going to have to tell Alec to find his own loft, but she does not want to deal with him right now. Figuring out how to dress for Nicholas is straining her coping abilities to the max.

Just to be on the safe side, she's keeping a careful distance between herself and the Thing which calls seductively: disappear yourself back inside where it's safe, sweet and endlessly fascinating. Her body will never forgive her if she passes up another chance to get horizontal with Nicholas.

Holding a figure-hugging lamé gown against her curvy body, Nevada shakes her head in bewilderment. Why did she let Alec buy this for her at Trashy Treasures: The Thrift Shop? He thought it was kinky and made her wear it when she modeled for his Lamé Goddess series and afterward, in bed. Would Nicholas find it erotic or would he prefer her to resemble a huge-breasted warrior in a brassiere made of shields? How can she possibly guess? She hardly knows the man. Anyway, lamé makes her itch. Longing for soft, meadow-dried cotton, she throws the golden dress on the bed.

A brassiere made of shields would probably itch, too. Just thinking about what Nicholas might like is giving her a rash. She'd better think about something else before she's beyond the help of the witch hazel in her medicine chest. In her satin slip, she wanders into the loft to say farewell to Alec's paintings. She'll miss them much more than she'll miss him. They fill her eyes with dreamy light-washed greens, creamy cloudy skies, delft blues, coolly beyond the reach of emotion. He filled a huge wild space in her bed—a mountain lion masquerading as a tabby. His unclipped toenails mark territory as effectively as cat piss, and don't retract.

Alec is like the marmalade cat who slept square in the middle of her Nyack bed. Somehow she could never bring herself to shove that cat over. She would hunch herself around him all night like a question mark, his sleep a more sacred space than her own. The cat's sleep was white, mysterious, holy. Her own sleep, she knew all too well, was a trashy jumble of dreams about boys and candy.

Nevada wanders back into the bedroom and hooks a white lace garter belt around her waist. Shoving a cat out of bed is something her mother would have done without a moment's regret. Sentimental notions about the sacredness of an alley cat's sleep? Throw that cat out of bed! Better yet, shove it down to the foot where it can make itself useful as a furry water bottle. And the cat

would have respected her for it, wouldn't have eyed her disdainfully and demanded its smelly sardines before she drank her first
cup of coffee.

Nevada runs her hand lingeringly over the velvets and sand-
washed silks in the back of the closet. Nicholas will be shocked to
see her in a dress, but she wants to keep him on his toes. She
doesn't want him to start thinking he can make assumptions
about her, that he can fit her in a neat, too-small box, the way her
mother, Alec, and Claire love to do. It's become everyone's favorite indoor sport—*Nevada in a Box*. Let's see what shape we can
make her this time! Flatten her head? Lop off an arm? She won't
miss it—she has two!

She's just starting to regain her natural contours after the
long Alec years, her Nevada shape—the blue-black silhouette of
Western mountains against the last dark red stain of sunset. And
she's getting her own colors back after being subsumed in Alec's
palette. She takes a crushed velvet gown out of the back of the
closet, gleaming subtly with cranberry, forest green, gold, and
midnight blue. Slipping into it feels almost as good as crawling
naked in the Thing. Could these colors serve as a portable Thing
for her as she travels through the city?

Nicholas wanted to pick her up, but there's no point in ex-
changing Alec's protection for Nicholas's. Even if Nicholas seems
like a more reasonable protector than Alec, cocooning in him
would not be a step forward. Her mother's been ashamed of her
long enough. Not that she's ever actually said it, but weakness
isn't very popular in her mother's household. Surely she can handle a mile and a half across the city on her own. If she can't, she
might as well put herself back in jail and hand Alec the key. She
shudders and prays for strength. Now that she's recovering her
colors, she *could* make herself a Huichol prayer stick. When Alec

brought one back from a retreat, she'd felt incapable of freeing herself from his colors. If you can't make a prayer stick with your own colors, there's no point in making one at all.

Quickly she gathers up some branches, seedpods, and leaves from the entry of the Thing. Yarn she gets from the knitting bag Claire left after her last date with Alec. Alec does have it in him to make a woman forget her knitting. Nevada sighs. Why should she regret Alec's charm? Her knowledge of its toxins is too encyclopedic. She just hopes Nicholas's charm is not as compromised.

Considering how different Claire's hair and skin are from hers, it's amazing how similar their colors are. Or maybe Claire just bought out the yarn store. Nevada's eyes drink in the colors as she chooses midnight blue, forest green, cranberry, harvest gold, winter white.

Setting her treasures on the oak kitchen table, she starts writing her prayers on parchment left over from the goddesses' journal project:

Please help me to walk across the Village and be able to take it all in—whatever it is—without shutting down. Help me to surrender to what is. Help me to hold my fear with poise.

Nevada takes a deep breath. This feels good. She wonders which gods or goddesses might be listening. Do Huichol gods care about the prayers of someone whose face is as pale as hers?

Please help me love Nicholas without fear, without thinking of every terrible thing that can happen, without thinking of every terrible thing that has happened, without remembering when Jim was starting an affair and I was playing goodwife in Bay Ridge, waiting for him to come home, without remembering all the wretched movies I watched on that VCR, without assuming that Nicholas will do it to me, because Jim did. Help me to learn to trust. Help me to be worthy of trust.

She wraps those prayers around a peeling birch branch and binds them with cranberry and midnight blue worsted. Stained glass colors. Maybe the goddesses will intercede for her with the Huichol gods. She can't help being white.

Please help me love without losing my self.

When you're on your own, the clarity and crispness are like new fall apples, like autumn light and crisp air. You know where your boundaries are. You're lonely but everything is so fresh. Loving Nicholas, could she maintain that autumnal crispness and not melt into him?

Please help me to maintain my colors and shapes without having to become a hermit, without having to cocoon in my Thing like a nun of art.

She doesn't know if it's possible, but what can she do but offer up her prayers and wear her colors like a prayer flag?

Please help me surrender my perfectionism.

Nevada scratches her head with her quill. She'd better not become a perfectionist about surrendering her perfectionism—that's just the kind of trouble she's likely to get herself in.

If I can't let go of my perfectionism, at least help me enjoy it.

Nevada smiles and puts down her pen. Carefully she wraps the rest of her prayers onto the birch stick with forest green and winter white—the colors of the woods in winter. She can see rabbit tracks in the snow. Every so often she adds a seedpod or a leaf, wrapping their stems securely into the yarn. The forest rustles around her.

The heft of the finished prayer stick, the colors, the way the pods and leaves are woven into the design say Nevada. Nevada grasps the stick and starts dancing, shaking it first toward the Hudson River, then toward the earth, then the sky. Now she's supposed to burn the stick and send its prayers spiraling upward, but it's just what she needs to accompany her on her journey across the Village.

Carrying the stick, she walks over to the mirror. She looks perfect. Too perfect. Too blond and petite and pretty, too ready to manifest girlfriend, daughter, literary slavey. She goes to Alec's work space and squeezes indian yellow onto the palette. With a wide, soft brush, she zaps a jagged lightning streak across her face. Perfect! She's ruined her pretty-pretty image with one stroke. Shaking her stick and singing, she heads for the door.

CHAPTER THIRTY-TWO

Alec and I climb the stairs to my room, me trying to resist the impulse to skulk. I have every right to be here with my boyfriend. What we do behind closed doors is nobody's business. I just hope Alec will be quiet about it, whatever it is.

As we reach the landing I see Madame disappearing around the corner, looking like Hitchcock in drag. "Madame, wait a second," I call, running after her. "There's something I have to ask you." I'm hoping she can give me some insight into Alec's wild card nature, but she disappears into her room.

"What's going on with Alec?" I yell at the closed door, but all I can hear is a computer booting up.

I guess the joker's wild. I hope the joke isn't on me. I go back to my door, where Alec is patiently waiting. It looks like he'd wait there for a month if I told him to. But if Madame isn't behind this, I don't want her to see Alec looking like a human doorpost.

I open the door and shove him in. "Close your eyes," I command, and push him down on the bed. If breathing weren't an autonomic function, he'd probably die if I didn't command him to breathe.

I get my Dominatrix Shoppe bags out of the closet. I have to admit I'm getting a thrill out of bossing Alec around, especially after his obnoxious behavior on Eighth Avenue. If there's anything I hate, it's having my breasts called boobs. My breasts aren't *things*. They have a soul. Giving Alec the evil eye, I slip into a black leather corset that turns my breasts into weapons. I think he can feel it through his closed eyes, because he shivers and looks more happily abject than ever.

Dominating someone this size is like throwing the big guys in aikido. When I sent 250 pounds of muscle sprawling to the mat, I felt like a warrior queen. I pull on the thigh-high boots and stride over to Alec. "Lace my boots up, slave," I command, putting my spike-heeled foot on his chest.

"Yes, Mistress," he quavers. Eyes still closed, he clumsily pulls at my laces.

I move my foot up toward his throat. "Clumsy peon. Open your eyes. And be quick about it."

"Thank you, Mistress." Alec opens his eyes and hastily laces my boot. Surreptitiously he eyes me.

"Keep your eyes to yourself, slave," I say, and give him a little swish with my belt. I have to admit I'm getting a charge out of somebody obeying me for a change.

I've always thought of myself as a banana bread baker, a sweet girlfriend, a teacher who proffers grammar with unconditional love. I can't believe I have this dark power rising like lava from my depths. What would my parents say? What would

Nevada say? She'd probably cheer after what Alec put her through.

"Turn over, slave," I command. "And take off that repellent shirt."

"Yes, Mistress." Alec can feel that I'm not playacting. He looks as happy as a pig in mud. There's actually drool coming out of his mouth. I have never seen anything so repulsive in my life, and I have seen more than my share of repulsive. Pulling off his shirt, Alec flips over. As I start applying the studded belt to the pale skin of his back, power courses through my arm like electricity. I hear the lies Aaron told me when he was starting his affair with Vivian. I hear Vivian telling me that what she was doing to me, to the ideals of sisterhood, to the marriage vows was just fine, because she and Aaron "loved each other." I hit Alec harder. I hear Alec saying "boobs," his eyes hungrily following the hookers on Eighth Avenue. I'm beginning to draw blood when I start crying and throw down the belt.

CHAPTER THIRTY-THREE

Nevada walks out of Westbeth, prayer stick in hand. With the yellow lightning streak zigzagging across her face, she has the feeling she's going to be the weirdest thing on the street. Or is she underestimating her neighborhood? Probably no one will even notice her.

Her purposeful imperfection and her invocations to the local gods are creating a space of courage for her to walk in. She's armored in air. It feels as if she's wearing a red sand-washed silk blouse; the red is courage and is seeping into every pore. Fear has been her companion for so long. Is it really gone? Maybe it's relocated, pots and brooms sticking out of a wood cart pulled by a broken-down horse. Hopefully it won't wind up on Claire's doorstep.

Walking boldly up Twelfth Street, Nevada drinks in the violet light. For such an ugly city, New York certainly has exquisite light. In the spring twilight, it's an enchanted city. And here comes the Fairy Queen herself, in a yellow chiffon gown. In spike heels, she's 6'5" and has five o'clock shadow on her square black jaw.

"Love your stick, girlfriend," the Queen calls.

Nevada sends her a radiant smile. Drag queens have so much to teach her about style as portable Thing. This one wears her attitude like light-permeable armor.

Nevada continues down Seventh Avenue South as the sky darkens. There are so many people out who are way weirder than she is, weirder even than Alec. A pair of vampires in satin capes and thick theatrical makeup pass by.

"Can I taste your tattoo, pretty lady?" one calls, baring plastic fangs.

Nevada smiles. She really is a member of the human race! It's so long since her eyes have had the freedom to touch what they want with nothing to impede their curious joy. She just hopes Nicholas isn't planning to crowd her visual field. She doesn't want to start seeing things through his eyes; she doesn't want to have to explain everything she sees. She just wants to fill her eyes with the glorious, glorious world.

There are so many interesting verticals in the city. The way the buildings reach for the sky is so bold, she can't believe their courage. And they're not reaching for the sky like, "You yellow-bellied varmint, Reach!" They're just bravely and simply being vertical, willing to submit to the winds and rain and pollution and graffiti bandits and the piss of stray dogs, doing what needs to be done, modestly, without trying to advance themselves, unlike the buildings Uptown, which hold themselves so far above humanity.

Uptown is not a habitat for humanity. The Village is a friendly home to strays and oddities like herself; the buildings maintain a human scale, while remaining resolutely vertical. They don't lie down on the job.

CHAPTER THIRTY-FOUR

"Mmm, Mommy. I want some milk."

Alec's lying in my bed, looking like a big, long-haired baby. He looks so sweet and infantile, despite his size, that I want to hold him forever. Just as he promised, the sweet Alec comes back when I beat him. While that's not my usual MO, I'm hardly in a position to be fastidious.

"Sorry, baby, no milk. One side's tea, the other's coffee." I stroke his hair while he sees if I'm telling the truth. "If I were Italian," I murmur, "one side would be espresso, the other cappuccino."

"What if you were Irish?"

"Guinness Stout and Bushmills."

"Mmm, my kind of woman," Alec says, trying to taste both sides at once.

"Two, three," I murmur, keeping score for him, since I'm not a screamer.

"I wish I were a woman," Alec says wistfully, sitting back on his heels. "Just for one day, I'd like to feel what it's like to keep coming the way you do."

"It would be nice if you could come just once," I say, reaching for him. "Why don't you let me try?"

"Not in public." Alec jerks away from me.

"I'd hardly call this 'in public.'"

"I don't like to mess up a lady's sheets."

"Life is messy."

"That may be OK for life, but not for the sheets."

"Surely you've encountered that ancient technological miracle, soap and water?" I prop myself up on my pillows. This could be a long night. "That antique but still amazingly relevant invention? A half hour in the washing machine, and those sheets will come out pure as angel wings. Isn't it amazing how we can return the filthiest stuff to its original pristine state?"

"What if your landlady saw them?"

"She'd say, '*Mazel tov!*'"

"I thought she was French." Alec gets out of the bed and walks across the room. He pulls on his jeans and fastens his Grateful Dead buckle securely in place.

"Where the heart meets the body, Yiddish is the mother tongue."

"It's unseemly for a naked woman to spout aphorisms. Especially one who's had as many orgasms as you."

I smirk complacently. "You could have one too, if you'd let me try my witchcraft."

Alec starts lacing up his work boots. "You'd think I would

recall meeting someone as unusual as you. Are you sure you haven't been feeding me magic mushrooms?"

You'd *think* he would have forgotten our nonexistent former relationship by now. I know I'm sick of hearing about it. What is it with guys today? Doesn't he want to come? I certainly do, as many more times as I can. The number of orgasms the universe owes me rivals the national debt. Well, I may not be able to make him come, but that's no reason I can't drown myself in excess. I wonder how many times a woman has to come to die of pleasure.

"My love juices are an aphrodisiac," I say temptingly, "but I wasn't aware that they were a hallucinogen, or that they destroyed men's minds. Maybe you should get another good taste so we can assess their effect. I'll take notes."

"Sounds like a good plan to me," Alec says, unbuckling.

"I promise to maintain my objectivity," I say as Alec puts my plan into effect. And promptly break my promise.

From the reddish depths of my pleasure haze, I look out into my room. Clothes cover the floor and furniture like an early snow. Alec, looking like Charles Manson's angelic brother, sits naked and cross-legged in my bed. B&D paraphernalia snakes over, under, and around Madame's typewriter.

It's clear that this room is no longer the shrine of a wise virgin. Maybe I should get a shotgun apartment on Avenue A, shave my head, and throw out everything I own that's not black leather. Which is practically everything. I'm not sure I belong here anymore.

I reach out a limp arm for the cold coffee sitting on the nightstand. I can barely move, but I'm not satisfied. I think I'd have to be dead before I stopped willingly. "What *can* you do with that thing besides paint?" I ask Alec.

"I could teach you how to drive stick."

"That *would* be useful."

"You never know when you'll have to drive a race car. Put your hand here," Alec instructs. "No, hold it like this. Now here's first gear. Second gear is up here and reverse is over to the side."

"How do I know when to shift?" I ask.

"By looking at my face."

"You look like you're about to go into overdrive."

"Oh, not with you. I could never do that." Alec's gearshift is starting to wilt.

"You can do all that dirty stuff without an iota of shame, but you can't take your own satisfaction?"

"So? What's your point?" I don't think there is a gear to describe where his shift is at. Reverse, maybe.

"You're the most dirty-minded puritan I've ever met," I say.

"Don't talk dirty."

"What did I say?" I ask, struggling to put him back in drive.

"Puritan."

"You're weird."

"That's why you like me." Alec grins.

"Is it? I wonder."

"Sure it is, doll. You could never enjoy being with a regular guy after me. They'd give you one orgasm and turn over and go to sleep. You'd be bored stiff with someone like that, even when he was awake and talking. You need a man who can keep you on your toes."

"Strut your stuff, baby!"

Alec flashes me a grin.

"But," I say, "do you really think you've got my capacity for multiple orgasm in your breast pocket?"

"Who could do it to you as good as me?"

I play with Alec's long hair. It's been a long time since any-body's done it to me at all. But I do remember a time when I took my prodigious capacity as much for granted as the water coming out of my kitchen tap. However, there's no need to rain on Alec's parade.

"It sounds like you want me to keep you around." I wrap one of his blond curls around my ring finger.

Alec sits up, with an alarmed expression on his face. "Don't go getting any notions, woman. I'm allergic to marriage. Here, look. I'm already breaking out in hives." He looks down at his stomach and starts scratching frantically. "Just the word sets me off."

"You said the M-word, not me." I get out of bed and start pacing, dominatrix-style, around the room. "You men have some egos. What makes you think I'm husband hunting? Or that you would even be a candidate? I've been married. Once was once too often." I start scratching my arm. "Look, I'm breaking out in hives, too."

Alec stops scratching his stomach and pulls me back down onto the bed. "That's good, doll." He scratches my arm for me. "Just don't forget and start getting any ideas about me and mar-riage."

"I'd have to be out of my mind." I say coldly. "But, you know, if I command you, you'll have to do what I say."

Alec looks worried.

"Did you or did you not pledge to be my slave?"

Alec nods. He doesn't look too happy.

"This is not a game, Alec." I start striding. "You can't be my slave just when it suits you. You think you can obey my com-mands only when it's something you happen to want to do? I de-mand nothing less than total submission. When I command you to come, you're going to submit to my will. If I ever command you to marry me, you're going to put your head on the block with a smile."

Alec pulls the quilt up. I have never seen such a sulky, obstinate look on a man's face before.

"You thought servicing an insatiable woman was a cool jerk-off fantasy?" I snarl. "I'll make you wish you were dead and in hell before you've finished. Your calluses will get calluses. Your tongue will turn black and swell. That pathetic organ you men lavish so much attention on will submit totally to my control. And believe me, you won't like it."

Alec is starting to look interested in spite of himself.

I sit on the bed and start stroking him with my toes. "No self-respecting mistress would even touch you with her hands," I snarl.

Alec's gearshift is starting to perk up. I don't really understand why this is working. I don't know whether to laugh or to cry. This guy has worse self-esteem than I do.

"Don't eyeball me, slave."

Obediently Alec closes his eyes.

My toes are starting to cramp. Doggedly I continue my efforts. I wonder if he's worth it. Could I transform Alec into the man I want? He seems to enjoy submitting to my will. Why shouldn't I get something out of this besides prehensile toes?

"Tomorrow you're going to come take me out for breakfast," I say in a voice no slave could argue with. "And you're going to bring me a giant stuffed animal every day for a week."

"Yes, Mistress," Alec quavers.

I smile and switch feet. I can't wait till he starts being the Alec I like all the time.

CHAPTER THIRTY-FIVE

"Hi," Nevada says merrily, shyly, gayly to Nicholas as he opens his apartment door for her. Mozart and late-slanting sunlight spill out into the hall. "Hi."

"Hi." Nicholas smiles at her lightning bolt and draws her into the apartment. "Hi."

"Hi." Nevada stands in the tiny vestibule, grinning and inhaling the odor of beeswax. Nicholas must have waxed his floors. She would have done the same for him, but it's not many men who would go beyond changing the sheets. The dark wood has a subtle, festive sheen. Hopefully she and Nicholas will soon be rolling on it, oblivious to splinters and scraped elbows.

"Can I take your stick?" Nicholas smooths his vest over his operatic stomach.

"No. Thank you. I'd like to keep it with me."

"Of course."

"It's a Huichol prayer stick," Nevada explains.

"It's very beautiful," Nicholas says gravely.

"Thank you. I made it myself. Look at the colors. They're *mine.*"

"They're very pretty."

Nevada realizes that Nicholas has no idea what she's talking about. If he did, he would never use the word pretty about her colors. He probably doesn't realize how much she gave away to Alec. And there's no way she can explain it. Giving him a lecture on prayer stick colors and the recovery of her palette would spoil everything. She would so like him to understand without her having to make a long, windy speech. Maybe Claire could do it in a few well-chosen, conversationally toned sentences, but she's not Claire. There's no way she could tell him what it's like to recover the freedom of the streets. She'll just have to put it in her new sculpture.

They're still standing in the vestibule. Nevada decides that, despite the awkwardness of the moment, a kiss would not be inappropriate. Parking her prayer stick under a Russian Orthodox icon, she sticks her face in his direction just as he sticks his face in hers.

"Ouch," Nevada says as they bump noses. "Are we out of synch here or what?"

"Somewhat," Nicholas concedes. "But if we sit and hold hands for a while, our body rhythms are sure to come back into harmony."

"Do you really think so?" Nevada asks, rubbing her nose. She grabs for her prayer stick as Nicholas leads her into the living room.

"I'm sure of it," he says, seating her on the sofa and drawing her close. His alpaca vest feels soft against her bare arm. "I missed you. I hope you got a lot of good work done."

"I missed you, too," Nevada admits, but sidesteps his curiosity about her work. If she weren't sitting on a sofa with Nicholas, she could be starting her new sculpture. It feels crowded in the little apartment, with Nicholas sitting so close. She's been alone so much the last couple of weeks, and Nicholas is so big. Alec didn't intrude this much on her space or the silence she brings with her out of the Thing. Nicholas's gold watch, its heavy chain stretched across his stomach, ticks loudly in the stillness, reminding her of all the time that's rushing down the toilet of eternity. When you waste time sculpting, at least you have something to show for it. When you waste time relating, what do you have to show except a few incorrect scraps of memory? She draws away. "Is it stuffy in here or is it me?"

"I can't imagine your ever being stuffy, my dear. You're the freshest breath of air to blow through any man's life."

Nevada smiles dubiously as Nicholas gets up to unlock a window. His compliment tastes as mild and sweet as white chocolate. It turns her into *une jeune fille bien elevée*, sitting on an overstuffed sofa in her mother's parlor, listening to her suitor proffer vapid compliments. Why doesn't Nicholas ravish her? Alec would, to the best of his abilities. It would at least get things moving. She's not sure how long she can stay in this airless space, despite its sepia-toned charm.

As Nicholas pushes the window up, a scrappy East Village breeze and a couple of flies make it through the steel security gates.

"It's too bad about the gates," Nevada says. "It's so fresh out."

"We could go for a stroll in St. Mark's Place." Nicholas

brings out a cut glass decanter and matching goblets on a gold tray. "Or have dinner at the Peacock Cafe. They have outdoor tables in the back with striped umbrellas. Very charming and so romantic, you'd think you were in the Veronese piazza where Romeo drank wine with his cousins."

"It sounds like you're writing an opera." Nevada pours out the wine, non–goddess-blessed, but what can you do? She has to remember not to drink too much. Secular wine always gets her in trouble. "I have nothing against opera. But could you do me a favor and set it in the East Village? I want to try being where I am, for a change."

"That sounds like an excellent plan. The East Village can be very romantic, too." His arm rests heavily on her shoulder.

"I'm no longer interested in romance." Nevada wriggles out from under his embrace and grabs her prayer stick. It's in happy communion with a bonsai, but she needs to feel its fuzzy-rough textures. If she ever needs the strength to walk out of here, it will make an admirable walking stick. "Now that I finally have my eyes open and my feet on the ground, I don't want to get caught in that magic Opera web you're spinning."

Nicholas screws his face up in an expression designed to reach the topmost balcony. "My dear, you wound me. I had hoped to get your feet off the ground as soon as possible."

Nevada laughs. "As long as you promise not to blind me with Opera dust."

"I don't know if I can help it." Reverently Nicholas touches her gold hair. "When you're around, it's hard for me to think of anything but magic. I haven't been able to think about anything but you since we met."

Nevada eyes him uneasily. That's just how that mess with Alec got started—with obsession. That's how all her messes with men get started. If only she were plain, like Claire. Claire can get away with being invisible, which is what an artist needs to be. Only in the Thing can she be still and hidden as a hawk, her glittering eye on life's moveable feast.

Nicholas winds one of her blond curls around his finger. "You know, Nevada, what happened to me in your Thing was extraordinary. I don't know whether it was your artistry or your heart as a woman, but pain I thought I'd carry with me forever just melted away."

Nevada smiles at him uneasily. Alec used to claim only she knew how to ease his hunger and his hurt.

"Don't look so worried, my dear. I'm just trying to thank you, in my clumsy way."

"I hope you don't have any expectations about my doing it on a regular basis." Nevada shakes her hair free.

"I'm not going to force you to sign a blood contract. Why don't we just take it as it comes?"

"I know that's supposed to be the sensible thing to do, but in my experience, that means I end up with my arms tied behind my back."

"I'm not Alec," Nicholas says, letting the space between them grow visible. "Don't you know me better than that?"

"I'm sorry, Nicholas. I can't think of anyone less like Alec than you." Nevada stares at the fly buzzing around her glass. "But aren't you at all scared about getting involved with me?"

"Isn't it a little late for that?"

"We could still back out."

"Is that what you want?"

"No." Nevada waves at the fly.

"What are you afraid of?"

An image of her legs, pale against blue sky, pops into her

mind. She squeezes her mind so tight, the image pops. "Of having to fit myself into too small a box."

"Do you think I'm a small person?"

"No. I find you very spacious. It just seems to happen that way. Men expect women to be a certain way one hundred percent of the time—nurturing, cheerful, submissive, whatever—and they hate it when you want to be something else for five minutes. I don't want to have to fight for the space to have PMS—or ecstatic visions. Men find ecstatic visions very inconvenient when their girlfriends are having them. I think they prefer PMS!"

"You're a strong woman," Nicholas says, stroking her forearm. "What's stopping you from being who you are? Let people think what they want. They will anyway."

Nevada touches her prayer stick. "I'll tell you what stops me—the feeling that, without love, life is one long bleak February day when it's been snowing forever and it's going to snow forever. When I was what Alec wanted, he was nice to me. Life was, if not like June, at least like late March. The blizzard was past and you could see some blue in the sky."

"It sounds like you're paying a pretty high price for a little affection."

Nevada nods. "Sometimes I wonder if it wouldn't be better just to be alone. When I'm in a relationship, I feel like I have to fight for my right to be human."

"Some of my fans project their unfulfilled romantic expectations onto me. I'd rather they just concentrated on the purity and power of the music, but romance sells tickets." He touches her face. "I love to surrender all that with you. I love to be soft. You don't expect me to strike heroic poses."

"We men and women have such magical expectations of each other," Nevada says. "It's a wonder relationships *ever* work out. If you do manifest your lover's fantasy, you wonder if the love they give you is as fake as what you're putting out to get it."

"I guess that's the other reason I've been alone so long." Nicholas glances at the picture of Eileen on the sideboard.

"I'm so afraid of that," Nevada says. "That if I insist on being my gritty, dark, ecstatic self, I'll end up all alone."

"Would that really be so terrible?" Nicholas asks. "I think you have to be comfortable alone, before you can truly connect."

"There you go being sensible again." Nevada taps him with her prayer stick. "Don't you ever get sick of being the voice of reason?"

Nicholas laughs. "Not when I think of the alternatives."

Nevada takes his hand. Between the wine and the music, she's starting to edge into comfort in the little room. His face and the touch of his meaty hand are starting to seem like home.

Was this big, blond, bearded man really inside her? Nevada lets her head rest on his shoulder. Putting his arm around her, he tucks her in close to his mountainous bulk. If he's sitting next to her in twenty years, will his face still seem this strange, this familiar?

"I find you so beautiful." Nevada starts pulling his clothing off. "I love the way your body fits together. It's all of a piece. It's so graceful the way your waist fits into your hips, the way your man parts fit in. Cutting that part off with clothing turns men into Ken dolls, ruins their power and grace. I couldn't have done a better job if I'd sculpted you myself."

Nicholas looks embarrassed. "No one ever called me beautiful before." Eileen was too obsessed with her own beauty to notice the beauty of anyone but her rivals. And on stage, he becomes the music; he's not Nicholas, he's not Nicholas's body. He's the body of the music. But music is bodiless. So he's bodiless, on stage at least.

"Your skin has this wonderful glow. Stand up and let me look at you."

Nicholas gets up and slowly revolves for her. He's glad he doesn't have to perform naked. It's hard enough to give himself over to Nevada's loving gaze.

He looks like a statue of a god, Nevada thinks, one of the husky ones like Thor. Despite what he said, he does have a larger-than-life quality. She can see why women would lay mythic expectations at his door. But she's going to try and love him for everything about him—his humanness, his compassion, his work with the homeless, his lack of pretensions, his sadness, his cooking, his insistence on being the unrelenting voice of reason and romance.

CHAPTER THIRTY-SIX

Alec walks into my room carrying a huge plush gorilla with a gingham bow around its neck. He's got that hangdog slave look in his eyes and looks like he might start drooling. There's something about that look that makes me want to rub him out of existence.

I sit down on the bed and look at Alec's present with a sick, dry feeling in my throat. I hadn't realized how disappointing getting a stuffed animal by coercion would be. This is not at all like when he brought me that teddy bear. This is dead matter, not something that can make me feel seventeen again and loved.

Could I find my way back to that sweet place in Alec's heart? I might wander through a fetid, overgrown jungle for the rest of my life, snuffling after a bit of honey. I can't force his heart open. If I had a psychotic break with reality and forced him to marry me, it would be a hundred times worse than my worst fantasies of being alone and horny for the rest of my life. This coerced love doesn't begin to touch the sad, lonely places in my heart.

"Put that animal down, slave," I say.

"Did I do good, Mistress?" he asks eagerly.

"Speak when you're spoken to," I say. "Take off your clothes."

Hurriedly Alec sheds his jeans and work shirt.

"I'm not wasting a lot of time on you. I'm giving you five minutes and then you're going to come. Do you understand me?"

Alec nods. I push him down on the bed and get to work. I'll have more control with my hands than I did with my feet, which have been cramping all morning.

When he catches a glimpse of the spider tattoo on my thigh, Alec gets even more excited. The stick-on looks very real and is a great accessory to my red leather corset. Am I finally going to succeed? If Alec can achieve release in a social context, he might be able to give me the love I crave.

As I work on Alec, I wonder what my grey plush gorilla thinks of all this. It has such a bemused, innocent expression on its furry face. Is it really part of the same script as my merry widow and spider tattoo? Maybe that's the problem—Alec and I think we're starring in the same movie, but we're actually reading different scripts, both trash. He thinks he's prancing through *Tall Men in Chains*, while I'm rehashing *Gidget Goes Ape*. Is tacking my stuffed animal fantasies onto his dominatrix longings my mistake, or is this always the way it is between men and women?

My wrist is starting to cramp. I switch hands. Nothing is happening. I've let myself get so hungry, I'm not even manifesting dominatrix. It takes a lot of energy to come from that place.

Halfheartedly I snarl at Alec, "You've got thirty seconds to come. After that I'm going to cut it off with a hacksaw."

That gets a little spurt of enthusiasm out of Alec. I wish I'd had a heartier breakfast. Café au lait and a croissant is fine for sitting around, reading Colette, but I'm going to need a Canadian lumberjack breakfast to get this job done right. Flapjacks and sausages and eggs and rivers of black coffee . . . I have to stop thinking about food. I'm losing my concentration and Alec's losing it. If Madame is writing this, I wish she'd write in some food. Anything. Even Fluffernutters on Wonder Bread, although I can't imagine she knows what that is.

I switch hands again. Alec's back in neutral. I sigh. Why am I doing this? Isn't there enough sperm blanketing the world? I wish I was back to manifesting banana bread–baking girlfriend. At least I'd have some banana bread. Although this is starting to feel exactly like manifesting girlfriend—that awful stuck feeling you get from doing something you don't want to do in order to get love, the barely repressed fury, the continual message you're sending your body that your feelings don't count, although everyone else's warrant endless worship.

I want to be in the world of the plush gorilla and a boyfriend who bought it for me of his own volition, and here I am manifesting dominatrix. Again. I feel like a prisoner of Alec's recalcitrant organ and this ridiculous red outfit, which I hope isn't giving me a rash. Aren't *I* supposed to be in charge?

Get me out of here, I call silently to Madame, just in case she is writing this, but nothing happens. Does she really want me to take responsibility for my own life? OK, then, I will.

I sit back on my heels. "I quit," I say, resting my hands on my thighs. "I'm going to get something to eat."

Alec's face contracts, and he spurts a weak white trickle onto his stomach.

"Wow," I say. *"Mazel tov."* What else is surrender the answer to?

Alec doesn't say anything. He looks green. I hope he's not going to throw up.

"You don't look too happy."

"Just because my body came, doesn't mean my heart did."

"Would it be so terrible to let your heart open to me just a little?"

"Could you hand me some tissues?"

"How come you're not calling me doll?" I pass Alec some Mansize Kleenex I bought specially for the occasion, though one of the pocket variety would have been more than adequate.

"I gave you what you want, but you women always want more, more, more. Could you please stop bugging me for five minutes?"

"You gave me what I want? This is your fantasy. Do you know how much I spent on these outfits?"

"No, and I really don't care. You've got a job." Alec gets up and goes into the bathroom, where I can hear him throwing up.

I'm starting to speculate about exactly what he's afraid of when I stop myself. The woman who's writing this book, whoever she is, doesn't need this crap.

"I'm going to get some breakfast," I call to Alec. "Let yourself out when you're done. And take your gorilla."

I don't need a man to feel good about myself. That's why the Goddess invented vibrators. And I know just where I can find a really good one.

CHAPTER THIRTY-SEVEN

"You really can imagine that Romeo was served wine here by the owner's great-grandfather," Nevada says. She and Nicholas are sitting on the terrace of the Peacock Cafe, eating goat cheese pizza. Soon the moon will illuminate the dusk that gathers like blackbirds in their tiny garden.

Nicholas smiles at her in a dazed way, drunk on her happiness.

"It's nice being somewhere other than The Orange Cat Bistro." Nevada spears a piece of endive, coated with honey-mustard vinaigrette. "That place was really starting to get on my nerves."

"Really?" Like heat-seeking missiles, Nicholas's fingers find the back of her neck. "When I'm there, I feel as though creatures out of old mythologies could step out of the kitchen, bearing steaming trays of mead."

"You sound like a good friend of mine," Nevada says worriedly. "But not like the voice of reason." If Nicholas stops being the voice of reason, anything could happen. Cows could fall out of the sky. Time could stretch, bend, and break, leaving her stranded on some forsaken island. There her time would run out of her like black, clotted blood.

"On enchanted Saturday nights with my beloved, I think it's permissible to take a vacation from logic."

"Don't you think that can be dangerous?" Nevada hitches her prayer stick closer.

"Romance?" Nicholas looks at her as though trying to memorize her face.

"That's just what I was trying to tell you at your apartment." Is Nicholas, despite his sweetness, just another guy who doesn't listen? Maybe being a mensch for the first couple of dates is all any guy can manage. She and Claire should open an institute for the propagation of long-term listening. "I said I wanted to keep my feet on the ground and the magic dust out of my eyes. Weren't you listening at all?"

"What can be the harm in a little romance?" Nicholas says. "I've finally found something to brighten the unending November my life became after Eileen died. Do you really want to snuff out that brightness with your obsession for reality?" He holds his hands up to her hair. "Be my sun."

"You sound like a real romance addict," Nevada says, but she can't help laughing at Nicholas's expansiveness. He must be wonderful on stage. If she really wants the unbending voice of reason and logic, she should date an accountant. Opera singers are neck deep in all that messy stuff the goddesses love.

"What do you expect from a baritone?"

"Someone who loves the power and the purity of the music." Nevada gazes at him levelly.

"You believed that?"

"Why? Is believing you a major mistake?" If Nicholas turns out to be as much of a truth-bender as her ex-husband, she's going to throttle Claire. But how has she let herself get so rooted in him? Forty or fifty years might be long enough to decide if he's trustworthy.

"No, dear," Nicholas says. "I just didn't want to admit to being a romantic fool."

"So you would have become a singer of Bach canons if you weren't addicted to the romance of opera." Nevada eyes him as she makes inroads on her goat cheese pizza.

"I probably would have become a partner in my father's tailor shop."

"Talk about the dreariness of reality!"

"Not really. The *stories* I would have heard about Mrs. Aiellos's granddaughter's illegitimate baby and Mr. Russo's gambling problems and the d'Angelos' fiftieth wedding anniversary! And I would have married a down-to-earth girl from the neighborhood, who, if she thought about anorexia at all, would think it was some kind of foreign food involving squid ink. Our children would be teenagers now." Nicholas looks sadly at the goat cheese oozing off his pizza.

"Playing rap at maximum volume and having screaming fights with you and your ignorant neighborhood angel."

"Probably." Nicholas smiles and sucks up the escaping cheese. "But would that really be so bad?"

"Sounds like hell to me. But I'm easily driven crazy by life's little irritations. I guess that's reason number three thousand and thirty six that I prefer it in my Thing."

"It sounds like you prefer romance to reality, too."

Nevada pauses for a second. "The Thing isn't about romance," she says finally. "What's in there is more real than anything out here, no matter what the *New York Times* says."

"We'll have to pick up the Sunday *Times* on the way home and see about that. You are coming home with me, aren't you?" Nicholas looks anxiously at Nevada.

"Not if you're going to force me to participate in the world of illusion the *New York Times* perpetuates. And the Sunday *Times*. We'll be depressed for a week!"

"I could get the *National Enquirer*."

"At least it would provide a little comic relief! Did you know laughter has the power to cure the most intractable diseases?"

"Even anorexia?"

"Why not?"

"Eileen never laughed much." Nicholas crosses his knife over his fork. "She was deadly serious about everything. She starved herself for her art, obsessed endlessly about her body. I tried to make her laugh, but . . . It's especially hard when your body is your instrument. There's no end to perfectionism on that road."

"After all you've suffered with Eileen, don't you feel nervous about taking on an agoraphobic?"

"Is it life-threatening?"

"Only if I refuse to leave my house when it's burning."

Nicholas smiles and picks up his fork.

"After all you've been through, aren't you just a little tired of crazy ladies? Wouldn't you like to find your ignorant neighborhood angel?"

"It's too late for that now."

"By now she's probably divorced with three children, stretch marks, and an attitude."

"Cynicism doesn't become you, my dear."

"Just call me Sunshine with an Attitude," Nevada says, glancing at the grape arbor that separates their garden from the street. Then she glances again at a tall, hulking figure scaling the wall. Could that possibly be Alec?

CHAPTER THIRTY-EIGHT

A lec trudges across the garden of the Peacock Cafe, lugging a stuffed gorilla.

"Hullo," he says and hands Nevada the gorilla. "I thought I smelled your perfume." He sits down and takes a piece of pizza.

"I'm not wearing perfume," Nevada says. Why is Alec bringing her stuffed animals? Did Claire finally kick him out of bed, or is he here to hassle her about the Thing?

"It must be those natural juices of yours." Alec kisses his fingers. "Sweetest stuff north of Houston."

Nicholas pushes back his chair and rises. "I really must protest," he says as Alec stuffs goat cheese in his face. "That's no way to talk to any lady, least of all my fiancée."

"Excuse me?" Nevada says, but is interrupted by Alec's snort.

"Your fiancée? This lady is my fiancée and I can talk to her any way I want."

"Hold the phone, boys." Nevada's chair scrapes against the patio bricks. "I'm not anybody's fiancée. You're both living in a delusional universe, though I doubt it's the same one."

"Didn't you learn anything from our time together?" Alec asks. "A delusional universe is the only place to live."

"The Way According to Alec?" Nevada snorts. "My book of that title is sure to top the best-seller lists. However the Thing is not a delusional universe. Your thinking that makes it even more obvious you're the wrong man for me." She squeezes Nicholas's hand. "And the things I learned from living with you, I would be ashamed to discuss in front of a gentleman." Nicholas, mollified, sits back down.

"Come on, Nevada. No woman can resist a guy who brings her a stuffed gorilla." Alec dances the plush simian around the table, knocking napkins and cutlery to the grassy bricks of the terrace.

"Is that what Claire told you?" Nevada says. "Did she also tell you that I have no use for leftovers, least of all hers. That is Claire's gorilla, isn't it?"

"Who told you about Claire?"

"She did."

"That two-timing . . .! You can't trust *anybody*, these days."

"You can say that again." Nevada glares at Alec.

Diplomatically Nicholas orders another bottle of Merlot. "You must be Alec," he says, holding out his hand. "I'm Nicholas. This is an awkward way to meet, but I want to tell you how much I admire your work. The translucent colors, the shifting shapes, what magic you create with a little latex."

"Where the hell did you see my work?" Alec stares at Nicholas's outstretched hand. He looks as though he'd rather start swinging than shaking. "And it's oils, you pompous old fart. I create a very different kind of magic with latex. Isn't that right, Nevada?"

"You call that magic? I can't remember the last time you even needed a condom." Nevada nibbles an endive leaf disdainfully.

"With Claire. I needed a condom with your friend, Claire." Alec glares triumphantly at Nevada.

"So Claire was actually able to pull it off." Nevada looks impressed. "So to speak. What does Claire have that I don't?"

"There's something about her."

"Endless, pigheaded patience, no doubt."

"That can be a very desirable quality in a woman."

"I'm sure you think so." Nevada puts her hand on Nicholas's back to let him know she knows he's still there. "If Claire is the Total Woman, what are you doing here?"

"Don't tell me you didn't miss me." Alec throws Nevada his most boyish smile.

"I can't tell you what a relief it was to be without you." Nevada looks at Alec as though he were a plate of picked-over, congealing chicken bones. "You're nothing more to me than Claire's leftovers."

"What about our artistic partnership?" Alec looks wounded but manages to down the wine Nicholas pours him.

"That's just a fancy way of saying I let you tie me up while you got off."

"I really don't think I should be hearing this." Nicholas starts to get up.

Nevada grabs his wrist. "Don't leave me alone with this maniac! And you"—she points a red fingernail at Alec—"stop upsetting my boyfriend. He's performing tomorrow and his vocal cords are very sensitive to stress."

"Don't worry about me, my dear." Nicholas touches

Nevada's hair. "It's you I'm worried about. Your body is such an exquisitely sensitive instrument. I don't want you retreating into your cocoon because of the clumsy machinations of this Neanderthal. Do you want me to dispatch him for you?"

"Dispatch yourself, buddy." Alec gets to his feet. He's got half a foot on Nicholas, but Nicholas has the weight advantage.

"Boys, boys, boys. This macho display is totally unnecessary. Alec has a new girlfriend. He doesn't want me."

"Nevada." Alec screws his face up into a passable imitation of the gorilla's goofy smirk. "You know how deeply I care about you."

"You're just afraid you'll miss out on the sale of the Thing."

"After all the years I subsidized its creation, don't you think I deserve something?"

"If you'd had to hire a hooker to do for you what I did, you'd have been bankrupt years ago!"

"You're going to have to sell the Thing unless this bozo is planning to pay your rent!"

"No one is going to pay my rent but me."

"Then you'll have to sell the Thing, and I have the connections."

"I don't like your connections."

"The Museum won't give you half as much as Hassiloff."

Nevada stands up and leans on the table. "America is obsessed with more, more, more, no matter what the human or environmental cost. I'm surprised that you, of all people, buy into that philosophy. Whatever happened to *The Way According to Alec?*"

Using his own arguments against him! Why did she have to pay such good attention to his rants? Alec slumps in his chair and lets Nicholas pour him another glass of Merlot. "So what are you going to do now?"

"I don't know. Start a new project. Go on tour with my fiancé. Maybe his company needs a set designer." Nevada looks inquiringly at Nicholas.

"Nothing could delight me more."

"You still want me after all you've heard about me and Alec, the gorilla-faced boy?"

"I've never wanted anything more in my life!"

"Let's go back to your place and celebrate."

"Celebrate for me, too," Alec says glumly, but he's already got his eye on a woman sitting under a red-striped umbrella, writing in a journal.

Nicholas calls for the check. "Are you really my fiancée?" he asks as he leads Nevada out to the street.

Nevada glances back at Alec, who's toting Claire's gorilla over to the journal writer's table. He doesn't wave good-bye. "Why not?"

"You no longer think romance is dangerous and foolish?"

"Of course it's dangerous and foolish. But you only live once, or maybe it's several thousand times. I forget which. It all comes to the same thing. Getting engaged fuddled my brain."

"My precious little girl. I would never let any harm come to you."

"That's very sweet." Somewhere garbage is burning. "Really it is. And I appreciate the thought. But just how are you going to accomplish that? Are you going to be my twenty-four-hour-a-day bodyguard? Are you going to carry a bigger gun than every bad guy on the street? And how are you going to reconcile your new career with your passion for the Opera?"

"I thought we were going to let ourselves be swept away by romance, at least for a little while," Nicholas says as they pass an artist sketching apocalyptic visions on the pavement with fat, colored chalks. "But you're already reverting to your fatal obsession with reality."

"Please don't use the word fatal about reality."

"I propose . . ."

"You did that already," Nevada interrupts.

". . . I propose a true marriage of reality and romance," Nicholas continues, beaming: "Sunday morning in bed, drinking cappuccino, cuddling, and reading the *Times*."

Nevada makes a face at him. "Can this marriage be saved? I'd better write Dear Abby."

"You'll have to buy the paper to read her reply."

"But not the *Times*," Nevada protests. "Some nice low to middlebrow paper, replete with grisly local murders and recipes for low-cal cheesecake. With a paper like that, you can really settle in for a cozy read. It's the perfect accompaniment to frozen fish sticks."

"The *Times* has grisly local murders and recipes for low-cal cheesecake."

"Yeah, but it always requires some special cheese you can only buy in one store in Little Italy and dried Black Forest cherries that can only be bought in Yorktown by a native speaker of German."

"There's a lot of entertainment value in reading a recipe like that. You don't have to make the cheesecake."

"I don't have to read the grisly murder stories."

"No, you don't."

"I suppose a cheesecake recipe that makes you travel from Little Italy to the Upper East Side is a good exercise for a recovering agoraphobic."

"Will you make it for me?"

"Of course, darling. I would do anything for you." And she would. But there's something she's got to do for herself first.

CHAPTER THIRTY-NINE

"I think my cunt is the most unaltruistic part of me," I say to Nevada. "It wants what it wants. It doesn't care about sacrificing itself for the sake of being loved or shoring up the male ego or mothering the universe." We're in a school locker room on the Upper East Side, getting ready for a Model Mugging class. We came early and there's no one here but us.

"The part of my body which most defines me as a woman would probably be labeled the least feminine. I can just hear the doctors saying, 'Young lady, your vagina is not very feminine.' It's a good thing they don't do clitoridectomies in this country. Or obsess about the vaginal versus the clitoral orgasm. Or define the simultaneous orgasm as the measure of all success. Remember all that crap from the fifties?"

"No," Nevada says. "And neither do you." She's sitting on a narrow oak bench, rooting in her gym bag.

"Well, I read about it. It was industry standard. It put the kibosh on women's sex lives for years."

"You are the most sexually healthy woman I've ever met," Nevada says, opening her locker.

"That was before Alec. They could write a casebook about me now." I unzip my flannel prairie skirt. Its buttercup yellow cactus flowers on forest green make me feel like a pioneer woman. In it I'm always striding freely through high grass.

"Don't be ridiculous. Everyone gets cut a little slack for experimentation."

"Still, I wish you'd warned me about Alec." The gunmetal grey floor feels smooth, shiny, and comfortingly institutional under my stocking feet.

"I did warn you."

"True, but I still don't understand how you could live with that man."

"Don't try to foist the blame for Alec off on me. He's the product of your fetid imagination." Nevada takes off her teal dress and hangs it in her locker.

"Thanks a lot," I say indignantly.

"Don't get your leggings in a knot. Everyone has a fetid imagination. If they have any imagination at all." Nevada pulls on a red and purple sweatshirt. Courage colors. I choose the same.

"By the way," I say. "Did I tell you how proud I am of you?"

"What for?"

"For coming up here on your own. You're at least five miles beyond your safety zone."

"My safety zone's expanding exponentially."

"I'll say. It used to be the size of your Thing."

"Yes, but don't forget my Thing opens onto infinite space."

"It's finite space that's the challenge for you," I say, pulling on purple leggings.

"Now I could go anywhere," Nevada says. "I carry my safety with me at all times."

"Like a turtle?"

"More like my body's a portable Thing." Nevada slips a red sweatband over her blond hair. "I'm proud of you too."

"Really." I grin. "How come?"

"For having the sense to break up with Alec twenty-one months sooner than I did. For writing this book."

"I'm not sure *who's* writing the book. But I will take credit for breaking up with Alec."

"Of course you're writing it," Nevada says. "Give yourself some credit. You're going to need something to feel good about when you go back out into the world of dating."

"Don't remind me," I sigh.

"Well, thanks for Nicholas, anyway," Nevada says.

"Congratulations on your engagement. I hope I can do half as well for myself."

"I'm sure you can," Nevada says. "But before you go back out there, I think you really should finish this book. You know you haven't begun to answer all the questions you've raised."

"They're age-old questions, Nevada," I say, pulling on a pair of purple slouch socks. "They don't have answers. It's just good to stir them up once in a while."

"That's such a teacher cop-out." Nevada slams her locker shut. "If you're going to raise them, I think you have a responsibility to answer them."

"Do we really have to get into this right now?" I ask as I lace up my running shoes. "We have a Model Mugging class to take."

Women are starting to filter into the dressing room. Most of them look scared. I am too. It's been a while since aikido. And we never went for knockout blows there. The aikido philosophy is to do as little damage as possible, just what's needed to restore harmony. Here the idea is to wipe the guy out. I hope this will answer at least one of the questions Nevada thinks I should have wrapped up by now.

I get up and head toward the gym, smiling at the other women nervously. I'm wondering, if I let the wild woman out of her cage, will I be able to get her back in?

CHAPTER FORTY

As we walk into the large, shining gymnasium, the instructors smile and hand us all knee and elbow pads. I try to reconnect with the calm centered place I learned to come from in aikido. I hope Nevada can handle this.

We do some stretching and warm-ups and then some centering exercises. This is all starting to seem reassuringly familiar when Moira, our instructor, starts showing us defensive moves—eye strike, knee to groin, side kick. This is very aggressive, very un-aikido. I take a deep, centering breath and practice the moves, while yelling, in unison with the other women, "No! No! No!" Yes is the aikido philosophy, yes even to injury and death. But yelling no with all my might feels wonderfully empowering. "No!" I scream.

After we've all learned the moves, Moira has us settle into a circle on the shiny gym floor and say why we're here. There are about fifteen of us, women of all ages. Almost every woman in the circle tells a story of rape, incest, or abuse.

Dottie, across the circle from me, was raped when she was four years old. Who would blame her for that, except for the man who did it to her, her father, who said she was asking for it, she shouldn't have been so seductive, she shouldn't have made his penis hard by her presence in his house?

Or what about Emily, sitting next to Nevada, who was raped by her fiancé's brother? He said he'd had too much to drink, as if that excused him, and told her he'd kill her if she told. After what he'd already done, she believed he was capable of murder. This is the first time she's told anyone. Imagine having to carry that inside you for twenty years, having to smile at your rapist at every family party, smile till you think you'll choke. For years she's felt as if her tongue is swelling, growing so huge, it will soon block her windpipe.

I can't keep the tears from streaming down my face as I listen to the common, common, nothing special pain, the daily bread of these women's lives. As I look at my classmates' faces, shining with tears, I realize that I can't keep blaming myself for having been raped, that I can't keep telling myself if I had been more careful, if I had lived my life differently, if I had embraced total excruciating respectability from the very instant I became a woman, I could have escaped this fate.

I'm not the only one crying, but Nevada tells her story in a monotone with a suspiciously blank face. I'm afraid for her. I have to remember to tell her that we should never, never, never blame ourselves for our agoraphobia. It's as clear to me as the moon shining in the big gym windows—a world where rape, incest, and abuse are this common is not a world we should blame ourselves for feeling fragile in.

Still crying, I tell my story about the man who still shows up in my dreams as a huge cockroach with a kitchen knife penis. The women on either side of me put their arms around me, which makes me cry harder. I wish Nevada could reach out for that support, too, but in her emotional blankness, she's beyond my reach.

After we take practice kicks at a padded pole, yelling, "No!" we're ready for our first confrontations. Moira demonstrates verbal defense tactics, using an authoritative voice and strong body language to make the attacker back off without a physical fight.

I'm the first up. I'm drawing heavily on my aikido training to keep from shaking. I've done this before, I keep reminding myself, or at least *something* like this. I've sent huge guys flying to the mat, but that was by turning their own aggressive energy against them. I rarely get in anyone's face, not even in the classroom, when I probably should. There's something about the idea of saying no that I'm having trouble with, that I've always had trouble with. It's a documentable miracle that I finally said, *"Enough!"* to Alec.

Robbie, one of the instructors, approaches me wearing a mask that makes him look like a slasher in a horror movie. I'm starting to shake. Who am I to say no to the universe? I try to take a deep breath, but suddenly there's not enough air in the gym. Robbie, acting as if he's on drugs, is circling close. I try to tell him to back off, but my throat's closing. I just know that if I draw my boundaries, if I finally learn to say, "No!", if I try to live my life on my own terms, not only will everyone stop loving me, my rapist will seek me out on psychic waves and rape me again, this time giving me AIDS and using that knife to incapacitate me permanently.

This is starting to sound so nuts, even to me, that I manage to shake off my paralysis. "Stand back," I squeak. Robbie comes threateningly close, mumbling profanities. I hear a voice in my head saying, "Placate him dear. You have to learn how to handle men. When he sees you're a lady, he'll want to protect you."

"Shut up, you stupid old bitch," I snarl. The voice squeaks like a haunted house door creaking shut. I assume my fighting stance, holding up my hand in a halt gesture. "Stop!" I say forcefully. "If you come any closer, I'll consider this an attack."

Robbie nods and moves away. A wave of exhilaration washes over my body. Defining your boundaries is even better than having a Thing to crawl back into. What else can I say no to? No to self-obsessed dates, no to goof-off students who want to eat up my time and patience with their lame excuses and need for extra attention because they weren't listening in the first place, no to friends who want to talk about their problems endlessly, but couldn't care less about mine. No to everything that isn't the life I want to live. I smile encouragingly at Nevada, who's looking extremely nonpresent. When her turn comes, she manages to hold her space, but still she looks untouched.

Everyone else successfully goes through the exercise. We take a break and then Moira demonstrates the moves we'll need to protect ourselves in a physical confrontation.

Numbly Nevada watches Jill, a delicate brunette in her twenties, get on the mat. Jill, who was alternately beaten and groped by her father, has a little white scar on her nose. She looks scared. Robbie, in a huge padded helmet and protective gear that makes him look like Everywoman's worst nightmare, throws her to the mat.

One thing Claire's right about, Nevada thinks, trying not to watch Jill go down, if her mother ever got raped (if she didn't manage to decapitate the guy with her meat cleaver which she sharpens faithfully every Friday), she would get up, brush her skirts off, and get back to work. How could she expect less of her daughter?

On the mat, Jill is doing an elbow strike to Robbie's helmeted face, followed by three knee strikes to the groin. Moira is on the mat, coaching, and everyone's yelling encouragement.

Nevada almost walks away from her place at the head of the line. There's nothing she wants more than to be back in the cool empty locker room, putting on her street clothes. And the street, so recently a place of terror, seems so much sweeter and cooler a place than this, so infinitely desirable a place to be. But something makes her stay, maybe not wanting to make an ass of herself in front of Claire, maybe thinking if she can't get past this wall, she might as well stop being her mother's daughter.

She's up next. Everyone's cheering for Jill, who's achieved a knockout. Nevada walks up to the mat, her arms and legs stiff as wooden poles. She hopes she can get them to work. Robbie looms at her from the other side of the mat, huge and terrifying in his protective gear.

As he approaches, Nevada starts shaking. She drops to the mat and watches him come toward her. Only he's no longer Robbie. He's the hunter who threatened to put out his campfire with her back if she didn't please him, who swore he'd torch her mother's house if she told. She can smell the woodsmoke and her own fear and realizes, for the second time, her complete helplessness. There's *nothing* she can do, she's *too* small, her will is as frozen as Siberian winter.

Nevada turns her face into the mat. Letting herself feel this way again, how can she keep going? It would be better to cocoon in her Thing forever than to feel, if feeling means feeling this.

She's on the mat, shaking and sobbing. Robbie's on top of her, crushing the air out of her body. Moira's beside her saying,

"You can do it. Look for an opening." Her classmates are scream-ing encouragement. "Eye strike, eye strike," she hears them call. Nevada looks up at Robbie and sees it as clearly as though there's a big red X painted on his mask. She jabs her fingers at the X and he falls back. She knees him in the groin twice, hard. As he comes at her groggily, she drops into position for a side kick and smashes her foot into his head. Robbie gives the signal that, if he weren't wearing protective gear, she would have knocked him out. Moira blows her whistle. The class cheers and Nevada walks back into line grinning and receiving hugs of encouragement.

She feels light as angel cake, strong as a sabra striding through the desert. Is it really OK to get this much joy from learn-ing to beat the shit out of men?

CHAPTER FORTY-ONE

Nevada and I burst out of the school doors into the spring night. The air is cool and exhilarating on our flushed faces.

"Good-bye, good-bye," we call to our classmates. "See you next week."

We set off down Lexington Avenue. It's only three miles down to the Village, and the air is too intoxicating for us to entomb ourselves in the subway for even twenty minutes. You'd think we would be exhausted after a five-hour class, but I feel as though I could walk to Far Rockaway.

"I can't wait till next week's class," I say, swinging my bag.

"I can't wait for some man to look at me cross-eyed," Nevada says.

"If you try taking on a group of guys hanging out on the street corner," I nod at some men passing around a bottle in front of a lighted deli, "I want you to know I'm not going to back you up. We're not that good."

"Yet," Nevada says. "But can't you just see red Xs on their soft spots?"

"Yes," I admit. "But I'm also remembering what I learned in aikido—when you initiate an act of violence, you put yourself off-balance. And when you're off-balance, you're vulnerable."

"I'm never going to use the 'V' word about myself again," Nevada says. "I love feeling like I could beat up any jerk walking down the street. Why didn't anybody tell us violence was so much fun?"

"Well I'd be very happy if you never think of yourself as a *victim* again. But if you can't embrace your *vulnerability*, I don't think you can be truly brave. The way to transform fear to fear-lessness is to be willing to feel your fear and keep going."

"Don't be a drip, Claire," Nevada says. She's striding along, her cheeks glowing red. I feel like I'm watching *The Seven Samurai*, recast with women in the leading roles. Why should I rain on her parade? Except that I'm remembering at least four of the seven died by the end of the movie. And they devoted their lives to the Arts of War.

"The way I feel now," Nevada says, "I'm definitely going to take the Multiple Attacks and Weapons classes."

"You want to be a woman warrior?"

"Why not?"

"You want to be a female Steven Seagal?"

"Absolutely."

"You want the men in your movies cowering under your protection?"

"I don't know if I'd go that far."

"You know the things about those movies, the hero is always

invulnerable. No one ever fights as good as he does. He's super-naturally good."

"That's Hollywood."

"That's exactly right. That's Hollywood."

"Are you trying to make me acknowledge that just because we've taken session one of a Model Mugging class, we're not invulnerable?"

"Give the lady a cigar."

Nevada shudders. "I haven't become *that* macho."

"If this were Hollywood, there'd always be a John Wayne or Steven Seagal around to rescue you when you were about to get raped. It's a nice fantasy, isn't it?" I say wistfully, as we swing by Thirty-fourth Street.

"Isn't that exactly what keeps us from learning to protect ourselves?" Nevada says, eye-striking at the cool air. "We're always waiting for John Wayne to ride up. Those movies make us think it's sexy to be helpless. If I ever have a daughter, I'm going to put her in martial arts classes as soon as she's out of diapers."

"That's when my parents started me on ballet lessons," I laugh. "I looked really cute in my pink tutu."

"Well, at least you developed strength and coordination."

I nod. It's almost midnight, but I'm not sleepy. "Do you want to come over for a pajama party?" I ask, admiring the aurora borealis the Empire State Building casts on the night sky. "We could make hot chocolate and stay up all night."

"I'm too full of energy to sit still. I'm going to go home and work."

"You're starting your new project?"

"I cannot *believe* how long I've been carrying that garbage around with me," Nevada says, eluding me once again. "I feel a hundred pounds lighter."

"I know what you mean," I say, letting her go about the sculpture. I've been promising myself I would show more respect for Nevada's space. "I wanted so much to be brave," I go on, "but I don't think I knew what the word really meant. I wanted to be a brave soldier. I've been telling myself for years that I was lucky. When I got raped, he didn't give me AIDS or kill me outright. I was lucky. I wasn't a virgin, so it wasn't my first experience with sex. I was lucky. It wasn't that bad. I got up and brushed off my skirts and got on with my life. For years I told myself I was lucky. I tried not to let it get to me. I didn't know how I was going to live my life if I really let it in."

Nevada puts her arm around my waist.

"I told myself," I say, "how can you take one little rape so seriously with all the suffering in the world? Look at what the guys coming home from Vietnam had to go through. I told myself with all the hunger and homelessness, with war zones where rape is as common as unexploded grenades, how can I make a big deal out of one piddly little rape? And that's what kept me from dealing with the pain."

"After I was raped," Nevada says, "the only possible thing to do seemed to be to find a large man to protect me. I tried to live a totally safe life, and I ended up bricking myself into a tomb."

"Trying to be totally safe is even more dangerous than trying to be a brave soldier," I say as we swing by Union Square Park. There's quite a lot of activity in the dark bushes. "We are absolutely not going to walk through the park and take down drug dealers," I say firmly.

"Give me credit for having a *little* sense, Claire. At least as much as I was born with."

"Sorry." I rub the sore places that are starting to come in on my back. "Wouldn't it be nice if we were Wonder Woman and Cat Woman and *could* do something for this poor city?"

"I think we should finish the Basics course before we start making our costumes."

"Since when did you become the voice of reason?"

"Nicholas must be rubbing off on me." Nevada laughs.

"I wish I had someone to rub off on me." I sigh.

"Watch out, you might get what you wish for."

"I could handle it, now that I've had a lesson in saying no." My legs are starting to feel like overstretched rubber bands.

"But when do you say no and when do you surrender to what is?"

"What makes you think I know the answer to that question?"

"I bet you've been thinking about it."

"Remember what I said in the locker room?"

"You said a lot of things in the locker room."

"The thing about how they're age-old questions and don't really have answers? It's just good to stir them up once in a while?"

"I'm sick of all that liberal crap," Nevada says, practicing two-handed groin punches as we round the south end of the park. "I want some *answers.*"

"Hmm," I say. "You want to beat up half the human race *and* get absolute, inscribed-in-stone answers. Perhaps you'd like to be apprenticed to Idi Amin? Or how about Jim Jones? He had lots of answers. Oh, that's no good. He's dead."

"Stop being right!"

"Sorry," I say. "I'll try not to do it again."

"I'll let you off this time."

"Saying no feels so wonderful," I say as we stride west on Twelfth Street. The air smells so fresh, the only clue that we're in

New York is the smell of pizza on the breeze. "Imagine the joys of saying yes when you really mean it!"

"I know what you mean, girlfriend," Nevada says.

"Are you thinking of saying yes to having a baby?"

"You never know."

"With Nicholas?"

"Stranger things have happened."

"It would be nice to have a baby to hold," I say wistfully.

"You can be my first daughter's godmother."

"Cool." And it is. After taking responsibility for my beleaguered characters, not to mention my multiply wounded students, I don't have the energy for my own child! "I don't know if I even want to meet another man. Sometimes I think I'd like to live in those soaring high places permanently, make my life a hermitage of art."

"I know what you mean," Nevada says. "But having a boyfriend keeps you connected. It keeps you from flying off totally into weird outer space realms from which you might never return. You make dinner together, eat, tell each other what happened during the day. You make love, you wash the dishes. It keeps you connected to your body. But even if you do want to meet someone, being happy on your own is a very strong place to come from."

"Maybe outer space is where you need to be to be a great artist and saint," I say, trying to make out the stars in the washed-out city sky.

"What would you write about?"

"How the stars shine in the darkness."

"How long do you think that would keep your interest?"

"A couple of weeks. A couple of days. A couple of hours."

Nevada laughs. "People *are* hard to relate to, but I think they're worth it."

"I can't believe I'm hearing you say this."

"I can't believe it either," Nevada says. "But as far as being a deeply spiritual person goes, do you know if you become a monk or a nun, it brings you more deeply into the world than ever? You're constantly dealing with the details of feeding and sheltering the poor, the administration of running a meditation center, etc."

"How do you know that?"

"I read a book."

"That can be dangerous."

"Not as dangerous as writing one."

"Ain't that the truth."

CHAPTER FORTY-TWO

Sitting at my desk, I gaze out the window into the dark, fragrant garden. Now that this book is done, I'm finally starting to understand how Nevada felt about finishing her Thing. How raw, how devastated, how abandoned by her world. How she has to stand raw and naked out in the real world with no place to retreat to. Acid rain is falling on her hair, her face, and she has no umbrella, no hat, no home, she just has to submit to the rain, she has to surrender to exposure, to homelessness. There's nothing to crawl into; she's just out there on the heath, all alone, surrounded by ugly dead vegetation. There aren't even any dogs, just dog turds. I'm nowhere.

How can I abandon her for the sake of completion? I *could* just keep writing this book for ten or twenty or a million years. But then I'd be back to cocooning. I don't want to set a bad example for Nevada.

To come from nowhere, be nothing. To take that chance, step out into thin air. Maybe thin air would be a good place to be. I would let go of being the author of this book, dissolve it into thin air and see what turns up next. It might not be so bad. There *are* other sacred spaces.

CHAPTER FORTY-THREE

Nevada turns her key in the lock and pushes open the door of her loft. She turns on the light and walks through the big empty echoing space. Her space. Throwing her jacket and bag on a kitchen chair, she brews a pot of smoky Lapsang tea.

The blackness is starting to shine. She puts on a white tee that's soft as sleep from years of laundering. Fastening her overalls, she takes a new drawing pad out of her supplies cabinet and sits down at the drafting table.

What she wants to make is a big piece, a bold piece, a piece unafraid to claim space. A people-friendly interactive goddess habitat. She starts sketching a plaza of black lava, a material that's both primitive and sophisticated, shiny and rough. The shiny blackness shapes itself into tiny waves under her soft pencil. Taking a sip of smoky tea, she sketches a fountain in the center of the plaza, with a raintree that spouts water on the upturned faces of children splashing in the basin. They'll see the sky in a whole new way because they're seeing its shapes and colors through the wet, glistening branches of her raintree.

The fountain makes her long to stand naked under running water, but holding herself to her desk, she sketches places for the earthbound to dream in the arms of huge goddesses. Like artists, they'll be in the landscape, yet removed from it. She'll hand-carve rough stone steps curving up the backs of the goddesses' skirts like Scottish castle stairs, whose curving indentations reveal the footsteps of ancestors ascending.

The moon is shining crazily into her big cold black loft windows, calling her to howl, be a lunatic, do a witches' dance naked beneath its shining. But she holds herself to her desk. She'll do her dancing in her design and invite the city to dance with her. The crowded, silently screaming city needs cathedral-like spaces in nature where people can find the shape of their bodies, the voice of their howls.

Her paper is receptive as fresh-plowed earth gleaming black under the moon. She sketches a tree house grove where city dwellers, shut off from sky, can dream airy dreams, gazing through gauzy branches at the sky's architecture.

When the silence sings, there's nothing she loves more than being alone in her loft. She sketches Nicholas as the spirit of a tree, a grand oak, watching over the grove. If she calls him Guardian of Discarded Children, she might even get him to model.

The darkness is really shining now. She sketches caves with stalactites and stalagmites, strange crystal structures, underground rivers, lichen that glow like stars in the darkness, so inhabitants of skyscrapers can dream earthy dreams. No caves that will suck you in like the Thing, just sanctuaries that welcome you into a realm

of refuge and fantasy, then let you back out into the world, re-
newed, to manifest your dreams.

Taking a block of modeling clay from her cabinet, Nevada
starts to work.